Playing for Keeps

BY JILL SHALVIS

Heartbreaker Bay Novels

Sweet Little Lies

The Trouble with Mistletoe

Accidentally on Purpose

Chasing Christmas Eve

About That Kiss

Hot Winter Nights

Playing for Keeps

Women's Fiction Novels

Rainy Day Friends

The Good Luck Sister (novella)

Lost and Found Sisters

Lucky Harbor Novels

One in a Million

He's So Fine

It's in His Kiss

Once in a Lifetime

Always on My Mind

It Had to Be You

Forever and a Day

At Last

Lucky in Love

Head Over Heels

The Sweetest Thing

Simply Irresistible

Animal Magnetism Novels

Still the One

All I Want

Then Came You

Rumor Has It

Rescue My Heart

Animal Attraction

Animal Magnetism

Playing for Keeps

A Heartbreaker Bay Novel

Jill Shalvis

HARPER LUXE

An Imprint of HarperCollinsPublishers

PLAYING FOR KEEPS. Copyright © 2019 by Jill Shalvis. All rights reserved. Printed in the United States of America. No part of this book may be used or reproduced in any manner whatsoever without written permission except in the case of brief quotations embodied in critical articles and reviews. For information address HarperCollins Publishers, 195 Broadway, New York, NY 10007.

HarperCollins books may be purchased for educational, business, or sales promotional use. For information please e-mail the Special Markets Department at SPsales@harpercollins.com.

FIRST HARPERLUXE EDITION

ISBN: 978-0-06-274190-5

HarperLuxe™ is a trademark of HarperCollins Publishers.

Library of Congress Cataloging-in-Publication Data is available upon request.

19 20 21 22 23   ID/LSC   10 9 8 7 6 5 4 3 2 1

Playing for Keeps

Chapter 1

#Suits

Sadie Lane walked through the day spa, closing up for the night, alone as usual. Her coworkers had left, but even if they hadn't, they'd just be milling around with their expensive teas, complaining about how hard this job was.

They had no idea how ridiculous that was to her, but as the lowest person on the ladder, she'd managed to keep her opinions to herself. She was sure it'd only be a matter of time before her mouth overtook her good sense.

Moving around shutting down the computers and dimming the lights, she fantasized about going home and stripping out of her daytime yoga pants and replacing them with her nighttime yoga pants. Unfortunately, even after eight hours on her feet, that wasn't in the cards for her.

Her phone buzzed an incoming call and a glance at the screen gave her an eye twitch. "Hey, Mom."

"You always forget to call me back. I've been trying to discuss your sister's wedding details with you for weeks now, and . . ."

Sadie listened with half her brain, the other half wandering off. Did she have time to grab an order of sliders and crispy fries from O'Riley's, the pub across the courtyard, before heading to her other job? Lunch had been eons ago . . .

"Mercedes Alyssa Lane, are you even listening to me?" her mom asked.

Being full-named always got her back up. It wasn't that she had anything against her name—okay, so she sort of did because who named a kid after the car where that kid had been conceived?—but more than anything, she had a whole lot against her mother's tone. "Of course I'm listening."

She wasn't. She was thinking about dessert after the sliders. Maybe cookies, maybe a brownie. Maybe both.

"Honey," her mom said, her voice going tentative.

"You're not feeling . . . *sad* again, are you?" She whispered *sad* as if it was a bad word.

And to be fair, for most of Sadie's teenage years it had been a bad word, along with *angry, misunderstood, sullen,* and *unhappy.* To say that she and her mom had a complicated relationship was pretty much the understatement of the year.

"Nope," Sadie said. "I'm fine." This was an automated response because she didn't want to deal with the *all you have to do to get over the blues is think positively* speech again, well-meaning as it was. But her mom was winding up for the big finish, so Sadie braced herself because in three, two, one—

"Remember what Dr. Evans always told you. To get over the blues, all you have to do is think positively."

Resisting the urge to smack her phone into her own forehead, Sadie drew a deep breath and sank into the cushy chair in her station, where her clients sat while she applied permanent makeup. This was her bread-and-butter job, seeing as the love-of-her-heart job—working as a tattoo artist in the Canvas Shop right next door—didn't pay enough yet. And call it silly and frivolous, but she'd grown fond of eating.

The problem was, all the time on her feet working way too many hours a day left her exhausted. And maybe the teeniest bit cranky. But not, it should be noted, sad. At least not at the moment. "Mom, you know it's not that easy, right?"

"To think positively? Of course it is. You just do it. Take your sister, for instance . . ."

Sadie closed her eyes and caught a few z's while her mom went on about Clara, whom Sadie loved and adored even if she was annoyingly perfect—

"Sadie? Yes or no?"

"Hmm?" She sat upright, opening her eyes. She'd missed a question, but pretending she knew what was going on at all times was her MO. If she couldn't blow her family away with her brilliance, plan B was always to baffle them with her bullshit. "Sure," she said. "Whatever you guys decide."

"Well, that's very . . . sweet of you," her mom said, sounding surprised. "And very unlike you."

Hoping she hadn't just agreed to wear a frothy Little Bo-Peep bridesmaid dress, Sadie let her gaze shift to the window. Over a hundred years ago, the Pacific Pier Building had been built around a beautiful cobblestoned courtyard that each of the ground floor shops and businesses opened onto, making it convenient for people watching.

One of Sadie's favorite pastimes.

Seeing as it was February in San Francisco, specifically the Cow Hollow District, a thick icy fog had descended over the dark evening with the promise of rain. She loved a good storm, the darker the better, and figured that love came from her own dark, stormy heart.

The lights had all come on, strung from potted tree to potted tree and along the wrought-iron benches around the water fountain. The area was usually a hub of activity. But tonight only the faint glow of the lights was visible behind the wall of fog, and there was no one in sight. Except . . . wait a minute. A form appeared out of the fog. A tall, leanly muscled form, his overcoat billowing out behind him like he was some sort of superhero.

Sadie called him Suits.

He had a real name, she knew. Caleb Parker. But she'd never said it out loud, preferring her nickname for him, since with the exception of the few times she'd run into him at a gym on the other side of Cow Hollow near the marina, she'd never seen him in anything but a suit. And though she herself wasn't a suit kind of girl, she could admit there was something about watching him move in gorgeous clothes that had probably cost more than her entire year's rent.

"Mercedes?" her mother said in her ear. "You still there?"

"Yep." She searched her brain for the conversation

she'd just missed. "Don't worry, I'll be on time for Clara's wedding dress fitting appointment."

"Did you get a date for the wedding yet?"

Sadie sighed.

"It's a wedding," her mom said firmly. "You'll need a date. And anyway, you're past due to find your Prince Charming. *Way* past due."

"Mom, I don't need a Prince Charming. Forest animals who clean, yes, but it's a hard pass for me on Prince Charming."

"Everyone needs romance," her mom said. "My book club just read the Fifty Shades trilogy and—"

"Those books aren't romance, they're erotica."

"Actually, they were very romantic. Christian Grey's a bazillionaire who falls in love with a regular girl. It's like a Cinderella story."

Sadie sighed. "*Fifty Shades of Grey* is only romantic because the guy's a billionaire. If he was living in a trailer, it'd be a *Criminal Minds* episode."

Her mom sighed. "I just don't know what you have against love."

"I don't have anything against it." Sadie hoped her nose wasn't growing at the lie. "I just don't need it right now." Or ever.

"But you haven't dated anyone since Wes, and that was three years ago. He was a good man."

An attorney, Wes had been sure of himself. Sexy, with an edge. Sadie was long past being hurt over what had happened between them, but she still wasn't feeling the need to let someone new in, mostly because she simply hadn't been attracted to anyone.

What about Suits? a voice inside her head whispered as she made her way from one window to the next in order to keep him in her sights. It was misting now and his dark hair shimmered with droplets every time he passed beneath a lamppost. Like Wes had been, he too was sure of himself. Sexy, with an edge . . .

He was everything she no longer let herself want.

Suddenly, he abruptly stopped between the day spa and the Canvas Shop. Crouching low in the now pouring rain, he stared at something she couldn't see. "I've gotta go, Mom. I'll call you back."

"You always say that, but you're fibbing. You're not supposed to fib to family."

"Uh-huh," Sadie said dryly. "Tooth fairy, Santa Claus, and the Easter bunny . . ." And at her mother's gasp, she gently disconnected, squelching a wince because she'd most definitely pay for that later. Her mom had a lot of talents, and one of them was being able to hold a grudge for a hundred years.

Sadie had a few talents herself, such as not sleeping

at night and enjoying chocolate just a little too much. And okay, so she also was talented at drinking tequila, preferably in the form of a frosty lime margarita.

Slipping her phone into her back pocket, she went back to window-gazing to see what Suits was up to. He was still balanced on the balls of his feet, the wind and now rain pummeling his back, seemingly unnoticed.

What the actual hell?

She knew a few things about him. Such as the fact that he had lean muscles everywhere you might want a man to have lean muscles, and that women tended to fall over themselves when he smiled. His eyes were a beautiful caramel, with flecks of gold that sparkled when he laughed. He was some sort of tech genius and used to work at a government think tank. He'd invented a bunch of stuff including a series of apps that he and his business partner had sold to Google. More recently the two of them had created a way of getting meds and medical care into remote developing nations via unmanned drones. He was innovative and inventive on a large scale, smart, charismatic . . .

Oh, and there was one more thing—he and Sadie rubbed each other the wrong way by just breathing. She wasn't even sure how it'd started, but there was an energy between the two of them she didn't understand.

At best it made her squirm. At worst, it sometimes kept her up at night.

Sadie's best friend, Ivy, who ran The Taco Truck parked outside the building, had decided that she and Caleb Parker shared an unrequited animalistic lust and nothing could convince her she was wrong.

But it wasn't lust, because Sadie no longer gave in to lust, animalistic or otherwise. Yes, he was fun, flirty, and charming, but she was highly suspicious of all those things. Her idea of fun, flirty, and charming meant being as sarcastic as possible. It'd done the trick too, scaring men off for years. But oddly, Suits seemed to be able to handle her sarcasm without so much as blinking an eye.

She had no idea what to make of that.

And what was he doing still all hunkered down like that in the rain? Was he hurt?

Driven by curiosity and the inability she had of letting anything go, she unlocked and opened the front door of the day spa and stuck her head out. "Hey."

Staring at the brick wall, he didn't turn her way or even glance over. He didn't do anything except to say "shh."

Oh, no. No, he did *not*, and she stepped outside to tell him what she thought of him and his *"shh"* and where he could put it. Sideways.

But with his gaze still on whatever was in front of him, he held up a hand, silently ordering her to stop where she was.

It was like he *wanted* her to lose her temper.

But then he was reaching out to the wall, and she realized over the noise of the storm that he was talking quietly to something.

Something that was growling at him fiercely.

"Don't be scared," he said softly. "I'm not going to hurt you, I promise."

The growling got a little louder, but Suits didn't back away, he just held eye contact with what sounded like a huge dog that Sadie still couldn't see in the dark shadows.

"Okay," Suits said. "Come here. Slowly."

Sadie realized with a start that he was talking to *her*. "What? No way. What is it?"

"Come closer and you'll see."

Damn him. And damn her insatiable curiosity because she stepped out from beneath the spa's overhang and immediately got wind and rain in her face for her efforts. Pulling out her cell phone, she accessed her flashlight app and aimed it at the wall.

"Don't," he said, wrapping his hand around her wrist, bringing the phone down to her side. "You'll scare it."

"Better that than getting eaten." She shrugged off his warm hand but went still when the growling upped a notch.

"I think it's hurt," Suits said. "Come here, baby," he coaxed gently. "Let me see."

Sadie bet that voice worked for him in the bedroom, but no way would it work here. And yet . . . the matted, drenched shadow scooted away from the wall, not nearly as large as she'd thought. Not a young puppy but not a grown dog either. Its tan-colored body was way too skinny, and amber eyes stared out from a black face. "Aw, looks like a young oversize pug," she murmured.

Suits shook his head. "Too big for a pug. It's probably got some bullmastiff in it though."

A skin-and-bones bullmastiff with only three legs, Sadie realized as it shifted closer, and her entire heart melted. "Oh my God." Moving toward it now without hesitation, she got only a few steps before the dog scrambled to escape her approach like a cat on linoleum, heading right at Suits.

With a surprised grunt, he fell to his ass on the wet cobblestones. "Okay," he said, hands up, backing up on those fine butt cheeks as if suddenly terrified of the dog trying to get into his lap. "Okay, see? You're safe now, right? Stay. Stay and sit."

The dog didn't stay. Or sit, for that matter. Instead, it leaned on Suits's bent legs, leaving dirty beige fur sticking to his pants.

He sucked in a breath and seemed to hold it. "I'd really like to be your person, but I can't."

"Arf!" Translation: *Too late, buddy, you're totally my person.*

"No, you don't understand," Suits said. "I literally *can't*."

Undeterred by this news, the dog continued to huddle close to his new human, even as that human shifted back, trying to avoid further contact.

Finally, Suits lifted his head and looked at Sadie. "Help."

Fascinated by this unexpected show of weakness in the man who'd always come off as invincible, she shook her head. "I think it thinks you're its mama."

He glanced around the courtyard as if to see who the dog might belong to, but there was no one.

"Arf!" the dog repeated and sat on Suits's foot.

"Oh, I hear you, and we're going to help you, I promise."

"I know you must mean you and the mouse in your pocket because *we*"—Sadie gestured with a finger between him and herself—"are most definitely not a *we*."

Ignoring that, he got to his feet, lifting his hands

at the dog, giving the universal gesture for *stay*. But the minute Suits raised his hands, the dog squeaked in terror and leapt back as if he'd been shoved. Off-balance with only three legs, it fell to its back, exposing its underbelly and the fact that *it* was a *she*.

Sadie didn't easily attach. To anything. But right then and there, she fell in love with her. Not partially, but all the way in love, because neglected and mistreated meant they were soul mates. "I'm going to kill her owner."

"Not if I get to them first." Suits's eyes flashed absolute fury, though his voice remained calm as he once again squatted low, trying to get his six-foot-plus frame as nonthreateningly small as he could. "It's okay, baby," he crooned softly. "We're together now, for better or worse, even if you're going to kill me."

"What are you talking about?" Sadie asked. "She wouldn't hurt a damn fly, much less kill you."

Proving that, the dog slowly once again scooted toward Suits, head down, her hind end a little wiggly as she crawled close, trying to get into his lap.

The sweet hope of it had Sadie's heart pretty much exploding in her chest.

With a sigh, Suits wrapped his arms around the dog and hugged her close. In response, the cutie-pie set her oversize head on his broad chest.

"Yeah, that's some killer," Sadie said, shoving her wet hair from her face.

"I'm allergic."

Suits said this so nonchalantly that she blinked. "Is that some sort of a euphemism for 'I hate dogs'?"

"No," he said. "Reach into my front left pocket."

She snorted. "You're kidding me, right? Does anyone actually fall for that?"

"If I pass out, you'll need my keys to play Nurse Nightingale."

She paused, staring at his face. She saw no sign that he was teasing—very unusual for the charming, easygoing guy she knew him to be.

"I'm trusting you to not let me die," he said as if he was discussing the weather.

"This isn't funny."

He met her gaze, his own more serious than she'd ever seen him. "If I don't make it, promise me you'll at least make up something really good for my funeral, okay? Like, I died heroically saving your sexy ass, and not because a sweet dog like this one hugged me."

"Okay," she said slowly, "I'm starting to think you're really not joking."

"I never joke about dying."

Chapter 2

#DogDays

Caleb Parker sat on the ground getting wetter by the second as the woman stared at him, her thoughts hooded. Rain had soaked through her gray sweater with the strategic cutouts, one across the top of her breasts and two others baring her shoulders, giving peekaboo hints of skin. Her jeans were jet-black and formfitting, hugged to her curves and tucked into a pair of high-heeled boots that gave a man ideas. Sexy-as-hell ideas. Her hair was half up and half down, the drenched strands teasing her cheeks, jaw, and shoulders. She wore enough earrings and bracelets to set off a metal detector.

Her name was Sadie Lane and she was spirited and

maybe also a little wild, but man. He never could take his eyes off of her.

Tonight though, he was distracted with the dog hugged up so close to his face that he was breathing in wet matted fur with each inhale. "My EpiPen's in my car," he said. "In the computer case on the passenger seat. Come on, you know you've been waiting for the opportunity to legally stab me."

Sadie shifted a little closer, every bit as wary as the dog. "You're making fun at a time like this?"

"What's the alternative?"

She shook her head. "If this is some sort of stupid come-on or something—"

"If this was a come-on, you'd know it."

She seemed massively unimpressed by this fact, her eyes deep and unreadable as always. And hey, maybe he'd only have an asthma attack. Maybe he wouldn't go into complete anaphylactic shock, in which case he'd only need his inhaler—currently also residing in his computer case. Which reminded him, he wasn't supposed to carry it in his case, it was supposed to be on his person. But it'd been years since he'd had any sort of serious asthma attack, even if the last one had landed him in the hospital practically on his deathbed. "I'm parked right out front," he said.

"You need more than an EpiPen if you think I'm going to reach into your pants pocket."

Rolling his eyes, he shifted the dog and pulled out the keys for her.

"If I do this, where am I supposed to jab you?"

"Upper thigh," he said.

"Not your ass?"

"Definitely not my ass."

She lifted her face to his. Raindrops were clinging to her long, dark lashes and glinting off the myriad of pretty little mismatched sparkling earrings she had running up the shell of her ear.

"Are you going to drop trou?" she asked.

He couldn't tell if she was asking with horror or fascination, and he let out a low laugh. "Not unless you take me to dinner first."

"Dream on, Suits."

And there it was, the reminder that she saw him as a know-it-all, a buttoned-up suit—literally—which he supposed was completely unappealing to the tattoo artist with the dark eyes, dark hair, and dark life. And he got it. They were polar opposites, not well suited, no pun intended.

And to be honest, he wished it was anyone out here in this storm with him tonight rather than the cynical smartass who seemed to take personal pleasure in driving him nuts.

They had some friends in common, so they ran into each other occasionally, and every time it was the same—an odd instant wariness he couldn't explain. There was also a healthy dose of irritation, at least on her end.

On his, it was mostly bafflement.

She stood there, hands on hips, probably waiting for him to stroke out. "You do realize that Lollipop's rubbing up against you and you're not sneezing or wheezing or anything, right?" she said.

"Lollipop?"

"It's the last thing I ate a *very* long time ago, and she seems as sweet as one," she said, still watching him carefully. "It fits. Are you or are you not dying?"

"You're hoping you get to use the EpiPen, aren't you?"

"Little bit," she said lightly, but her expression was still assessing, and actually, something else as well.

"You're worried about me," he said, surprised enough to smile. "Cute."

"Don't flatter yourself. I'm not worried, I just don't need you keeling over. I'd have to call Emergency Services and I'm not a fan of hospitals."

Well, they were in sync there. "I'm fine," he said,

a little shocked that it was true. Other than being drenched through and unable to feel his own frozen ass, he wasn't exhibiting any of the allergic reactions he'd been told all his life by his mom and four sisters he'd get if he allowed a dog to get too close.

Lollipop shivered and stared up at him with an expression that said she was maybe counting on him, which got him right in the feels. Interesting since he'd been utterly devoid of feels for longer than he could remember.

The thing was, he'd spent way too many of his own formative years as undersized, scared, weak, and vulnerable as Lollipop. Plus, of all the things he hated, including but not limited to tailgate drivers, loud chewers, and spam mail, people who abused animals were at the top of his list. He stood, still holding on to the dog. She was big enough to weigh at least fifty pounds, but skin and bones, she couldn't have been more than thirty. "Maybe I'm wearing too many clothes to get an allergic reaction."

"Your bare hands are on her and you have some fur stuck to your stubble," Sadie said. "Here, let me take her."

"No, I've got her. I'm feeling fine." For some reason, Sadie was the only woman on the planet who could set his head spinning without even trying. Some of it was a good spin, but most of it was a different sort of spin altogether, one that left him baffled and confused—two things he'd worked hard at never feeling. He pulled out his phone and snapped a pic of Lollipop that he could send to his contacts to see if anyone had any knowledge of her, before returning it to his pocket.

"I can't believe she just let you pick her up," Sadie said. "My boss, Rocco, said he'd seen a stray around, so I've been leaving out a bowl of water and food, but she must be waiting until we're gone to get to it. She doesn't trust humans." She cocked her head. "This would be a good time to tell me you're Batman or something."

"Batman's human."

She rolled her eyes. "My point is that you seem to have the touch." She sounded insultingly shocked at this.

"Hey," he said. "I have the touch in spades."

She laughed.

"Wow, you're judgy. I didn't see that coming."

"Excuse me?" She crossed her arms over her chest. "I'm the most un-judgy person on this entire planet."

He snorted and she looked taken aback for a quick beat, holding his gaze. Tendrils of her long, dark hair had slipped from her ponytail to cling to her face and throat. She had some blue streaks in it that matched her striking dark blue eyes. Yesterday, the streaks had been purple. The month before they'd been red. Her sparkling earrings caught the light and softened her edginess slightly—a fact he was sure she wouldn't appreciate. He knew this because all his life he'd soaked up the details of everything around him, categorizing the tidbits into his brain's filing system. Most people thought this trait defined him as a nerd at best, a weirdo at worst. He'd never cared much what people thought, although if he was being honest, he wouldn't mind his early childhood tormentors and bullies seeing his current placement on the *Forbes* Top 100.

But whatever Sadie thought of him, he knew she had to be drawn to him on some level because she always seemed to run into him.

Although that might've been wishful thinking on his part.

"Look, it seems like Lollipop's claimed you. I'm just surprised by that since . . ."

"Since . . . ?"

"Since you don't seem the maternal type. Or the kind of man who'd get emotionally attached." Her words hung in the suddenly tension-filled air.

"You think I don't have emotions or the ability to attach?" he asked.

"Maybe it takes one to know one."

His phone had been having a seizure in his pocket as the dog huddled up against his chest, eyes revealing a haunted hollowness that said she'd been through hell. And then there was the woman standing in front of him with . . . damn . . . the same haunted hollowness.

Uncomfortable with both, he shifted closer, hoping he wasn't risking certain death. "I've got to go." Soon as he figured out how to bring the dog to a business dinner with his attorney and not croak at the table.

Sadie held out her hands. "I'll take her."

Here was the thing. Caleb was more allergic to accepting *help* than he was to dogs and that went way back, deeply ingrained from a time he hated to revisit. The women in his life considered this a huge flaw in his system. He considered it just good sense. When he hesitated to let go, Sadie gave him a long look.

"You've gotta go," she said. "Don't worry, I'll take good care of her, dry her off, check for injuries, feed her, keep her warm. And anyway, if you're 'allergic'"—she put the word in air quotes—"you don't need the hassle. Have you ever even had a pet?"

"No."

"Not even a family pet?"

He shook his head, and he'd have sworn she actually felt sorry for him at that. He looked down at the dog, still staring up at him with those sweet amber eyes as if she totally trusted him, and again something pinched inside his chest.

PLAYING FOR KEEPS • 23

"She'll be fine with me for the night," Sadie said. "You have stuff to do, like world domination or something."

He opened his mouth to protest, which made no sense at all, but she took Lollipop, and with a look he wasn't equipped to read, she vanished inside the day spa.

Sadie walked through the darkened spa, holding Lollipop as close as the thing would allow. "That was a close call," she murmured softly. "You almost had to go home with a boy."

Lollipop licked her chin.

"Aw, thank you. I bet you're chilly. It's a cold night already." Sadie grabbed her discarded scarf from the employee room and wrapped it around the too-skinny dog, holding her to her chest for extra warmth. "There, how's that?"

Lollipop blinked slow as an owl, remaining a little stiff in Sadie's arms, and she had to laugh. "You *wanted* to stay with Suits, didn't you?" She shook her head. "Trust me on this, a hot-looking package like that who's too smart for his own good and who's never had a single taste of failure . . ." She shook her head. "He's pedigree. A purebred. And you and me, we're mutts."

Lollipop sighed and Sadie could hear the disappointment. "Fine. You liked him better than me. I get it." There'd definitely been something about the way his arms had so carefully and gently held the dog that had opened Sadie up to him for a moment. But only for a moment.

She startled at the sound of a knock on the front door. Peering out into the stormy night, she saw the tall, dark, and drenched Caleb Parker and reluctantly opened up. "What?"

He smiled, and this disconcerted her until she realized he was smiling at Lollipop.

Not her.

And Lollipop was bicycling her three paws like crazy, trying to ride the air over to him.

"Can I?" he asked, but then reached out and took Lollipop without waiting for a response.

The dog immediately set her head on Caleb's shoulder and Sadie saw something she had never seen before.

Caleb Parker softening.

She was shocked. She'd never seen any sign of softness from him, ever. Amusement, yes. Cynicism, yes. Charm, yes. And on top of all of that, there was also always a sense of impenetrable . . . maleness. He was at the top of the food chain and he knew it. Since she had no idea what that was like, it put her at a disadvantage, which in turn made her feel on edge. "Maybe she's drawn to your perfume," she said.

"I don't wear perfume."

"You sure?" She sniffed. "Because you definitely smell like . . ."

A very sexy guy, dammit. No matter what she told herself, she was not indifferent to him, not even close. In fact, she was hugely attracted and didn't know what to do with the unexpected rush of heat he always caused.

He gave her a look, silently daring her to speak her thoughts. As if she would. "Expensive," she finally said.

He laughed. *Laughed.* "Don't judge me by my clothes," he said mildly and snuggled the dog close.

Snuggled. The dog. Close.

A phone buzzed. Hers this time. Thinking it was just her mom, she pulled the phone from her pocket to hit ignore but it wasn't her mom. It was a text from her first tattoo client of the night. She was letting Sadie know she was nearly at the Canvas Shop. She shrugged. "Having a job's great until you actually have to go," she quipped, tucking her phone back into her pocket.

Caleb kissed the top of Lollipop's bedraggled head. "You're going to be okay."

She licked his nose. "Ruining your breed's badass image," he teased. "Remember to guard the pretty lady for me, okay?"

"The pretty lady guards herself," Sadie said.

Caleb, still looking into Lollipop's eyes, smiled. "Yeah, she's as badass as you are and I've got no doubt she can take care of herself, but have her six anyway, alright?" He ruffled Lollipop's fur. "I'm counting on you."

"Hand her over," she said. "We both have to go." When he hesitated, she leaned in. "Is that a rash on your neck?" She pretended to take a closer look, when instead she was trying to inhale that unique scent that might as well be orgasm in a damn bottle. "Yeah," she murmured, "it is. Is your tongue getting thick? Are you breathing funny? You are, right? Gimme your keys."

Caleb gave her an impressive eye roll and handed her Lollipop.

"Why did you come back anyway?" she asked.

He pulled money from one of his pockets and handed it over to her.

"Whoa," she said, taking a step back. "What the actual hell?"

"For Lollipop. Food, bed, whatever."

"I don't need your money."

Taking advantage of her full hands, he stuffed the money into one of her front jeans pockets. The sensation of his fingers sliding in made her go utterly still as their gazes met.

And held.

And then, with a self-mocking half smile, as if he was in on a joke that she'd missed, he turned and vanished into the night.

Several hours later, Sadie had finished with her clients and was curled up with Lollipop in the Canvas Shop with a bag of popcorn she'd nuked in the back room. Nothing said self-care more than absurd amounts of ranch-flavored popcorn with extra butter. She was happily munching through it when she got a text from a number that wasn't recognized by her phone. It said:

Proof of life pic?

Suits. Wanting to finish her *How I Met Your Mother* episode on her laptop first, she ignored him. The problem was that TV shows like this often made her feel as if everyone could come clean with their real feelings, but in reality people swallowed their feelings and let them rot them from the inside out.

So she switched it up to a murder documentary. "Nothing better than cuddling with your dog and watching stories about people getting their heads cut off with a steak knife," she told Lollipop.

Ten minutes later she got another text.

When someone doesn't text me back within five minutes, I assume they're dead and will send out the proper authorities.

Sadie snorted, snapped a pic of a freshly bathed and fed and sleeping Lollipop, and texted it back to him. She then entered him into her contacts as Do Not Even Think About Falling For This Guy.

Not thirty minutes later she was scrolling through Instagram when she saw a pic that Ivy had liked. It'd been posted by one Caleb Parker. It was the one he'd taken of Lollipop in the courtyard earlier with the caption: *Was mugged tonight by this vicious killer and fell for her hard. Not sure what I've gotten myself into . . .*

Sadie found herself smiling and ordered herself to stop it. Because the truth was, she wasn't sure what she'd gotten herself into either.

Chapter 3

#TemptationWalking

Since he wasn't dying, at least not tonight, Caleb made his dinner meeting at a restaurant in the financial district with his attorney, who also happened to be one of his four sisters. The restaurant had a view of the bay and great food, but his mind wasn't on either.

Hannah looked at him in shock. "Why are you all wet?"

"Because it's raining."

"Smartass." She handed him a stack of files and ate his nachos while he signed several new contracts for various partnership and new venture agreements.

"Could've done this in the office in the morning," he said, pushing the files back to her.

"But then I couldn't have eaten your nachos."

"I pay you a fortune. You can buy your own nachos anytime."

She shook her head. "My own nachos would come with calories. If I eat yours, the calories don't count because they're yours. You see?"

He stared at her. "Where did you get your law degree again? Online?"

"You know where. Stanford. Because you paid for it." She scooped his last chip, stuck it in her mouth, and licked the cheese off her thumb. "Thanks for that, by the way. How's Naoki?"

"Going to see him after this."

"Long day," she murmured.

"They all are. I'm fine," he added when she started to open her mouth again.

"But—"

"Hannah." He put his hand over hers. "We dreamed of this, remember? Of not living week to week? And here we are."

She let the worry drain from her eyes and smiled. "And here we are."

Thirty minutes later, Caleb hit his last stop of the day. This one was personal, and something he did as often as he could. The steep streets were no joke in the Russian Hill neighborhood, not that he could get a spot on the street if he wanted one. He pulled into the small alley spot reserved for him next to a Victorian building, took a deep breath, and headed inside.

The woman at the reception counter smiled in welcome. "Mr. Parker, he's waiting up for you."

"Caleb," he said, as he did every time. "How's he doing?"

Her smile faded a little. "Depends on the day. You got today's doctor's report?"

"Yes." And it hadn't been good. "He's comfortable?"

"Absolutely," she said with conviction and he nodded with relief and headed down the hall.

The old mansion had been renovated several times in the past hundred years, most recently about five years ago, and turned into a very cushy top-notch retirement home.

One of the night nurses met him in the hallway. "Just brought him his tea," she reported. "Thanks for having it sent special from the UK, since we couldn't find it here for him." She patted his arm. "Don't worry, it came in anonymously. Your secret's safe, Mr. Parker."

"Caleb," he said. "And how did you know I'd sent the tea?"

"Because I've seen you with him. You'd do anything for him." She paused. "Including buying this facility and renovating it to higher specs for specific needs so you could ensure the best possible home in which to keep him safe." She smiled. "He's lucky to have you."

Actually, she had that backward. Caleb had been lucky to have Naoki in his life. When the nurse continued on her way down the hallway, he entered the room.

The old man was sitting in the chair in front of the window, a throw blanket across his legs. He turned and eyed Caleb with suspicion. "Who are you?"

A pang pierced through Caleb, the same pang he got every single time at that question. Why, he had no idea. Naoki hadn't remembered him at first sight in at least two years.

Caleb stepped into the room. He'd left his still-wet suit jacket and tie in the car. He unbuttoned his shirt and pulled it off.

The old man's gaze dropped to Caleb's torso, slowly taking in the tattoos. Naoki had many himself, a lot more than Caleb, but the living trees on the backs of their left shoulders were a near-identical match. So was the Japanese character just beneath them. Naoki, whose name literally meant *tree*, smiled at the sight of it, which cut through the barriers of dementia and age-battered memories.

Caleb returned the smile and shrugged back into his shirt, covering his own family emblem on the inside of his left bicep and the lettering down his right side that read *Carpe Diem*. He took one of the chairs at the small table near the bed and brought it to the window, then turned it around to straddle it as he eyed his old sensei.

"I know you?" Naoki asked, his voice tremulous with age.

Caleb nodded. Once upon a time, Naoki had saved his life. Actually, he'd saved Caleb's life many times over if he was keeping count. And Caleb always kept count.

"You have some of the same tattoos as I do," Naoki said.

"Yes."

"You're . . ." The old man's eyes crinkled with a smile. "You're the boy who ran into my dojo because other boys, bigger and meaner boys, were chasing him."

Hating the memory, Caleb nodded.

"You were beat all to shit," Naoki remembered. "You had no idea how to defend yourself."

Caleb nodded again. *"Beat all to shit"* was putting it mildly given that he'd had a broken arm, a battered face, and a concussion—that time.

"I taught you to fight," Naoki said.

"You did. It took a while." He'd been small. And asthmatic. And weak.

"You're big and strong now," Naoki said, eyeing Caleb's build. "I bet no one messes with you anymore." He seemed pleased by this. "What became of you? I never saw you again."

This wasn't true. Caleb had gone to that dojo every single day that year. And the next year. And the year after that. He'd learned discipline, he'd learned self-control, he'd learned so damn much from this very small, very frail man that it hurt his heart to be here.

But he came anyway. Because once upon a time, this man had been everything in Caleb's small life, and now for the rest of his, he'd want for nothing. "Do you need another blanket?" Caleb asked. "Are you warm enough?"

Naoki waved this off. "Tell me about my dojo. No one here can tell me anything about my life, and—" He shook his head. "I can't remember. The dojo's still there, yes?"

"Yes, and it's very successful." Only a partial lie. Naoki had been forced to sell the dojo back when Caleb had been seventeen due to financial problems in a downturned market and shitty economy. The place had been turned into a gym and gone through many owners before Caleb had been able to buy it back almost a decade ago.

Naoki yawned. His eyes drifted shut and his head fell forward.

Caleb watched him sleep for a few minutes and then stood up to help him into bed. The minute he moved, Naoki's eyes flew open and once again narrowed on him.

"Who are you and what do you want?" he demanded.

A nurse entered the room before Caleb could speak. Naoki pointed at him. "I told you, no male nurses!"

She smiled easily at Naoki. "I'm sorry, sir, but he's not—"

"No worries." Caleb moved to the door. "I'll leave you in good hands. Sleep well." He paused in the hallway, reminding himself he'd gotten a good five minutes this time. It was more than he'd had in months.

Not ready to go home, he ended up at his offices, which occupied a ten-story building in the financial district. All was quiet and mostly dark. He encouraged his employees to go home after eight hours. It had nothing to do with paying overtime and everything to do with making sure his entire team had a life, which was hopefully made easier by generous benefits packages, including paid leave for philanthropy efforts.

His office was on the tenth floor. He went straight

to the tall windows overlooking the city and wondered where Sadie and Lollipop were now. Were they dry and fed?

And why did he care?

He was rubbing his aching forehead when he heard someone come into his office.

"You look exhausted."

He turned to face his oldest sister, Sienne, who was his right hand when it came to work.

And his left. "I'm fine," he said, wondering how many times a day he told that to one sister or another. "And busy," he said pointedly.

She snorted and came in. "You'd say you were fine even if you had a limb falling off. When you were little and bullied all the way home from school, you'd stagger into the house bleeding at seven years old and say you were 'fine.' When you were so sick you couldn't get enough air in your lungs, leaving you with black circles under your eyes and perpetually short of breath, you were 'fine.' And now, these days, with your world worth so much and a billion balls in the air at all times, you're still 'fine.'"

"And I'm neither bleeding nor wheezing for breath," he said.

"I'll call Mom if I have to."

He dropped his head and laughed while rubbing

the back of his neck. "I'm thirty-two and you're forty, and you're really going to call Mom and tattle on me?"

"Hey," Sienne said, "I'm thirty-nine for two more months and you know it, so say *forty* again and die. And yeah, I'd call Mom. She's the only one who could ever talk any sense into you."

"Mom's on that cruise in Greece, the first vacation we've talked her into ever. Leave her out of this."

"*You* talked her into it by buying her the ticket and guilting her into going by saying you didn't want the money to go to waste." Sienne gave him a reluctant smile. "Which was incredibly deceptive of you. I feel so proud. It was also sweet, given that you spend a fortune supporting all of us these days."

"You earn your keep," Caleb said. "But even if you didn't, it's my turn, remember? I was a hell of a burden on you guys." For years. And he could say they'd all moved on without being scarred, but he'd be lying. He knew this was where his inability to accept help or let anyone take care of him in any way came from. He took care of himself these days, thank you very much. "I'll never forget all you did for me."

She set her head on his shoulder and together they both stared out the large window at the San Francisco night. "You were never a burden, Caleb."

He shook his head. "The doctor and hospital bills said otherwise, as did Mom's bankruptcy."

"You were a preemie with medical problems, and then an asthmatic little kid who wheezed for every breath and was beat up for it, and when I think about those days," she said, fisting her hands, "I *still* want to murder people."

"Sienne."

"Well, I do," she said fiercely, her hand entangling with his. "I know you work so hard because you want to give back to us. You think we sacrificed so much for you—"

"You did."

"What we Parkers do for each other, we do out of love," she said, voice still iron. "And don't you dare taint it by suggesting you owe us."

"Sienne—"

"No. And one more thing before I shut up. None of what happened when you were young, not you being sick and not us barely being able to afford your medical care, none of it was your fault."

He squeezed her fingers and met her gaze. "It wasn't any of yours either, and yet you all put your life on hold for me." They'd done whatever they'd had to, including working as many jobs as it took to keep them all together.

Sienne opened her mouth, but he pointed at her. "You promised to shut up now."

"I lied."

"Knew it was too good to be true."

She smiled. "I'll change the subject to work, how's that? Two things. You're updated with today's progress and tomorrow's meetings." She nodded to the iPad on his desk. "Check your files for all the reports."

She was his director of operations. Not an easy job, and neither was working for him. But compared to some of the things they'd been through together, the job and his business were a walk in the park. "Thanks."

"Just trying to earn my ridiculously high paycheck," she said. "Don't want to be a burden, or have you sacrificing resources for your sister."

He slid her a glance. "Sarcasm?"

"No. Irony. I don't want to ever hear again that you feel guilty thinking we sacrificed for you. Are you going to tell me what's wrong?"

"Nothing's wrong."

She studied him a beat. "I think you actually believe that." She shook her head. "But I see a restlessness in you lately. You're not happy."

He turned back to the window, uncomfortable that she could read him so well. "I'm not *unhappy*."

Her voice softened. "You're working too hard. You logged something like eighty hours last week. You need to pass some of that work down to the rest of us. Take some time for yourself."

"I'll think about it."

"You always say that," she said. "You need to stop thinking and do."

"You need a life too."

"I've got one," she said with a secret little smile that told him things were going well with her husband, Niles. "It's your turn."

He thought of Sadie in the courtyard tonight, hair and clothes plastered to her with rain, her eyes holding all her secrets. She was as independent as they came, fiercely so, and didn't need anyone. That was damn attractive to a man like himself. And then, as if he'd conjured her up, his phone buzzed with an incoming FaceTime call from her, making his heart leap. "I've got to take this."

Sienne nodded and headed for the door. Turning his back on her, he answered and found Lollipop staring at him through the screen. She was dry and her eyes were bright, tongue lolling. She seemed much happier than she had earlier.

"She wanted to say goodnight," came Sadie's amused

voice. "I told her that you were likely out on the town with a date, living the high life to match your suit, but she still wanted a goodnight kiss from Daddy."

Caleb smiled. "Are you using our child to ask if I'm seeing someone?"

Sadie's face appeared behind the dog's. She too was dry, though she didn't seem nearly as happy to see him as Lollipop. "I'm most definitely not asking," she said.

He smiled.

"I'm not!" she exclaimed. "I don't care if you're seeing someone."

His smile widened.

She pointed at him. "Knock it off. It's absolutely none of my business who you're with."

"Because you don't like me, right?"

"Oh good, you know. That makes it way less awkward."

He laughed, but at the sound behind him, he had to shake his head. He should've known nosy-as-hell Sienne wouldn't actually leave.

"Um, don't look now," Sadie said, eyes on something over his shoulder. "But there's a woman behind you wearing an expression that says maybe you *are* on a date."

"Ignore her," he said.

"Don't be rude." Sienne pushed her way in closer to look at Sadie. "I'm Sienne Parker, Caleb's sister. And you are . . . ?"

"Now who's being rude?" Caleb murmured. "Sadie, my sister Sienne. Sienne, this is Sadie, who works in the Pacific Pier Building."

"So this is about . . . work?" Sienne asked.

"No," Caleb said and didn't further explain, hoping to cut off his sister's curiosity at the knees. "And you were just leaving, remember?"

"Yes, but I forgot to give you this." Sienne handed him a food container and a fork. "My famous home-made baked mac and cheese."

He slid her a look. "You know I'm not ten anymore, right?"

"Physically, no. Mentally?" She smiled. "There are whole days . . ."

He snorted and took the container *and* the gesture for what it was. The mac and cheese was his comfort food, always had been. There'd been times when they'd lived off boxed mac and cheese because it'd been cheap. When things had gotten better, Sienne had learned to make it from scratch, though these days she usually had to be bribed to do so.

Sienne gave him a long look he couldn't quite decipher and left.

"Arf!"

Lollipop was back on the screen, demanding attention. Caleb certainly had enough women in his life demanding attention, but he felt a pinch in the region of his heart and smiled at her. "Hey, baby, how you doing?"

Sadie poked her head around Lollipop's. "We'd be doing better if someone had made *us* mac and cheese."

"I deliver," he said without thinking and . . . the call disconnected and his screen went dark.

Sadie grimaced and shoved her phone into her pocket. "He was going through a tunnel," she told Lollipop. "Bad connection."

Her phone buzzed.

Crap.

She pulled the phone back out of her pocket and looked at the screen. Do Not Even Think About Falling For This Guy was FaceTiming.

She bit her lower lip. "Dammit," she said and answered. "I've got bad reception."

"Clearly," Caleb said dryly.

He was still in his office, a big-ass fancy one at that, with floor-to-ceiling windows behind him and an incredible view of the city at night. And he was kicked back in his chair, coat and tie gone, sleeves rolled up, eating the mac and cheese, and making her mouth water.

"Wow," she said, going for sarcasm rather than revealing how it'd felt to get a glimpse into his and his sister's relationship, which seemed far more real and open and honest than she'd ever had with any of her family. "Spoiled much? I mean you can get a box of mac and cheese for what, a buck?"

But her teasing quip had the very opposite effect than she'd imagined. Caleb's face closed up to her, including his warm eyes and contagious smile. All gone in a blink.

"You don't know enough about me to go there," he said lightly.

"Go where exactly?" she asked. "I was just teasing."

"You were judging. Again."

Since that might very well be true, she shut her mouth and put Lollipop back in front of her. "Just say goodnight."

"Because, let me guess, you have to go."

Okay, so he was onto her. Still, she held his gaze and stood her ground because holding her ground, small as it might be, was what she did. "I do have to go, I've got an early morning. And . . ." She blew out a sigh. "I'm sorry. For hanging up on you."

"But not for the judging?"

Dammit. "Maybe a little for the judging. But I'm not going to lie," she said. "I'm probably not done judging you. I mean I'll try to work on it, but it'll be a process."

His mouth quirked. "Fair enough."

"And you're sorry too, right?"

"For . . . ?"

"For assuming the worst of me when I was just kidding around."

He stared at her for a beat. "I do tend to assume the worst and then go to a dark place to mull that worst over." He paused and some amusement came back into his eyes. "I'll try to work on it."

She gave him a small smile of her own. "It's okay. I've been to some pretty dark places myself." An understatement. A huge understatement. And why she'd even told him such a thing about herself, she had no idea. It made her itchy because really, what the hell was she doing? Flirting with him? It sure felt a whole lot like exactly that and this made her even itchier.

Flirting led to intimacy, even love. But she'd never been loved for who she really was and she was pretty sure she never would be. So she wasn't about to go looking for it, and in fact she probably wouldn't even recognize it if it hit her in the face. It was why she'd given up on men three years ago. And in those three years, she'd not found herself interested, not once.

She'd promised herself she'd take a long break from hurting people and getting hurt. She'd needed to figure out her own shit.

And yet here she was, tempted by a hot smile. "I've really gotta go." And this time when she disconnected, she also turned off her phone to avoid any further temptation.

A temptation she hadn't seen coming.

Chapter 4

#SharkTank

When Caleb finally dropped into bed at midnight, he was reeling in a lot of ways, not the least of which was why he couldn't take his mind off a certain pair of deep, haunting eyes.

Not the dog's, though her eyes had been pretty great.

But Sadie . . . Sadie and that wary, hooded, steely blue gaze that said *don't get too close.*

It made him want to do just that.

It was confusing. They'd had interactions in the past, none of which had been anything like tonight. She was both what he'd expected and also . . . not at all what he'd expected. He'd seen a side of her that he'd never seen before, that fierce protectiveness over Lollipop, as well as her own vulnerability—which she'd done her best to cover up with a toughness and a sarcasm that he knew and expected.

The night had been one surprise after another. He'd forgotten to ask Sienne or Hannah why he hadn't been allergic to the dog. He supposed it was possible he'd simply outgrown the allergy. The bigger question was . . . what was he going to do about this strange and bewildering and undeniable attraction he had for one Sadie Lane?

It was four a.m. when he gave up on the pretense of sleep. He checked his phone because yes, his world started early, but he was really just hoping for another pic from Sadie.

Nothing.

He wasn't big on social media. He didn't use Facebook or Twitter, but he had an Instagram account so he could keep up with his family and friends, and occasionally post, as he had last night. He searched for Sadie and found her account.

It was filled with her own sketches and pictures of the tattoos she created.

Her work stunned him. She was an incredible artist.

But there was nothing about her personally, and nothing more on Lollipop. He then got distracted by a text from his cousin Kel. They were the same age and had gone to school together through fifth grade. When Kel's mom had been tragically killed, Kel and his sisters had been shipped off to relatives in Sunshine, Idaho. Kel was now a small-town sheriff and rancher who worked even more than Caleb did, if that was possible. They tended to keep in touch via short, usually obnoxiously rude texts.

KEL: **I suppose you already banked seven figures on the day that's barely begun.**

CALEB: And I suppose you've already chased a few cows away from the single intersection in Sunshine.

KEL: **Going for donuts next. My work's never done . . .**

CALEB: You're going to go soft. Hope your women don't mind.

KEL: **I'll show you soft next time we step into the ring.**

Caleb was grinning when he switched to work, making his way through a long list of e-mails that had come in overnight. He employed entrepreneurs, investment bankers, financial advisers, research analysts, investors, business process developers, and more all over the world. After skimming through, checking in on various projects, he scanned through the day's headlines for articles, interested mostly in his portfolio companies, competitors, and the industry in general.

Since he was by now wide-awake, he checked in on Naoki's status and then hit the gym for a quick workout. He'd renovated the place, but hadn't returned it to the dojo it'd once been because it wouldn't be the same without Naoki's presence. He had a few different sparring partners. Today it was Spence. They'd met a decade ago in the government think tank they'd both been recruited to right from college, and had gone on to be occasional business partners.

But today they were partners of a different sort. They each had thirty minutes, and they used every one of them in the ring pummeling the shit out of each other. They were both trained in martial arts and fairly evenly matched, but today Spence was taking a beating. When he hit the floor for the third time in a row, Caleb stood over him, hands on hips. "What's wrong with you?"

Spence grimaced and remained flat on his back. "I don't know."

"I bet I do." Caleb stepped back. "You and Colbie ran off and got hitched in the Bahamas and stayed there for two weeks. You've got honeymoon-itis. Translation, you've had your brains—and brawn—fucked out."

Spence grinned up at him unabashedly. "Good deduction, Sherlock."

Caleb shook his head and turned away. "You're no good here. A twelve-year-old could take you today—"

That was the last word he uttered before Spence hooked a foot around his ankle and tugged. In the next breath, Caleb was eating the mat.

"You were saying?" Spence asked mildly, still flat on his back.

"Shit." Caleb stared up at the ceiling and had to laugh. "We've both lost our minds."

"Well we know where mine went. What's your excuse and does it have anything to do with that cutie-pie tattoo artist?"

Ignoring the question, Caleb rose to his feet.

"It does," Spence said smugly as he stood too. "Colbie said that Molly said that Elle said she saw you in the courtyard with Sadie last night in the rain looking pretty cozy." He made a move to once again knock Caleb's feet out from under him, but Caleb struck first and leveled Spence flat.

"Touchy." Spence gasped and sucked air back into

his lungs. "And also, I *am* right. I love being right." He sat up, holding his hands out in front of him, signaling a peace treaty. "Look, it's been a while since you've had a woman in your life, right? And I'm not talking about that hot start-up CEO in New York you hooked up with last month or the sexy pilot you boinked for like a week the month before that. I'm talking about someone you attempted to keep around and be with—out of bed as well as in it. And trust me, I know. It's not easy."

Caleb knew that Spence was referring to the troubles he'd had before he'd met Colbie. Women had come after him for either his connections or money. Caleb too had some of that in his past, but he had a secret weapon called The Coven—aka, his sisters. Ever since a woman had stalked him years ago after a blind date, they'd taken to vetting anyone new in his life to within an inch of theirs. They'd become professional stalkers, weeding out the bad seeds with an eager ruthlessness that would've scared Caleb if they hadn't been on his side.

"But it's no reason to just give up on any kind of a real relationship," Spence said.

"Marriage isn't for all of us."

"I get it," Spence said. "You're opposed to daily sex and someone fawning over you day and night."

Caleb gave him a *get real* look. "Colbie 'fawns' over you day and night, huh?" He pulled out his phone. "Let's just ask her . . ."

Spence winced and pushed Caleb's phone down. "Christ, don't call her. Okay, so maybe she doesn't fawn. Maybe sometimes she wants to kill me. Whatever. It's still a lot of sex, man."

And sex was good. Actually, sex was great. For a while after Caleb had first found success, women had suddenly wanted a piece of him. And after being the asthmatic geeky loser all his life, he'd definitely made the most of it. But eventually he'd realized it wasn't about him, but about what he could do for someone, and that had gotten old.

It wasn't as if he yearned for someone to take care of him. That was the last thing he wanted. So he'd taken a step back and now he didn't even really see the opportunities anymore. He just sort of flirted and charmed his way through life, and he was good with that.

A trainer had come through and tossed them each a towel. "I wouldn't mind having a lot of sex," he said wistfully. "There's this woman who comes in for weight training and she acts like she's into me, but I never know how to start a conversation with her without looking like the annoying dude trying to hit on her while she works out."

"You could always drop a weight on your foot and ask her to take you to the hospital," Spence said.

"Or," Caleb said, "you could let me drop a weight on your head, seeing as you must have forgotten that I expect you to never hit on a woman in this gym where you work, *ever.*"

The guy winced and nodded like a bobblehead. "Right. Got it. Okay, I'm just gonna . . ." He gestured vaguely to another area of the gym and scampered off.

Spence slid him a look. "Not a bad idea, you know. Sadie's come here before, right? You could drop a weight on your foot and—"

"Shut up."

"Or on your head," Spence said.

"Okay, we're done here." Caleb exited the ring.

"Hey, I'm just trying to be helpful—"

"You're the opposite of helpful, Spence."

"You could just wish on the fountain in my building."

Spence owned the Pacific Pier Building, and hell no would Caleb be wishing on it. Setting aside that the fountain was only one hundred feet from where Sadie worked, there was also the myth associated with that fountain that said if you wished for true love with a true heart, it'd be granted. It'd happened to enough people he knew to be worrisome, including Spence and Colbie.

So yeah, he'd be staying *far* away from that fountain.

He took a quick shower in the locker room, dressed for his workday, and then headed to the Pacific Pier Building, making a quick stop and a phone call. Walking through the cobblestone courtyard, he stared at the fountain. It wasn't that he had anything against the idea of love. Exactly. But love tended to come with things like responsibility and an openness he didn't have time for right now.

He knew what he was worth monetarily. He had accountants for that and reports. What he didn't know and couldn't tangibly measure or print a spreadsheet for was what he was worth *emotionally*. By his own calculations, not much.

Not that it mattered, since he wasn't going there. As for where he *was* going with this inexplicable attraction to Sadie, he had no clue. So much for being a so-called genius.

The day spa wasn't open yet, and neither was the Canvas Shop. But he could see a glow of low light coming through the slats in the drawn shades.

Someone was in there. It wouldn't be the shop's owner. It was only six thirty a.m. and Rocco had never met a morning he liked. Caleb stepped closer to the window and cupped his hands around his eyes for a better look.

The interior of the tattoo shop was unique, which lent to its success. The place was done up in soft warm soothing colors, the walls filled with the artwork of the artists who worked there. There was a half wall separating out a waiting/reception area with comfy love seats and a coffee table with tattoo art books and magazines. A glass-front refrigerator was against one wall, filled with water, juices, sodas, and snacks, available to all. Beyond the half wall was the work area. There were six lux chair beds, three on one side of the room, three on the other. The overhead lighting was a combination of hanging open lanterns and strings of white lights that gave off both a warm glow and enough light to work efficiently.

He could just barely see the lower half of the worktable in Sadie's corner. And a leg and a bare foot with midnight blue toenails and a tiny delicate silver ring around one of those toes.

Sadie.

Caleb hesitated before knocking, not wanting to startle her. But he was on borrowed time, so in the end, he knocked as lightly as he could.

The foot jerked.

Barking sounded.

Then the foot hit the floor, attached to the rest of the body that came with it.

Sadie, wearing loose-fitting black pj bottoms with skulls all over them, a heart-stopping pale gray camisole top, and a deranged expression on her face that said she'd been sleeping and sleeping deeply and was slightly confused.

The dog at her feet wasn't. Lollipop caught sight of Caleb and came running toward the window at a surprising speed given she was working with only three legs. She scratched at the door to get to him, wide-awake and clearly trying to bark the situation under control.

Sadie continued to just stare at him as if in a stupor, making no move toward the door.

Clearly she was sleeping in the shop for whatever reason, and he wished he knew why. If he came right out and asked, he knew she'd shut down so he did his best to look nonthreatening. He held up the two coffee to-go cups he'd picked up from the courtyard coffee place. He sipped one, licked his lips, and smiled enticingly.

Apparently caffeine was the way to her heart, because that's what got her moving to the door. When she turned back for a moment, as if to look and see if he'd been able to watch her sleeping, he caught sight of a small, almost dainty infinity sign tattooed on the back of her shoulder. Then she was holding his gaze again as she unlocked and opened the door.

"What the actual hell," she said, voice thick and raspy.

And sexy. He could see more of her than he ever had before, including the pretty script tattooed around her ankle. Thanks to his prescription sunglasses he was able to read, *The things that make me different . . .* That was all he caught before the words wrapped around her ankle out of sight, but he knew the quote from Winnie the Pooh.

The things that make me different are the things that make me . . .

Caleb set down the coffees on the magazine table and hunkered low to greet Lollipop. She was maybe thirty pounds of pure happiness given how she wriggled all over, trying to get closer to him.

"It's the middle of the night," Sadie said.

Caleb opened his mouth to speak, and was French-kissed by Lollipop. "Thanks," he said and then spoke to Sadie. "It's six thirty."

"Like I said, middle of the night. Why are you here?"

"Couldn't sleep."

"So you thought you'd make sure I couldn't either?"

He handed her one of the two hot coffees and found himself amused when she snatched at it like it was the elixir of life. After a few deep pulls of the magic potion, she drew a deep breath and let it out.

"So," he said. "Not a morning person, huh?"

"I would be if mornings started at noon." She drank deeply again and the rest of the fog faded from her eyes, replaced by surprise. "You added the exact right amount of vanilla cream."

He nodded.

She was watching him carefully. "Feels like a bribe."

He raised a brow. "Why would I need to bribe you?"

"I don't know. You tell me."

Still balanced on the balls of his feet with the dog plastered up against the front of him, he shrugged. "I wanted to see you."

"You mean you wanted to see Lollipop?"

He lifted his gaze and met hers. "Her too. And I'm not sold on that name."

"She's a stray. What would a guy like you care about her name?"

He paused, stroking Lollipop, learning how she liked to be touched—which was basically in every way possible. "A name's important. Has she eaten?"

"Yes," she said. "About four times her weight. Then she pooped twice that."

Caleb rubbed his jaw to the top of Lollipop's soft

head, which she tucked into his neck. "You bathed her," he said.

"To help warm her up last night. We showered together. It was quite the adventure."

Annnnnnnddd now he was picturing her in the shower. Lollipop squirmed to be freed and he let her go.

She immediately set about chasing her tail. She bashed into a wall and then a chair, which didn't slow her down.

"Why is she chasing her tail?" he asked.

"Because she can."

Lollipop stopped chasing her tail and toppled over. She panted for a few beats and then . . . went back to doing wheelies, stopping every few circles to smile up at him. She was excited to see him, he realized, and while she continued to go absolutely bonkers, he felt that same odd tightening in the region of his chest as he had last night. When she toppled over again, he scooped her up.

She immediately started swimming through the air with her three legs, trying to get to his face, so he pulled her closer. She settled right in and set her head on his shoulder, and his heart rolled over and exposed its underbelly. He actually didn't even know what to do with all the feelings. How the hell did people do this?

"I thought I'd take her to get checked out," he said. "Make sure she's okay, and then—"

"I'm not giving her back to whatever asshole deserted her on the streets," Sadie said.

"Agreed. But I want to get her to a vet and go from there."

"How are you going to get her into a vet this early?"

"I've got her an appointment at seven."

She just stared at him. "I can't have this conversation in my pj's."

"And you're in your pj's because . . . ?"

"Give me five minutes," she said instead of answering.

He had no idea what kind of conversation required a change of clothing, but he'd grown up with four sisters. He wasn't stupid. He just nodded and she vanished into the back. But five minutes, his ass. He'd never met a woman who could get ready to go out the door in less than an hour.

But sure enough, five minutes later, she reappeared in a soft-looking black sweater and jeans snugged to her curves with some strategic frayed holes in one thigh and the opposite knee, giving him peekaboo hints of skin. They were tucked into kickass boots that made a man think about what she'd look like in just those boots. She'd added some makeup and piled her dark hair on top of her head, her blue highlights once again emphasizing her blue eyes.

"Impressive," he said while thinking *why are you sleeping in the shop?*

"You have your superhero armor," she said, nodding to his suit, "and I've got mine."

He wondered why she needed armor. He wondered a lot about her. "I was referring to the fact that you really only took five minutes to get ready for your day."

She shrugged. "I'm different."

She absolutely was. And he was starting to realize how much he liked it. "Are you living here?"

"No."

"You clearly slept here last night," he pointed out.

She shrugged. "I do that sometimes when I work really late, that's all."

Okay. But he knew she rented an apartment in the Tenderloin, which wasn't very far away. But if money was the problem, she'd no doubt be worrying about the cost of a vet and probably also about having another mouth to feed.

Another pang in his chest, except this time it was for the two-legged female in the room. He wanted to offer to help in some way, in *any* way, but she was so damn prickly, he didn't dare risk her pride. "How about I take her? The vet's a friend of mine who owes me a favor."

"What did you do, get him on QVC or something?"

He had to laugh. "Just what exactly is it that you think I do for a living?"

"You're one of those genius *Shark Tank* investors who backs cool inventions."

He laughed. "That's actually shockingly accurate."

She shrugged. "Ivy told me about some of what you and Spence have done together, and that now you're also doing something for NASA. You're working on a trash pickup system for space." She paused, seemed to be embarrassed that she knew so much about him, and crossed her arms. "Or whatever."

He went brows up. First, he'd never seen Sadie anything but utterly comfortable in her own skin. And second, Ivy was a friend of his as well. She operated The Taco Truck outside the building, and her food was amazing. When she'd recently run into some trouble with the person who'd owned the truck before her, Caleb had offered a lucrative business deal. Now she was the sole proprietor and he a silent partner on a deal that had turned out to be beneficial to them both. She got to be her own boss and he got the best food on the planet whenever he was here at the Pacific Pier Building.

He'd known Ivy and Sadie were tight, that didn't surprise him, but what did was that he'd been the topic of discussion between them. "Until yesterday, you and

I have barely said two words to each other. Why would you be gossiping about me?"

"It wasn't gossip." But she looked away, unable to hold his gaze.

Even more fascinating.

"My point being," she said, "that you're probably too busy taking over the world to go to the vet."

"I've made the time."

"I don't know," she said. "What if you pass out from the still-to-be-seen dog allergy?"

"I'll manage." Lollipop gave him a cheerful lick on his chin.

"I'm coming with."

"Why?"

She shrugged. "If you stop breathing, who's going to give you mouth-to-mouth?"

He stopped and met her gaze. "Are you saying you would?"

"I'm saying I don't want you dead, is all."

He'd take it.

Chapter 5

#HelloKitty

Sadie had no idea what she thought she was doing. Apparently she'd decided on love at first sight with Lollipop, and no matter that she had zero business adopting a dog, she was going to do it anyway.

But if the guy wanted to take Lollipop to the vet, she should let him. She didn't need to go.

But she wanted to.

The reasons for that were far too complicated to contemplate so she grabbed her bag and her keys. She was hugely grateful to Rocco, the owner of the Canvas Shop, because he had a full bathroom here, including a very tiny shower. This was mostly because Rocco lived an hour south of San Francisco with some of his motorcycle club brothers and didn't always go home after being out all night doing his thing and before coming to work.

No one was supposed to sleep here but he'd broken that rule for her a few times now and she knew he didn't mind. He understood the problem with being a young tattoo artist. You didn't do it for the money, you did it for the love of the art. And in her case, the need to help other women like herself, who had scars they wanted to keep hidden, whether from abuse, surgeries, accidents, self-harm . . . whatever. The reasons weren't nearly as important as the work itself.

But it didn't pay well, at least not yet.

Hence her second job at the day spa. She'd promised herself it was temporary and only until she built up her clientele at the Canvas Shop, but working two full-time jobs was harder than she'd thought.

And yet it was necessary. Her rent had just gone up several hundred dollars a month and her car had decided now was a good time to need a new everything. So she'd used her utility money for a mechanic, which meant taking buses until her car was finished. To pay the bill, she'd given up cable and turned off her heater, which was the real loss. TV she could do without. But no heat in the coldest February in San Francisco on record was a new low, even for her. Not to mention everyone else she knew was pairing up and buying homes and starting families, and yesterday she'd gone to sleep at eight so she wouldn't have to buy dinner.

Sometimes life really bit a girl on the ass. Thankfully she had enough padding there to take the hit. Still, she'd slept in the Canvas Shop two nights running in order to not freeze to death, hoping no one would notice.

Rocco had tried to give her an advance on her pay. It'd been an incredibly sweet thing for him to do, which was funny because Rocco wasn't sweet. In fact, he'd gotten seriously pissed off when she'd called him that, growling something about how he'd *"put a lot of fucking time into training her and just didn't want it to go to fucking waste when she fucking froze to death in her fucking stupid apartment."*

She checked her bag to make sure she had her wallet, which she did, but unfortunately, breakfast had not mysteriously appeared. She lifted her head to say she was ready and found Caleb sitting on the floor roughhousing with Lollipop without any apparent care for yet another undoubtedly insanely expensive suit.

One, she would never understand rich people. Two, when had she started to think of him as Caleb and not "Suits"?

And three . . . she had a correction. He wasn't

roughhousing with the dog. He was actually being very gentle and careful with her as she rolled on her back in clear ecstasy at the attention, a wide smile on her adorable face.

And what girl wouldn't be smiling at having Caleb Parker's hands all over her?

Her. That's who, she reminded herself. "Let's get this over with." Her stomach growled, loudly, and she tried to talk over it so he didn't notice. "I've got to be at the spa by eight thirty."

Caleb glanced at his watch, scooped up the dog, and without use of his hands still rose easily to his feet. Sadie had made a makeshift leash, a length of rope she'd found in the back. Caleb took the leash and opened the door for them, pausing to let Sadie pass through first. She wanted to say *stop being nice to me, I don't know what to do with nice!* But that was far too revealing, so she held her tongue.

They made a pit stop at the pet shop at the other end of the courtyard on their way out. Willa, the store owner, greeted them with a sweet smile and a warm hug for Caleb. A careful warm hug because her pregnancy bump was just starting to show.

"I can't thank you enough," she told him, brushing a kiss to his jaw. "You're a miracle worker."

"The website's working then?" he asked.

"Working and making me a mint! Taking this shop online was brilliant. I owe you."

"You don't," Caleb said firmly. "You paid for the work."

"There's no way I paid your guy his real price. I got a discount, a deep one."

"You can pay me back with dog advice," Caleb said. "We stopped by for some supplies for this cutie here."

Before Willa could respond, a huge Doberman came galloping from the back and jumped up on Caleb.

"Oh shoot!" Willa cried. "Carl, down! Caleb's allergic, don't touch him!"

"It's okay." Caleb staggered back a step from Carl's weight. "Apparently, I've outgrown the allergy."

"Well I'm still sorry you got jumped," Willa said. "I'm dog sitting today."

"No worries. If I get taken down by a hundred-pound mass of happiness, then that's how I go."

"*And* slobber," Willa said, pulling a napkin from her pocket and surreptitiously swiping it down Caleb's trousered thigh. Then she spent a few minutes gushing over Lollipop before getting down to business, showing them what they'd need. "And think about one of these carriers," she said, pointing to doggy backpacks. "With only three legs, she's bound to get tired quickly, and then you can carry her home when needed." She hugged Caleb again, sent Sadie another friendly but curious smile. "Is this . . ." she waggled a finger between Caleb and Sadie ". . . something?"

"No," Sadie said.

"Yes," Caleb said.

They stared at each other, Sadie with her eyes narrowed, Caleb looking amused. "We seem to have rescued a dog," he said to Willa, eyes still locked on Sadie's.

"But not *together* together," Sadie said and sent Caleb a dirty look.

"A very important distinction," Willa said, smiling.

Dammit. "No, really," Sadie said. "We just rescued her last night, haven't even talked about what's next. We only need a few things . . ." Damn. She was saying *we* an awful lot . . .

Willa rubbed her baby belly and met Caleb's gaze. "The reluctant ones are always the best, trust me." Then she was gone, off to help another customer.

Sadie stared at Caleb.

Caleb raised his hands. "Hey, don't look at me."

"She was matchmaking."

"That's what Willa does."

"Not for me. I'm not . . . matchable."

"Noted," Caleb said. "But for the record, I disagree. You're 100 percent matchable."

Because that made her feel both flattered and incredibly wary, and because she never knew what to do with either of those emotions, she turned to dog backpacks and pulled out a shiny neon pink one.

"No way," he said.

With a shrug, she went for a leopard print next.

"Seriously?" he asked.

With a small smile, she picked up the one she'd had her eyes on the whole time. A black patent leather one with a large white cat face sticking its tongue out at the world. Underneath in bold print it said *Hello Kitty*.

Caleb just looked at her.

"What?"

"It says *Hello Kitty*."

"It's an ego thing, right?" Sadie asked. "You're afraid to risk your masculinity, even if it means this poor neglected sweetheart has to walk past her comfort level—"

Caleb snatched the backpack from her hands and added it to the pile that was getting worrisomely large. She laughed and pulled out her wallet, hoping her credit card wasn't going to be rejected, but Caleb smoothly beat her to it like some sort of Knight In Shining Credit Card Armor.

Her rescue dog now officially had more possessions than she did.

When they finally got to Caleb's car, Sadie stopped

short. It looked sleek and fast and supremely spotless. "Maybe we should Uber," she said.

"Not necessary."

"Look, one of us isn't exactly potty trained."

"She'll be fine. Get in."

"Alright, it's your dime." She sank in the front passenger seat and nearly moaned. Soft supple leather cradled her, more comfortable than her own bed.

Caleb put Lollipop in the back in the crate they'd just purchased. Correction. *Caleb* had just purchased. He'd purchased a hell of a lot more than just a crate too. Bowls, food, leash, halter—both in matching Hello Kitty black patent leather—doggy toothbrush, toys, bed . . .

She waited until he slid behind the wheel to voice the question that had been on the tip of her tongue since he'd dropped his black AmEx card back at Willa's pet shop. "Why are you investing so much on this dog that isn't yours?"

He didn't answer. Instead, he pulled out his phone, which was vibrating. "Excuse me a minute," he said and got out to take the call. He stepped away from the car for a few minutes, completely out of sight, but before she could figure out where he'd gone, he was back and handing her a bag that smelled suspiciously like muffins. And not any muffins either, but Tina's muffins from the coffee shop, which meant they were made by Tina, the shop's owner. Tina made the best muffins on the planet and Sadie's mouth began to water. "What's this?"

"Breakfast. To tame the beast," he said, starting his car. "The rumbling's driving me mad."

She pressed her hands to her belly, horrified and embarrassed because it was true, it'd been rumbling since he'd woken her up, but she'd hoped he hadn't noticed. "I don't know what you're talking about."

"My stomach." He pulled out into the street and flashed her a wry smile. "I was at the gym before this and I'm running on empty. Hand me one?"

The muffins were bite-size, meaning they were perfect. She pulled out what looked like a blueberry one and handed it to him.

Keeping his eyes on the road, he shook his head. "I don't like blueberry. You eat that one."

Happily, she thought and popped it into her mouth, letting out a low moan of pleasure before she could stop herself. She reached into the bag and pulled out a poppy seed muffin next and held it out, ignoring the fact that his eyes had something new in them now.

Heat.

"I don't like poppy seed either," he said softly and watched her as she shrugged and popped that one in her mouth as well. When she tried to hand him a lemon muffin and he again shook his head, she finally caught on.

He was feeding her.

On purpose.

Dammit.

Before Sadie could blast him for that high-handed manipulation, Lollipop began to whine. Sadie craned her neck to see the dog, who was ears and tail down, looking sad. "Think she's jealous of the muffins?"

"No. She's scared." Caleb pulled over and turned to face the back, reaching in to unhinge the crate. Lollipop immediately leapt at him. Once in his lap, she set her front paws on his chest and licked his face from chin to forehead in thanks.

He stroked her, and a bunch of fur rose off the dog's body to float around in the air, inevitably landing on the spotless leather upholstery. With an easy laugh, Caleb plopped her into Sadie's lap. "For the way home, we'll figure out how to use the harness seatbelt we bought, but for now do your best to hold on to her good."

"Not we. *You* bought everything." But Sadie

wrapped her arms around Lollipop and tried to cuddle her in, but the dog's eyes were on Caleb, as if maybe the sun rose and set on his broad shoulders.

Reaching over, he patted her on the head—the dog, not Sadie—and started driving again.

Lollipop immediately began whining and trying to get back into Caleb's lap.

Without taking his eyes off the road, he reached out to pet her. This helped until he stopped touching her. Soon as he did, Lollipop held up a paw in his direction like, *keep petting me!*

Caleb took her paw in his big hand and kept driving.

While holding the dog's paw.

Lollipop relaxed, even smiled as she turned in Sadie's lap to face the windshield, now appearing to enjoy the ride.

"Are you serious?" Sadie asked.

"I think she is."

"I meant you," Sadie said.

"Hey, she stopped crying, didn't she? Do me a favor and shift into third gear when I ease into the clutch so I don't have to let go of her hand."

Huh. Over the past year or so since Caleb Parker had first come into her orbit, she'd amused herself by coming up with all sorts of stories about him, like he probably only dated supermodels, maybe even two at a time, and she bet he didn't leave tips when he ate out, things like that.

But the stories were starting to crumble beneath the weight of the truth.

He was actually kind of a really good guy, one who fed people he thought needed feeding and risked an allergic reaction to rescue a scared, lonely, abandoned dog. She glanced over at him. He was still holding Lollipop's paw.

"What?" he asked, catching her staring. "Want me to hold your hand next?"

"Funny, but I'm not whining, so . . ." she quipped with a teasing tone that was in complete contrast to the way her heart kicked hard at the thought of a physical connection to him.

What the hell was happening to her?

"You nervous about something?" he asked.

"No. Why would I be nervous?" And how was he reading her at all? She had a world-class poker face that she'd worked her entire life to perfect.

"I don't know, but I smell something burning." He pulled into the underground parking for the vet center. "What's got you thinking so hard?"

"Maybe I'm just a quiet person."

He laughed softly and she had to smile. "Okay," she admitted. "So I'm not quiet. I'm opinionated and stubborn and I like to think I know what I'm doing at all times."

"All excellent qualities."

Not where she'd come from. Her parents had tried all her life to squelch those very tendencies, to no avail. She'd never met anyone who could handle her at her best, much less her worst, so his comment really threw her. "Look, we're barely acquaintances, much less friends. You don't have to say things that aren't true just to be nice."

His smile faded at whatever he saw in her expression. "I never say things that aren't true," he said.

Sensing a serious moment, Lollipop squeezed her face in between theirs and barked.

Caleb smiled. "You want attention too, I take it. But your mama first." He hadn't taken his eyes from Sadie. "We good?"

Was he kidding? Her head was spinning, but she nodded. It was her automatic response, one that she gave without even thinking because she'd never admit to not being good.

He called her out on her lie. "Now who's saying things that aren't true?" he chided.

"How do you do that?" she demanded, baffled. "Read me like that?" No one else had ever been able to, she'd seen to it.

Lollipop barked again and jumped from her lap to Caleb's and he opened his door and got out.

She followed. The vet center looked very expensive and she went back to worrying about that. But not as much as Lollipop, who up till now had been trotting happily along on her new black patent leather Hello Kitty leash beside Caleb. He should have looked ridiculous. Instead, he looked incredibly sure of himself, and damn. That was sexy.

At the door, Lollipop stopped short and froze, and then flattened herself to the ground, refusing to go another step.

"Someone just realized she got played and is at the vet," Caleb said and picked her up.

Lollipop licked his chin and together they entered.

The vet who owed Caleb a favor turned out to be a tall curvy brunette with a sweet, welcoming smile for Caleb that had Sadie rolling her eyes. But Dr. Vicki Consuela gave Sadie the same sweet, welcoming smile and was so kind and good with Lollipop, Sadie got over herself and the fact that clearly these two had been lovers at some point—or maybe even still were.

Okay, so she didn't get over herself, not even close. But she could keep that close to the vest. In fact, she could hold a grudge until the end of time if she wanted, and she'd come by that ability naturally from her mother, but even she wasn't bitchy enough to do so against a woman who was genuinely a pretty great person.

Turned out, Lollipop had been born with only three legs, so she didn't know anything else and she had no idea that she was disabled. She was a bit undernourished, but otherwise healthy. She didn't have a microchip. Dr. Consuela got her up to date on her vaccinations and administered a deworming treatment among a few other things, each making Sadie more panicked than the last because . . . The Cost.

But watching Caleb with Lollipop, clearly enjoying his first real connection with a dog, was oddly . . . intense, and not in a negative way, much as she'd like it to be so.

"You really should microchip," Dr. Consuela said and looked between Caleb and Sadie. "Who's adopting her?"

"Me," Sadie said at the very same time that Caleb said, "I am."

Chapter 6

#BlindFaith

Shocked to the core, Sadie stared at Caleb. "What? No. You can't adopt. You're allergic. Look, I appreciate the ride here, very much. And I'll pay you back for everything, I promise, but—"

"You could co-parent," Dr. Consuela suggested.

"But we're not together," Sadie said for the second time that morning.

Dr. Consuela shrugged. "That doesn't matter. Co-petting's a new craze, actually, making it easier for people who work and have very full lives to have a pet. Sharing alleviates half of the day-to-day responsibility."

Sadie turned to see Caleb's reaction to this ridicu-

PLAYING FOR KEEPS · 81

lousness, positive she'd see a smile curving his mouth at the thought of them sharing the dog.

No smile. Just a thoughtful, inward expression. He was actually considering this.

"Are you off your rocker?" she asked.

"No more than you, I imagine. Do you want to keep her?"

"Yes."

"Me too," he said. Quiet steel. "I don't know what I'm doing obviously, but I'm drawn to her, very much. So . . . we doing this?"

She blew out a shaky breath. "You don't have time in your life for a dog."

"That's my call. Yes or no, Sadie?"

She already loved Lollipop with all her black heart and couldn't imagine being without her. But if she said yes, she was tying herself to Caleb as well as the dog. *Say no.* "Yes." *Dammit.*

Dr. Consuela smiled. "It's official then. Welcome to parenthood. You can check out at the front desk."

Sadie looked at Caleb, whose gaze was warm and did something funny to her belly. Oh boy . . .

Two minutes later they were at the front desk. They'd been offered a custom tag for Lollipop's collar and had come up against their first joint decision— whose address to use on the tag.

"I'd like it to be mine," she said, her need for control coming over her.

Caleb shook his head and her warm fuzzies vanished.

"Why?" she asked. "I had her first."

He didn't dispute that, even though she knew he certainly could've made the argument that *he'd* had her first. He just looked at her with those fathomless caramel eyes.

"What?" she asked a little temperamentally. She couldn't help it. When he looked at her like that, like he could see all of her, the good, the bad, *and* the ugly, she had the urge to bury her head in the sand because again, no one had ever seen all of her. "Give me one good reason why it shouldn't be my address on the tag."

"Okay," he said quietly, apparently refusing to engage her temper with his. "You don't appear to actually be living at your place."

She held up a hand as a surge of something ugly went through her. Pride, she knew, and ego. Both were a bitch. "Where I live and why is none of your business."

"We're going to have to agree to disagree there," he said. "But for now, my point is that if Lollipop goes missing, it needs to be an address where one of us is actually living." He reached out and covered her hand with his. "We also need a phone number listed and that can be yours. It *should* be yours, because as you said, she was yours first and I know how much you care about her and would want to hear right away if someone found her."

Her anger abruptly drained for something else entirely and left her feeling off-balance and exposed and uncomfortable. She didn't understand it, but when she was with him, she felt like she was in a lightning storm over open water. Aka, possibly in mortal danger.

"Aw," the vet tech behind the front counter said with a smile. "This is one lucky dog. You guys are so great together."

Sadie opened her mouth to say for the third time that day that they weren't together, but Caleb beat her to it.

"We're not together," he said easily as he handed over his fancy credit card.

She stared at him and he ignored her staring at him.

Five minutes later they were back in Caleb's car. He'd quickly settled the bill and neither of them spoke another word as he belted Lollipop into her Hello Kitty dog harness seatbelt.

"You guys are so great together . . ."

Sadie knew why that had freaked her out more than a little bit, but she had no idea why Caleb had suddenly backed off. All she knew was that the more she thought about it, the more it chapped her ass. She was a damn catch!

Well, she would be a damn catch once she got her life together. Not that she wanted to be a catch . . .

Good Lord. She was so messed up in the head.

Caleb, who hadn't yet started the car, was watching her think too hard, one hand at the back of her head-rest, the other on the steering wheel. "Okay, spill it," he said. "First you were annoyed when I suggested we were a team for Lollipop, and now you're annoyed when I don't say it. Help me out here. What's going on?"

What was going on was that in the close, intimate interior of the car, the scent of him came to her. Sexy smelling soap, something citrusy and outdoorsy, and the man himself, which—dammit—was even better than the muffins he'd fed her for breakfast.

"Talk to me, Sadie."

"Arf!" Lollipop said.

Caleb smiled and his gaze flicked to the rearview mirror. "Not you." He turned back to Sadie. "*You.* You talk to me."

"Aren't you late for your morning world domination or something?"

His fingers left the headrest and wrapped around a stray strand of her hair. "World domination's on hold at the moment. Right now I'm doing this."

"This?"

"Yes, this. With you. Whatever the hell it is. I don't understand why you so carefully weigh everything you say to me. Don't hold back, Sadie. It's not like you. Just say your piece."

"Alright," she said. "I don't understand why you'd want to share a dog with me."

"Because I'm willing to take what I can get."

"Of Lollipop?" she asked.

He didn't answer that, just held her gaze, and her heart flip-flopped. He was willing to take whatever he could get of her? She had no idea what that even meant, or how to feel about it. "So why then were you so quick to tell the vet tech we weren't together?" she asked.

He raised a brow. "Should I have said otherwise?"

"Of course not," she said, though he sure as hell could've hesitated at least a little bit. "But just so you know, I'm a catch."

His mouth quirked, but his eyes stayed serious. "I have no doubt, Tough Girl."

Was that sarcasm? "Not that you'll ever find out. I don't date guys like you."

"You mean nice?"

"I mean gazillionaires." Though she hadn't made nice all that much of a priority either. Another reason she'd given up men. She had no nice meter, at all.

He let his smile through. "But you're thinking about it now. About us."

"Am not." Look at her with all the lies today. He was very close. And very big and sexy. He hadn't shaved for at least several mornings and the stubble on his lean jaw was scarily enticing. Also, that crackalicious scent of him should be illegal. And why her mind had gone down this path with him, she had no idea. "This is all your fault."

He laughed, the soft one that always scraped all her good parts. "Whatever you have to tell yourself to sleep at night," he said, and with one last playful tug on her hair, he started the car and pulled out into the street.

Lollipop immediately lost her shit, whining with escalating volume until she was sobbing.

"I can't," Sadie said, her heart cracked open. She reached back and clicked open the dog's seatbelt, and in a single blink, Lollipop was in her lap, holding out her paw for Caleb.

He took it in his hand and shook his head. "Apparently I'm highly trainable."

No way was that actually true. She turned away from the adorable sight and stared out the window. When they pulled up to the Pacific Pier Building, she reached for Lollipop's leash, but Caleb put a hand on her arm.

"How were you planning on dividing up the days for Lollipop's custody?"

She bit her lower lip. Much as she didn't want to admit it, especially to him, she was grateful to have someone to share the responsibility with. "We could switch off days," she suggested, wanting to be fair. "I could keep her for twenty-four hours and then you do the same. Does that work?"

"Sure," he said. "I can take the first shift. You've got a full schedule today, right?"

"Yes, but I'm sure you do too."

"We'll be okay," he said easily.

"You've never had a dog before," she reminded him. "Trust me, it's harder than it looks."

He shrugged, clearly not worried.

Fine. She let go of the leash. "Send proof of life pics."

"Sure."

"No, don't just placate the silly dog lady," she said. "Promise me."

He met her gaze, his own solemn now. "Something you should know about me. When I give my word, I give my word. I don't go back on it."

There was something in the air now. Tension. A sexual tension, but also . . . more. "Never?" she breathed.

"Never."

It'd always been important to her that she hold her own and go toe-to-toe with . . . well, everyone. But especially Caleb, a guy used to running his world and getting his way. Still, she looked away first because she didn't believe him. Couldn't. *No one* kept their word all the time.

With a gentle hand on her jaw, he brought her face back around. "You don't believe me," he said. "But you will. You can trust me, Sadie. I'll have Lollipop back to you tomorrow morning."

And then he was gone.

She put a hand to her jaw where he'd touched her and stood there like an idiot for a long beat. What had just happened? Nothing, she decided. Nothing at all, and with fifteen minutes to spare, she headed for the southeast corner of the building where The Taco Truck was parked.

Ivy was in her truck. A five-foot-two-inch dynamo of a cook with a personality much bigger than her petite frame, she was sassy, funny, smart, and a taker of absolutely no bullshit. Sadie knew she could count on Ivy's opinion straight up.

"What'll float your boat this morning?" Ivy asked.

Sadie eyed the chalkboard menu on the side of the

truck. Every single thing on the menu was amazing, which she knew from experience. "An egg, cheese, and bacon soft taco—make that *two*, and a side of what do you think of Caleb Parker?"

Ivy froze in surprise. "Well," she finally said. "I think he'd go better with today's special, which is my spicy chorizo and fried egg breakfast taco."

Sadie rolled her eyes.

"I'm not kidding," Ivy said. "Caleb Parker's ridiculously hot. You know that feeling when you meet someone and your heart skips a beat?"

"Yeah," Sadie said. "It's called arrhythmia and you can die from that shit."

Ivy laughed. "Why are you asking me about Caleb?"

No use keeping it a secret. There were no secrets in this building. "Because we rescued a dog and I think we're going to share her."

"You're going to adopt a dog with a man you've been calling Suits all year in order to avoid saying his name?"

"Ridiculous, right?" Sadie shook her head. "I'd rather catch a Razor scooter to my ankle twenty-five times in a row than ever catch feelings for anyone ever again, and yet . . ." She spread out her arms. "Here I am, feeling all the damn feelings," she admitted.

Ivy set her knife down. "You're serious. Okay. Wow. That doesn't happen often. You're so picky, I thought you'd never want another guy."

"Yeah, yeah, I'm picky," Sadie agreed. "Too picky. But last night I watched my new dog look for the perfect place to poop for like thirty minutes, so I've decided to rethink some things."

"Good to know," Ivy said. "And the dog's adorable by the way. I saw Caleb's post. Let me make you my special—on the house—and we'll talk, okay?"

"But I don't know if I'll like spicy chorizo and fried egg breakfast tacos."

"Have some faith, woman. I'm making it, which means you'll love it. So let's hear it. Don't skip anything."

Sadie sighed. "I don't know where to start."

"With the feelings!" Ivy demanded, brandishing her knife for emphasis.

"But I don't know what to say about the feelings. It's like on the outside, I'm cool as a cucumber. But on the inside, I'm more like . . . a squirrel in traffic." When Ivy laughed, Sadie shook her head. "It's dumb. I feel dumb."

"Hold on." Ivy's smile slowly faded. "It's not dumb. It's just that you've never shown much interest in any guy in all the time I've known you, so it struck me as funny that you'd then pick a guy at the highest level of expertise end of the spectrum, that's all. I mean just last week, you told me to never be the chaser. To always be the one who's chased. That I'm the tequila, not the lime. I loved that because it implied you were badass enough to never let your feelings get in the way. But, Sadie, feelings aren't always bad."

"They are in this case," Sadie said. "Caleb's so far out of my league that I can't even see the league."

"No. *No*," Ivy repeated softly. "It's not that, not even close." She drew a deep breath and looked around to make sure no one was near. "I mean yes, he's shockingly easy to look at, but he's also—"

"Oh hell," Sadie said. "He's an asshole, right? He kicks kittens? Doesn't leave tips? Wears lifts in his shoes? Don't tell me he wears the male equivalent to Spanx. *Is* there a male equivalent to Spanx?"

"God, I hope not." Ivy shuddered as she worked on Sadie's order. "Honestly? He's just a good guy."

Sadie shook her head, even though she'd been thinking the same thing earlier. "Not possible. Nice guys are urban myths. They're extinct, if they ever even existed."

Ivy shrugged. "I'm inclined to agree with you, but one apparently survived."

"He's got flaws. He can't be perfect."

"Oh, I didn't say perfect," Ivy said. "No penis-carrying human is perfect. But in spite of his flaws, or maybe because of them, he really is just a good guy. He'd be a good guy for you."

"How do you know?"

"I have this test," Ivy said and handed Sadie a basket with her two tacos. "No matter how rich or intelligent you are, how you treat an animal tells me all I need to know about you. And look at how he treated your dog."

Damn. That was a good rule. Sadie took a bite of her breakfast taco and moaned. "Oh. My. God."

"Right?" Ivy asked with a smile.

Sadie couldn't get enough or stop eating. "I want to marry these tacos and have their babies. And seriously, you believe Caleb's a good guy, just like that?"

"Yeah. Call it blind faith."

Sadie shook her head. "I don't have the capability for blind faith."

Ivy watched her inhale the second taco she'd claimed to not want and smiled. "I think you might be wrong about that."

Chapter 7

#AreYouKiddingMe

Caleb headed into work, which had always been his happy place. He could lose himself there, solve problems, create solutions, whatever was needed, and not give his personal life—or lack of one—a single thought.

Not the case today. Today he couldn't multitask to save his life. All he could do was think about Sadie. The people in his life tended to fit into mental compartments. Employees. Friends. Dates. His family. And in spite of the overabundant richness his life had turned out to be, and all the good people in it, he was alone. He'd never put it into words before, the restlessness in him, but he did so now.

He was sick of being alone.

And Sadie knew what that was like. He'd seen it with how she interacted with her coworkers and friends. They cared about her, but they didn't understand her, and because of that, she kept a part of herself from them.

He recognized that. He understood that.

As a general rule, he didn't do denial. He was attracted to her, hugely so. What he didn't know was what to do with it. The things in his life balanced and added up. But not Sadie. She wasn't an account or a number or a company. She was a complicated person who represented a puzzle that he couldn't seem to solve.

Some of it was just sheer physical chemistry. But it was also more. He . . . *liked* her, a lot. He wanted to know more about her, wanted to spend time and see where this thing went.

Did she feel the same way? He had absolutely no idea. She was very good at hiding her emotions when she wanted to—even more than him, and that was saying something.

She, unlike anyone else he'd ever met, had him off his game. She was fiercely independent and incredibly private and had a lot of walls built up around her, hiding he had no idea what. Walls she had no intention of lowering for him.

And now they owned a dog together.

He'd brought Lollipop to work with him because he hadn't wanted to leave her alone at his house all day, but also to introduce her to his sisters and find out why the hell he wasn't allergic to dogs. Unfortunately, Sienne and Hannah were off-site today. Kayla was on maternity leave, busy growing her second baby. And Emory was in New York, having finally gone after her dream of going to graduate school.

His two admins helped him by dog sitting during his meetings, and Lollipop soon had his entire staff in love with her. As often as he could, he sent Snaps to Sadie. She didn't reply to any of them but he could see by the notifications that she opened each one immediately.

After work, he drove Lollipop home. Holding her hand, of course. When they got out of the car, she did her business on his front lawn. In three different spots. Seemed his dog liked to walk and poop at the same time.

"Maybe we should change your name to Poops A Lot," he said.

She sat at his feet and panted up at him, quite pleased with herself.

Luckily for him, at that very moment his house-keeper and her teenage son came out of his place, clearly just finishing their weekly cleaning. Reaching into his pocket, he came up with two twenties and offered the dough to the kid to clean up after Lollipop. He turned to take her inside and found her eating something from the flower beds.

"Some other dog's poop," the kid said.

Caleb pulled out another twenty and the kid made sure the entire yard was a poop-free zone.

He was going to need more twenties.

Inside, he set up Lollipop's bed in his living room, and then turned on the TV to make her feel comfortable. He checked his phone and found a text from Sadie.

Don't let her sleep with you, it's a bad habit you can't undo.

No problem, since he had zero intention of sharing his bed. At least not with Lollipop. But not two minutes into an episode of one of his favorite car shows, Lollipop had figured out how to jump up onto the couch by climbing his legs like a jungle gym. With a proud-of-herself huff, she set her head on his thigh. "Okay, but don't tell your mom."

At eleven, he carried Lollipop to her bed, told her to stay, and then tried to escape to his bedroom.

Lollipop followed him.

He walked her back to her bed and then looked into

her huge golden eyes. "You stay here and guard the house, okay?"

She whined softly, her tail tucked.

Hell. "Okay, I'll guard the house. And I'll watch TV with you for a little bit longer . . ."

Back to the couch they went. Several hours later, he found himself deep into a really great dream. A woman was in his lap.

Sadie.

She was licking her way along his jaw to his ear, whispering all the things she wanted to do to him. Oh yeah. He was all in. He opened his eyes and . . .

Came face-to-face with Lollipop, who wriggled her butt when he made eye contact.

"Okay," he said seriously. "We need to talk. I might not have grown up with dogs, but I know I'm not supposed to cave to you. I'm the adult." Rising from the couch, he once again walked her to her bed. "Goodnight," he said firmly and then ruined it by kissing the top of her head.

But as it turned out, Lollipop had zero intentions of staying in the living room. It also turned out that his house was way too big. After walking the hallway from his bedroom to the living room with her no less than a hundred times, he finally figured out that his dog could out-stubborn him to the end of time. "You got that from your mom," he said, setting up her bed next to his. He crouched down to meet her gaze. "You're going to stay now, right?"

Lollipop panted her doggy breath in his face, smiling from ear to ear. It was impossible not to smile back. "You're a nut," he said fondly. Rising, he stripped out of his clothes, took a quick shower, and came out to find Lollipop watching with a worried expression that said she didn't like nor trust water. He brushed his teeth, dropped his towel, tucked her back into her bed, and then climbed into his. He closed his eyes and . . .

Lollipop whined.

"You're okay," he said in the dark. "I'm right here."

But like the backseat of his car and her bed in the living room, she wasn't having it. He heard her move to the side of his bed and attempt to jump up.

And miss.

"Shit." He leapt out of bed and scooped her up. She was fine, but he'd just had a heart attack. Giving up, he got back into bed. With her. She curled up against his side and was snoring before he laid his head on his pillow.

He was such a sucker.

He slept for a few hours, waking just before dawn with Lollipop asleep on his chest. He managed to check his phone without disturbing her and found a text from Sadie from around midnight the night before.

WHERE'S MY PROOF OF LIFE?

He snapped a quick pic of Lollipop and sent it off. Two seconds later, his phone rang.

"Who belongs to the abs my dog is sleeping on?" Sadie wanted to know.

"Me," he said.

His phone buzzed. Sadie had switched to FaceTime. He hit accept and there she was, hair wild around her makeup-free face. Her eyes were . . . well, amazing. "Hey," he said and felt a stupid grin come over his face. "You're in my bed."

"Funny," she said, her tone making it clear she didn't find him funny at all. "What the hell are you doing?"

Chapter 8

#GetAGrip

Sadie didn't know where to look, his bare chest, those broad shoulders, the abs that she wanted to lick . . . It was a complete feast for her eyes. But no way was she going to admit such a thing.

"Morning," Caleb said with a lazy smile and a gruff morning voice that gave her a secret thrill.

Get a grip! she ordered herself. So he looked sexy as hell first thing in the morning. So what. And so she was thinking things, really erotic things. He didn't need to know this. "Sleeping with my dog on your bed is the exact opposite of *not* letting my dog sleep on your bed," she said.

His mouth curved. "Our dog," he said. "And she wouldn't sleep unless she was with me."

"But you're naked."

He shrugged. "That's how I sleep."

Oh boy. She was torn between relief and disappointment that his sheet was pooled low on his hips, hiding his goodies.

"You look pretty," he said.

She was in an oversize T-shirt and sweats. No makeup. And she knew damn well she had circles under her eyes and was pale. Stress. But here was the thing. This gorgeous man, naked or not, impeccably groomed or not, was staring at her absolutely meaning what he said. He thought she looked good and she was going to own that. But it was going to take her a moment.

His eyes darkened and a bolt of electricity came through from his phone to hers and directly to her good parts.

Huh. Maybe she wasn't going to need a minute after all.

"Wow," he murmured in that husky morning voice. "Mark the date. I just rendered Sadie Lane speechless." He paused and his eyes took her in the way she looked at red velvet cupcakes. And then his smile spread. "You want me bad."

"Wrong. First, it's the middle of the night and my brain isn't running on full power."

The combo of humor and heat in his eyes said he was onto her but too polite to call her a liar. "And second?" he inquired.

Dammit, she'd forgotten the rest of her point. "You know what? So you have superior genes. That's just good luck. Don't let it go to your head. Either of them." And then she disconnected.

She needed a cold shower.

Her phone rang as she rose from her bed a few minutes later. She expected it to be Caleb again, but it wasn't. It was her boss at the day spa, reminding her that though she thought Lollipop was very cute, she wouldn't be allowed in the spa.

Something Sadie already knew but had hoped for anyway. She looked at the time. Damn. And then she took a deep breath and thumbed to recent calls and hit Caleb's contact.

Which meant it was a FaceTime call instead of a regular one. He answered wearing a whole lot of wet, sleek, sinewy skin and a towel wrapped dangerously low on his hips. He shook his head and drops flew into the steam around him. "What's up?"

"Um," she said brilliantly, operating on maybe two brain cells.

He smiled. "Tell me the truth. You just wanted to see me naked again."

She bit her own tongue hard to get it to behave. No sense in giving information to the enemy. "You're not naked, you're wearing a towel."

"I could lose the towel."

"Not interested," said her mouth.

Her brain though, it was telling her a different story.

He just grinned. He knew. Dammit. She forced her gaze off his body and into his eyes.

But that was almost worse because his body, great as it was, didn't hold her as much as his eyes did. There were secrets there, and a dark edge that gave her a shocking thrill. Caleb Parker was a man of power and wealth, and he was always, *always* in control. But a part of her wondered what he might be like if he lost that control . . .

Nope. Not going there. With anyone. "I need help," she said. Not an easy admission. "Lollipop isn't allowed at the day spa. I need to get her from you early so I have time to drop her off at doggy day care with Willa."

"Why don't you save the money and leave her with me," he said. "She can stay here for my morning meetings. I'll pick her up and get her to you before your shift at the Canvas Shop."

"You don't have to—"

"I want to." He suddenly stilled and looked around him. "Shit. Hold on." He apparently tossed the phone down on a counter because then she was looking up at steam swirling around the ceiling. She could hear him calling for Lollipop and her heart stopped.

"Did you find her?" she asked.

Nothing.

Ten long seconds later, he picked up his phone and turned it out so she could see his room. One of his pillows had fallen to the floor and that's where Lollipop had made herself comfortable, curled up on top of the pillow like she owned it.

And him.

"Oh my God," she said. "See? Now you're never going to get her out of your bed."

He scooped up the dog and went nose-to-nose with her. "You're cute," he said. "I'll give you that. But listen carefully. Last night was a one-time thing."

Sadie snorted.

Lollipop licked his nose.

"No, I mean it," he said.

This got him another lick and he turned to look at Sadie. "She's not listening."

What female would when faced with the sight of him

standing there in just that towel? Then she realized he was staring at her. "What?" she asked.

He gave a slow shake of his head. "Nothing. For a minute there, I thought you were softening for me." He smiled. "But that was my imagination, right?"

She cleared her throat. "Definitely."

She knew that he knew she was full of shit, but he let her get away with it. "Do you want to keep her company while I get ready for work?" he asked.

Well, hell. If she hadn't softened before when he'd run through his house looking for the dog, she did so now for giving her the few extra minutes. "Yes, thank you."

"Anytime," he said, and though people said that word all the time and didn't mean it, she somehow knew he did.

Caleb set Lollipop back on the bed and grabbed his fallen pillow to prop the phone up so she could see. Then he grabbed his clothes and went into the bathroom to change.

Which was a bummer. How scary was that?

Three minutes later, he reappeared in a suit looking ready to take on the world. She had no idea how he did that, but even his expression was different.

Caleb Parker was in full business mode.

"Hold on a sec," he called to her and vanished. A minute later he was back with a length of wood, which he quickly rigged up like a makeshift ramp against the bed for Lollipop to get safely down.

Sadie was floored.

He then showed Lollipop how to use it. "Okay, so you're going to hang out here for a few hours. I'll come back for you at lunch. All you've got to do is nap and . . . do whatever dogs do during the day."

He gave her a quick kiss on the snout and caught Sadie's raised brow. "You want a kiss too?" he asked.

Yes . . . "In your dreams."

"You're already there," he said and that shut her up.

He dreamed about her?

He scooped up the phone and moved through the house.

"The ramp," she said carefully. "That was . . . something."

He flashed a smile. "Something good, right?"

Try amazing . . . "You're the biggest sucker I've ever met," she said.

He laughed, obviously seeing right through her.

And he was right. She was touched beyond belief by what he'd done for Lollipop, and damn. She was having feelings, so many feelings. "You're different," she said.

"So I'm both the biggest sucker you've ever met *and* different. So many compliments today."

She rolled her eyes. "Like you need compliments from me." She paused. "You're . . . analytical, which makes you more cut-and-dry than the average person. You're a tactical thinker. One who can build a ramp for his disabled dog on the fly and be a sarcastic smartass at the same time."

He laughed. "Sarcastic smartass. Well, it takes one to know one." He looked at her, eyes warm. "And you're different too. Different good, by the way. You're a puzzle, one I can't seem to solve. That doesn't happen often."

"You can't solve a woman," she said.

He laughed again, and she thought she could get very used to that sound. Even addicted. So not good.

With their FaceTime call still connected, he went out what she assumed was his front door. She couldn't see much but she had no problem hearing the sudden howling. And not just little howls either, ear-splitting howls of death. "Oh my God," she said. "What's wrong, what happened to her?"

Caleb quickly unlocked the door and stepped back inside. The howls immediately stopped and Sadie heard the pitter-patter of uneven paws as they skidded across the hardwood floors. And then Caleb was mobbed.

"She okay?" Sadie asked as he crouched low and hoisted the dog in his arms.

"Yes. I think she was just sad that I left. Listen," he said to Lollipop. "You can't howl like that. People'll think I'm killing someone in here." He set the dog down and rose to his feet, and then suddenly Sadie's view went topsy-turvy.

He'd dropped the phone.

It hit the floor, bouncing close to Lollipop, who leapt straight up into the air and, with a terrified expression, went scrambling out of sight.

"Shit," Caleb muttered and then he called out to Lollipop in a gentler voice. "It's okay, baby, it was just my phone . . ."

"Someone must have thrown things at her," Sadie said, her chest tight.

"I know." He was already moving, clearly going after her. "Lollipop?"

A noise alerted them both, a whimper really, and tugged at all of Sadie's very new and very raw emotions.

"She's under my bed," Caleb said and dropped to his knees.

Lollipop was back as far as she could get, huddled up against the wall, cowering.

"Aw, no, baby," he murmured. "Don't be scared. No one's going to hurt you, I promise."

Lollipop just stared at him with those huge soulful eyes and Sadie could hardly breathe.

"I get it now," Caleb said softly. "You don't like to be alone. And some asshole wasn't nice to you and probably threw things at you. That life's over, okay? You can come with me to work. You liked it there, remember? My admin has that beef jerky you love."

Lollipop didn't budge except for the very tip of her tail which wagged once. She wanted to believe but she couldn't.

Sadie's throat burned. She knew just how the dog felt.

Caleb set the phone down low so Lollipop could see Sadie. "Talk to her," he said. "I'll be right back."

He reappeared in less than a minute with some deli meat and cheese. After coming out from beneath the bed to scarf it down, Lollipop appeared to forget her trauma.

Caleb met Sadie's gaze via the phone. "So she can be bribed."

"You just fed her a fortune in fancy cuts of meats and cheeses," she said. "Anyone could've been bribed with that. Hell, I'd have jumped into a stranger-danger van for that."

He smiled. "Good to know that too. I'll bring you some when I bring Lollipop."

She rolled her eyes and disconnected.

And then proceeded to think about him for the rest of the day.

A few minutes later, Caleb and Lollipop were in his car, finally heading to work, holding hands, one of them smelling like turkey and cheese and drooling on the passenger window.

Twenty minutes later they were in his building heading for Sienne's office instead of his own. Hannah was there too and he gestured to the dog at his side in her harness and black patent leather Hello Kitty leash. "Take a good look at this," he said to his sisters. "What is she?"

"You have an MBA from Stanford," Hannah said. "I think you know what a dog looks like. Did you hit your head at the gym this morning? And why are you in possession of a dog?"

"The question isn't why," he said. "It's how am I able to be with a dog in the first place. In the same room. Me not dying." He squatted down beside Lollipop and she wriggled in happiness at him. "I mean, look at her. She was abused, abandoned, and has not a single clue that she's got an owie. Also, I just used the phrase 'she's got an owie.' What the actual hell?"

They both just stared at him, boggled, as they shook their heads.

He drew in a deep breath and studied his closest confidantes. "Someone tell me why I'm not allergic to dogs." He pointed to Hannah. "Go."

"Um . . . you outgrew it?" she asked.

"Bullshit." He turned to Sienne.

Sienne shook her head at Hannah and then moved to Caleb. She squatted low to pet Lollipop, who surprised everyone by affecting a protective stance in front of Caleb and growling low in her throat.

Sienne didn't take it personally. She smiled and rose. "She doesn't want another woman touching her man."

"I've known her all of two days," Caleb said. "It's not that—" Before he could finish the sentence, Lollipop sat on his feet.

"Cute," Hannah said. "She's claimed you."

Out of patience, he shook his head. "One of you has a business MBA and the other was third in her law class. I want answers."

"Okay, fine," Sienne said. "You were allergic to everything back then. You eventually outgrew most of your allergies. It was more that a dog didn't fit our lifestyle."

He stared at her as the truth hit him with the force

of a two-by-four. Back when he'd been a kid, they couldn't have handled even one more mouth to feed. His mom and sisters had had their hands full just keeping a roof over their heads and him healthy and alive. And like always when he remembered what it'd been like, he felt a gratitude fill him that those days were long over. Letting out a breath, he nodded. "Well, she fits my lifestyle now."

"You're really going to keep her?" Sienne asked.

"Yes. Well, half of her," he corrected. "I'm sharing custody."

Sienne's eyes sharpened. "With who?"

"Whom," Hannah corrected.

"*Whom* isn't relevant," Caleb said.

"So it's a woman," Sienne said. "Just tell us."

He laughed. "Are you kidding me? Last time I was interested in someone, you put her through all your search programs and cyberstalked her." No way was he subjecting Sadie to that.

"Which turned out to be a good thing, since she was also cyberstalking you," Hannah said. "She was looking to get herself an MRS degree and become Mrs. Parker so she could spend your money."

"Maybe," he allowed. "But I was still just having a good time, until you went all Sherlock on me and delivered the report about her every indiscretion, including the time she'd cheated on a spelling test in the third grade."

"Well, I thought you should know," Sienne said in her best fuck-off-and-die voice.

"Sienne." He squeezed her hand. "Just the other day, you told me it was my turn to get a life. Did you mean it?"

"Of course I did."

"So then, maybe that's what I'm doing."

"Maybe?"

"Definitely, so back off."

"Caleb—" Sienne started and he shot her a look that told her he was done talking about this. He had no problem defending his feelings for Sadie, but they were too new right now and not for public consumption. His phone was vibrating in his pocket, but he waited for Sienne to acknowledge that he was serious. She stared back and then let out a sigh.

"Fine," she said. "It's your life."

"Try to remember that." He took Lollipop to his office. The dog made herself at home.

With a nod, she left. Hannah followed. Lollipop had made herself at home and was sprawled out on the floor beside his desk, her Hello Kitty leash flashing in the light as he answered Spence's phone call. "Sorry," he said. "I was in a meeting."

"With The Coven?" Spence asked.

"Half of them. Introduced Sienne and Hannah to the new woman in my life."

"Sadie?"

"Lollipop. Jesus."

Spence laughed and said something that Caleb missed because Lollipop started barking at something beneath his desk. He got down and looked.

"Problem?" Spence asked.

"There's a Skittle under my desk. She's apparently convinced it's the enemy, but she isn't sure, so you can imagine the stress she's under."

Lollipop headed to the door, in a sudden hurry.

"Oh shit," Caleb said, rising. "Gotta go—"

Too late. Lollipop was hunching into position on his rug.

"Oh shit?" Spence asked.

Caleb sighed. "Literally."

Just before lunch, Sadie checked her phone, wondering how Lollipop was managing. Actually, that was a big fat lie. She was wondering how Caleb was managing. He'd left her a text.

DO NOT EVEN THINK ABOUT FALLING FOR THIS GUY: **Poops A Lot is living up to her name.**

SADIE: I'm trying to imagine you in those fancy suits, scooping poop.

DO NOT EVEN THINK ABOUT FALLING FOR THIS GUY: **Attractive, right?**

DO NOT EVEN THINK ABOUT FALLING FOR THIS GUY: **And she just farted so loud she scared herself. She got upset when I laughed. My attorney and director of operations are demanding hazard pay because the stench is so bad.**

SADIE: Are you making your attorney and your director of operations dog sit while you rule the world?

DO NOT EVEN THINK ABOUT FALLING FOR THIS GUY: **I only rule the world on the odd days of the month. And my attorney and director of operations are two of my four sisters. They're older than me, so I'm not sure they really get the hierarchy here. One just told me she's going to tell our mom I was rude to her.**

Sadie laughed and a couple of her coworkers stared at her in shock. She rarely laughed here at the day spa.

Honestly, she rarely laughed in general. But Caleb brought it out in her. He was nice to dogs. He employed his sisters, and not just as office staff, but in high-powered positions. He'd fed Sadie. He'd paid for her dog's vet bills.

Their dog's vet bills, she reminded herself.

It was a struggle to remember he was practically still a stranger. Everyone had their armor. Hers was obvious, it was her bad attitude, and she'd been unapologetic about that.

Your bad attitude isn't your only armor, a part of her brain whispered. And that was certainly true. She hid behind the colorful streaks she liked in her hair, behind the shiny sparkly jewelry she favored, behind the clothes that said *back the eff up* . . . Even her tats hid something—her old cutting scars, for example. And the not so old ones.

DO NOT EVEN THINK ABOUT FALLING FOR THIS GUY: **Just took Lollipop on a quick walk at a pet park on our way to you. She chased someone's cat. I don't think she meant to, she just lost her mind for a second. She nosed the cat in the ass and got bitch-slapped. She's not hurt, not that you could tell by her sobbing. She's having a rough**

**day, currently sitting in my lap holding my
hand. Be there in a few.**

He'd taken Lollipop to a pet park. He held her hand
whenever she got scared. Damn. The man was dangerous to her heart and soul.

Which made him the very opposite of perfect . . .

Chapter 9

#DogKissesSolveEverything

A few days went by, during which Sadie had too many hours on the job and not enough hours sleeping. Tired didn't come close to describing how she felt. She'd just spent about ten hours on her feet, leaning over clients, more than a little uptight about getting everything just right. Being an artist was one thing. So was selling your art. It was subjective, and that was okay.

But being an artist and selling the art that you literally inked *onto* a person's skin couldn't be subjective.

It had to be perfect.

She'd texted Caleb asking if she could have Lollipop tonight even though it wasn't her night. The truth was, she felt lonely and needed the company. It was unlike her to admit she needed anything, but somehow texting Caleb didn't make her feel as vulnerable as she might have with anyone else.

Which made no sense.

He'd let her know he would meet her at eight p.m. near the pub.

At ten minutes till, she walked the length of the courtyard, slowing to wave at Old Man Eddie, who lived in the alley. Spence, his grandson, had tried unsuccessfully to relocate Eddie to an apartment in the building, but Eddie preferred the alley. He waved back. "How's it going, cutie-pie?"

This was his nickname for most of the females who passed by. Probably because he couldn't remember any of their names. "Good," she said. "How you doing? How's the new girlfriend?"

He scratched his head, his wild Einstein hair standing on end. "She dumped me. Twice. Women should come with instructions."

"What would be the point of that?" Sadie asked. "I've never actually seen a man read any instructions."

Eddie was laughing as she walked on.

And a minute later, she found Caleb looking pained as he watched Lollipop on a leash chasing her tail until she fell over.

And though Sadie had thought it was Lollipop she needed that night, she knew she was at least partially wrong. Because it wasn't the dog who caught her attention and held it, but the man.

He'd shucked his suit jacket and shoved his sleeves up his forearms. No tie, top few buttons undone, the material stretched taut over his broad shoulders. With his build and the way he had of making her feel like the only person in the room, she had no doubt that if he'd been the lonely one tonight, he could flash his very easygoing, laid-back smile and draw in all the single females in the entire city.

Tonight though, standing there by himself and not "on" for any reason, he seemed . . . different. He had an air of being as exhausted as she, and maybe also a whole lot on edge, which was a very unusual look for him. And also ridiculously, disarmingly sexy.

Especially when Lollipop stopped twirling in circles and leaned against him. He squatted low and opened his arms and the dog walked right into them.

And Ivy's words came back to Sadie. "*No matter how rich or intelligent you are, how you treat an animal tells me all I need to know about you . . .*"

She took a deep breath and admitted to herself that watching Caleb with Lollipop told her a whole hell of a lot about him.

He looked up and held her gaze prisoner in his for a beat. "Hey," he said, voice low, a little rough. "You okay?"

"Why? Don't I look okay?" The instant 'tude was an auto response.

But he didn't back off. "You look . . ." He gave a quick head shake and a small smile. "Well, if you knew what I was thinking about how you look, you wouldn't still be standing there, you'd be running for the hills."

Something quivered low in her belly. Dangerously attracted, she stayed right where she was.

"I'm asking," he said, "because you look tired. You had a long day."

She had. And how long had it been since anyone had noticed, much less worried about her? "I could say the same thing about you."

Another small smile. "So we're both overworked."

"Yes," she said. "But only one of us is underpaid."

He came toward her. "I'm assuming we're both starving though, right?"

She nodded. She was starving. She just wasn't quite sure she was starving for food.

"I was thinking tacos. Ivy's open for the street fair tonight." He looped Lollipop's leash around the back of a wrought-iron bench and turned back to Sadie. "But first, I opened a credit card account for us."

She blinked. "What? Why?"

"For Poops A Lot. She's cute, but she's expensive as hell." He pulled a credit card from his pocket and held it out to her.

She stared at the card without taking it. It had her name on it. And it wasn't any old card either, it was a black AmEx card. "What the actual hell?" she asked calmly.

Okay, not calmly. Not even a little bit calmly.

"A dog's expensive," he said. And he did manage calm, as always. "This way if you have to buy stuff, you're covered."

She thought about strangling him. Instead, she said, "I cover myself."

"I know." Damn him for being so reasonable when she couldn't seem to manage anything close on the best of days, of which this wasn't one. "I'm not trying to piss you off," he said. "There's just no reason for you to have to cover her when I can do it."

Okay, so he was aware he was pissing her off. Brownie points for that. But he lost points for being a stupid male. "We agreed to fifty-fifty."

"As it pertained to physical custody," he said. "But not monetarily. You've got enough on your plate right now, working two jobs and trying to build up your clientele."

He probably had no idea that he'd just stomped right on her rawest nerve and secret fear—that no matter how hard she worked, she wouldn't ever make it. Stepping closer, she poked a finger in his pec, which was a lot more solid than she'd anticipated. "I agreed to share custody," she said, "but to be clear, Lollipop is the rescue, not me. I'm not a charity case."

He grimaced and shoved a hand through his hair so that it looked like he'd just gotten out of bed. It should've made him look silly, but it actually had the opposite effect.

"You're not a rescue or a charity case," he said. "In fact, you're one of the strongest, most capable women I know. But—"

"No," she said. "Stop right there. Nothing good ever comes after a but." Unable to listen to reason, her fragile ego already bruised, she poked him again, harder this time so that it actually hurt her finger, which caused a flare of irritation in his eyes. He grabbed her hand in his and held tight.

Dammit, he really did have an edge to him and that was dangerously attractive.

No longer dating the wrong-for-me guys, she reminded herself. "This is a bad idea," she said. "A *colossally* bad idea."

"The shared custody or getting food?" he asked.

"Both. But especially going to eat."

"Why?"

"Because a guy like you doesn't . . ." She broke off, unwilling to finish the sentence she never should have started.

"A guy like me," he repeated. "Doesn't what?"

What part of this wasn't he getting? "You could have anyone," she said. "Which means *not* someone like me."

"Wow," he said quietly even though his eyes flashed anger, proving once again he was much more efficient at managing his temper than she was. "Impressive. You just managed to insult both of us in a single sentence."

She closed her eyes. "Yeah. I'm real good at that when I don't know what I'm doing. I lash out. I tried to warn you." She opened her eyes and gave him this truth at least. "I think I do it to make sure I don't have an audience for the occasionally *really* dumbass things I do—which I usually don't realize are dumb until right after I've done them."

He surprised her by letting out a self-deprecating laugh, like he maybe did the same thing, which she highly doubted. Then he gave a little tug on her hand, which he was still holding in his, so that she was forced to take a step into him. "You aren't conceited enough to think you're the only one of the two of us who has made mistakes, right?" he asked. "Because we've all made mistakes, Sadie."

He didn't say her name often, but when he did, the sound of it on his lips stilled her. There were other reactions too, but nothing that should be happening out in public.

"You think we're too different," he said.

"To be co-dog owners?" She shook her head. "No."

"You know that's not what I mean. You think we're too different for this." He waggled a finger between them and her stomach jangled some more.

"There's no this," she said.

He let out a low laugh. "Did you know that when you lie, you break eye contact? It's your tell." He waited until her gaze flew back to his, her temper renewed, before quietly saying, "You don't know enough about me to make that decision. And I get it. You don't want to know enough about me, because then you might be interested."

"Seriously," she murmured. "Are you some kind of mind reader?"

He wasn't feeling playful. "I've had a really long day, and I'm going to guess you did too. So while I get a kick out of bickering with you, I'm too hungry to keep it up, so can we agree to disagree until after we get food?"

"I didn't agree to food," she said.

"You don't like tacos? No problem. You pick."

She eyed the alley, thinking that was her shortcut out of here, but he tightened his grip on her hand.

"Don't run off," he said.

"I don't like it when people tell me what to do."

"I get that," he said. "And same. Also, I try very hard to *never* tell anyone what to do. But I think we need to finish this. *Please.*"

Another quiver from deep inside her. "I keep telling you, there's no this."

"Are you sure?" Very slowly and carefully, clearly giving her plenty of time to get away if she really wanted, he stepped into her, making her extremely aware that she now stood hemmed in between the alley wall and his body, neither quite touching her.

But she wanted him to. She actually ached to close that last inch between them. She didn't do it. Instead, she lifted her chin. "I could make you a eunuch right now if I wanted." The threat was minimalized by the fact that she whispered it, but suddenly holding on to her temper was difficult. So was talking. "Don't think I can't."

"I have no doubt," he said, still holding one of her hands. He took the other as well and squeezed gently. "I think you could probably do anything you set your mind to."

No one had ever said those words to her, not ever, and when she felt the back of her eyes sting unexpectedly, she closed them in self-defense.

"Sadie."

She shook her head.

"Look at me. Please?"

It was the damn *please* that had her opening her eyes. He'd closed the gap so that if she so much as took a breath, they'd be touching.

So she did just that. She took a deep breath, and then their bodies were up against each other, his warm and hard. Everywhere. "What's happening?" she whispered.

"I believe you're deciding between kicking me in the nuts and kissing me." One side of his mouth curved very slightly as he lifted their still joined hands above her head, against the wall. "But that last part might just be in my dreams."

"Yes," she whispered.

"Yes, it's just in my dreams?"

She meant to say yes again, she really did. She even opened her mouth to say it, because this was insane, this incredible . . . *craving* she had for him. It made no sense. Less than no sense, and yet . . .

She went up on tiptoe and touched her mouth to his.

He froze for a single beat, and then he was kissing her back. And in that very moment, it suddenly made perfect sense. As his hands dropped hers and his arms came around her, she felt . . . moved, more moved than she could ever remember. It was like her entire body had just come alive, and even more terrifying, her heart had come along for the ride. Again her throat tightened and her eyes prickled, but she didn't pull away. She did the opposite. She tried to deepen the kiss but Caleb pulled back a fraction to look into her eyes, using his thumb to swipe at a tear she hadn't even realized she'd shed.

"What's this?" he asked very quietly, cupping her face in his big hands.

She shook her head. "I've got something in my eye."

"Try again."

"Arf!"

They both looked down at Lollipop, who had pulled the leash as taut as she could to sit on one of Caleb's feet and was staring up at them impatiently.

"I think she's jealous," Sadie murmured.

But Caleb wasn't interested in a subject change. "Sadie."

"What?"

"You know what."

"Look, I don't know what that was, okay?" She lifted a shoulder. "Temporary insanity? Stupidity? Pick one."

He didn't laugh. Instead, he gave another slow head shake, like maybe he didn't know either, but then, with her face still sandwiched in his palms, with Lollipop on his foot, he kissed her again.

And then again.

Sadie . . . melted. That was the only word that worked for what happened to her. It was just that his body heat soaked into her and he smelled good, way too good, and she got drunk on it. She could feel herself curling closer, and then closer still for more. She wanted to take her mouth on a tour of his entire body, wanted to feel his muscles ripple and roll beneath her hands as she touched him. She wanted a whole hell of a lot of things, and each and every one of them shocked her.

This time when he pulled back, it took her a long moment to focus, but when she did, she found him looking more uncertain than she'd ever seen him.

"You're right," he murmured. "That's definitely insanity—temporary or otherwise." Then he took her by one hand and Lollipop by the leash and they walked down the alley to the street and to Ivy's taco truck.

Ivy grinned and waved at the sight of them, but as per the girl code, she didn't say anything embarrassing. She did however surprise Sadie by coming out and giving Caleb a warm hug.

"Thanks for the software update," she said.

"Anytime."

Ivy turned and hugged Sadie too, whispering in her ear, "That's a good look for you, the happy glow."

Whoa. Was that really the look she was projecting?

Ivy hopped back into her truck, all business now. "So. What can I get you?"

Caleb turned to Sadie, gesturing for her to go first. "Um . . ." She eyed the menu she had memorized. Nerves demanded she go for comfort food. "Two trailer park tacos," she said, mouth watering at the idea of the eggs, hash browns, cheese, and maple bacon tacos.

"Double that," Caleb said. "And add a side of grilled chicken for Lollipop, no heat."

They ate sitting at one of the two picnic benches near Ivy's taco truck, their view being the marina at the bottom of the hill and the bay beyond that. Sadie was jaded about a lot of things, but she never got tired of that view.

Afterward, Caleb offered to drive her and Lollipop home. She panicked. The forecast was for icy rain and record low temps, so she'd planned on sleeping in the Canvas Shop again for heat. "Why?" she asked.

He was surprised at the question. "Because I have a car and you don't?"

"I have a car, it's just being fixed," she said.

"And . . . I'm not going home yet. I've got some things I want to do in the tat shop." Liar, liar, pants on fire. What she wanted was another heart-stopping kiss. And then there was the 90 percent of her that wanted to invite him home and jump him. Okay, make that 75 percent because she couldn't remember if she'd shaved her legs that morning. Or what kind of undies she had on.

Caleb walked her and Lollipop to the courtyard and seemed to be planning on escorting her all the way to the Canvas Shop. "You don't have to walk me to the door," she said.

"I want to." He looked at her and smiled. "Afraid you won't be able to resist me?"

"No." *Yes.* She went for nonchalant, but on the inside she was trying not to collapse from the look of desire that crossed his face as they got to the door. He slowly slid one arm around her waist and pulled her into him as he cradled her head with his other hand. He lowered his mouth to hers and kissed her with a tenderness she'd never before experienced.

When the kiss ended, she just stared at him. "Still don't know what that is."

He didn't look concerned as he kissed her once more, not gently this time. She was panting when he pulled free and turned to go.

"Are you serious?" she asked his back. "You're just going to leave it like that?"

He faced her. "Like what?"

Unbearably turned on. And she could see he was too, hard for a man to hide it. "You could come in," she said, the words escaping her before she could stop them. "Everyone's gone for the night."

He walked back to her and her heart skipped a beat at the thought of what was going to happen now. And when he kissed her again, deeper this time, it was so good that she heard herself moan.

But then he pulled back again. "Not yet," he said.

She gaped at him.

One of his thumbs stroked over her bottom lip. "You haven't decided if you like me or not," he said and then he dropped his hands from her, bent to kiss Lollipop on top of her snout, and walked off.

"And what does me liking you have to do with anything?" she asked and heard his low laugh as he vanished.

Damn. Her heart was still pounding, body aching for things she was absolutely not going to give in to. Ever. The ratfink bastard. "It was definitely insanity," she whispered to Lollipop. "Temporary insanity."

Chapter 10

#WhatAboutSadie

A week later, Sadie was sitting in the bridal shop on the ground floor of the Pacific Pier Building listening to her mom, her aunt Thea, and her older sister, Clara, go on and on—and on and on—about Clara's upcoming wedding.

The shop was new and tastefully decorated. The owner of the shop, Addie, was actually a client of Sadie's. She'd tattooed over some scars Addie had wanted to not have to look at anymore.

Sadie had recommended the shop to Clara, but now she felt a little sorry for Addie, who was stuck dealing with the chaos that was the Lane family women.

"Sadie, are you even listening?" her mom asked.

"Of course." She totally wasn't listening. She was eating from a big bag of salt and vinegar chips and day-dreaming about the way Caleb had kissed her against the Canvas Shop's door last week. No, wait, she'd kissed him. She'd kissed him and it'd been . . . She shook her head, still dizzy from the feel of his mouth on hers.

It'd been a-maz-ing.

Every time she thought about it, she got a hot flash. Either she was going through the change of life at twenty-eight, or she had it bad.

Neither option appealed.

So she stuffed another chip into her mouth and went back to daydreaming about how it'd felt to be hauled up against Caleb's hard body, his hands gripping her like he didn't want to let her go, and his mouth, God, that mouth—

"Well then?"

Sadie jumped a little and glanced up at Clara, who was in her bridal gown looking . . . well, white. And perfect as always.

A seamstress and Addie, as well as Sadie's mom and aunt, fluttered around the bride, all of it reflecting back at Sadie, the sole audience, through the six huge floor-to-ceiling mirrors in a half circle around the bride-to-be.

"Yes or no?" her mom asked Sadie.

"Um . . ." She'd zoned out thinking about Caleb and wondering why she'd been stupid enough to avoid being alone with him for a long week. To stall, she made a show of looking around. "Anyone have ranch dip? No? Maybe a margarita?"

Her mom sighed. "Will you be serious for once?"

"I am serious. I'm starving."

"You keep eating those chips and we'll have to order up a size when we order your bridesmaid dress."

Addie sucked in a little breath of shock, but managed to say calmly, "We don't size-shame here."

"It's okay," Sadie told her. "I'm fairly un-shameable." And that was true. For the most part, the things her well-meaning family said didn't get to her. Except for once in a great while, in the deep, dark of the night when she lay in bed, replaying every stupid thing she'd ever done instead of sleeping, including stress-eating a big bag of chips so that her yoga pants—which had never seen an actual yoga class—became too tight.

With a sigh, she set aside the chips and carefully picked off a few crumbs so as to not make a mess. The gesture made her miss Lollipop, who had turned out to be a great companion and a most excellent vacuum cleaner.

For the past seven days she and Caleb had been co-parenting the adorable three-legged dog by handing off custody each day, the time varying depending on whether or not she worked at the spa. It'd been shockingly easy. This morning Caleb had picked up Lollipop early, leaving Sadie without a buffer between her and her family at the moment.

Not ideal.

But she smiled at the memory of Caleb dropping to his knees to hug Lollipop hello, laughing softly at the sight of several lip gloss kiss prints that Sadie had inadvertently left all over the dog's face. "Lucky dog," he'd murmured and something had quivered deep inside Sadie as their eyes had met and held.

And she'd had to admit to herself that she wouldn't have minded having her mouth on that square scruffy jaw.

Or on his lips . . .

"Helloooooo!" Clara went hands on hips, accidentally dislodging the seamstress off the platform. "Bride here! Can you or can you not see nipplage through this dress?"

Sadie looked over her sister's perfect store-bought C's. "Yep, but if it helps, it's pretty nice-looking nipplage."

Her aunt Thea gasped as if personally affronted.

"Oh my God." Clara slapped her hands over her breasts.

"No worries," Addie said quickly. "We carry some strapless bras for just this very thing. We can sew it right into the dress." She produced one quickly and Clara sucked in a breath at the price tag of one hundred bucks.

"It's fine," her mom said. "We don't put a price on hiding our nipples."

While the bride worked on getting herself into the bra, her mom looked around. "Now. What about Sadie?"

Sadie froze with a chip halfway to her mouth, realizing the question was the refrain of her entire life in three words.

What about Sadie?

Once upon a time this would have sent her spiraling. But she'd learned to accept herself.

Mostly.

Clara turned her attention from her reflection to Sadie. "Did you pick out which style of bridesmaid dress you like yet?"

"Whichever you want me to wear," Sadie said.

"I want you to pick."

Sadie glanced at the rack of bridesmaid dresses that they'd all already gone through. She loved Addie, she really did, but none of the dresses were her style. "Today's about you. I'll come back to do that another time."

Clara shook her head. "We've shopped around for months. Why can't you just pick one?"

"I don't know," Sadie said. "Why do bras cost a hundred bucks and dresses cost a gazillion dollars and yet men's shirts come in a plastic pack of four for ten bucks? Just another of life's little mysteries."

"Do you have any new tattoos you'll have to hide with your dress?" Aunt Thea asked.

Since the subject of Sadie's tattoos had long been a bone of contention, everyone stilled.

"Well, I'm just saying," Aunt Thea said. "They're pretty permanent, you know."

"And you have four kids," Clara said in Sadie's defense. "Those are pretty damn permanent too."

"It's okay," Sadie said, not wanting this to turn into a fight. "I'll wear whatever you guys want."

Her mom sighed.

Sadie knew that sigh. It was the martyr sigh. The one that said Sadie was being difficult again. And since she wasn't actually trying for difficult, she gave a peace offering. "Really. Whatever you guys want, I like them all."

At this, her sister snorted. "No, you don't. You hate big fancy weddings and all the craziness that goes with them."

"And yet you made me a bridesmaid."

"Hey, you should be thanking me for not making you maid of honor. Can you just pick the dress that you hate the least?"

Since Sadie wasn't a fan of taffeta or satin, not to mention weddings in general, she wasn't sure that was possible, but for Clara, she'd try. "Are you sure you don't have a favorite yourself?"

Addie gently piped in here, clearly trying to be helpful. "Usually, a bridesmaid really wants to have a say in what she wears—"

"Oh, that's just Sadie," her mom said. "Don't bother pushing her, she doesn't care. You could tell her the world was coming to an end tomorrow and she wouldn't care about that either."

Sadie stuffed another chip in her mouth. She'd heard her mom say this before, many times. It wasn't accurate, it wasn't even close to accurate, but she could see how her mom had gotten there, since when it came to the Lane family, Sadie was the Which-Of-These-Things-Is-Not-Like-The-Others.

And she got it, she really did. She'd grown up in a very normal middle-America-type existence. A suburban home complete with white picket fence, two parents and a sister who'd happily played soccer, taken gymnastic lessons, and been a Girl Scout.

And then there was Sadie, the square peg that

couldn't fit into the round hole to save her own life. Growing up, she'd preferred being alone with a sketch pad and a pencil to sports, clubs, or birthday parties. She'd been quiet, and when spoken to by anyone she didn't know, she'd come off as sullen and uninterested.

The uninterested part might have been true. But she had always felt so out of place in her own skin and hadn't known how to express that. She'd used her art when she could, drawing in secret, refusing to allow anyone to see her work.

Complicating her existence was the fact that she also didn't look like anyone in her family. Her parents and sister were tall and lanky lean. They ate like birds and exercised to within an inch of their regimented lives.

And that was great. For them.

But Sadie had never been lanky lean, not from day one, no matter how she ate or exercised. Nothing changed the fact that she was . . . well, curvy. And fighting it by restricting her food intake and exercising herself half to death for way too many years had only made her hate life.

Her parents had not known what to do with her. She'd been fourteen when they'd sneaked a peek into one of her sketch pads and found some drawings she'd done of a teenage girl wielding a knife, and they'd freaked out. Her mom had contacted a psychologist, Sadie's school, and practically the National Guard.

This had put her on near lock-down with little to no privacy allowed. They might as well have cut off her hands because drawing had been her only outlet. Once that had become monitored, she'd started a new secret thing, one she *could* control. The *only* thing she could control.

Cutting.

And when that had been discovered two years later, her parents had institutionalized her. The nightmare had lasted only a few weeks, but to this day it'd been the worst, darkest time of her life.

She'd come a long way since then, but it'd been a learning curve. These days she didn't care much about what people thought. And that alone was the reason she was still here. She didn't live to make people happy, even if those people were her own family.

Needing a quick bout of happy at the moment, she pulled out her phone and brought up her pics, specifically the one from this morning when Caleb had come to pick up Lollipop. She'd run on her three legs right for him and taken a flying leap. The pic was live, showing Lollipop hitting Caleb's chest and then his arms coming around the dog, but it was the smile on both man's and dog's face that caught her.

"What are you smiling at?" her mom asked, sitting next to her. "Who's that?"

Sadie had played aloof so long she'd almost started to believe it about herself, but the truth was, there wasn't anything aloof about how she felt about the dog. She was starting to come to terms with the fact that she felt a whole hell of a lot for the man too. Or at least certain parts of her did. "No one," she said and slipped her phone away.

Her mom opened her mouth to press, but Addie interrupted and cemented a place in Sadie's heart for it.

"How about this dress for you?" Addie asked. "It'd suit you." She was holding up a long lacy bridesmaid dress that was actually pretty except for the fact that it was pink. But at least it was pale pink, almost a champagne color, and who didn't like champagne . . . "This is the right color, yes?" she asked Clara.

Clara nodded. "And it's great for Sadie's skin tone."

"Her tattoos will show," her mom said. "And what will we do about her hair?"

Sadie reached for the bag of chips again just as her phone went off with a text from the Canvas Shop letting her know her next client was in.

Perfect.

She stood. "Sorry, gotta get to work." She hugged Addie, and then on second thought hugged her sister, her mom, and her aunt too, even though the Lanes weren't exactly the hugging type. Stepping back, she let out a breath, officially hugged out for the rest of the year. She was halfway out the door of the bridal shop when she heard her mom.

"But seriously, what about Sadie—?"

She couldn't hear the rest of the question, but chances were that it was a valid one. No one ever knew what to do with her.

Three minutes later, Sadie entered the Canvas Shop. Rocco gave a jerk of his head to the back room. His version of asking her to talk for a minute.

She followed him.

He leaned back against a counter and stared at her. His black hair was wild as always and months past needing a cut. His jeans were torn up, his kickass boots battered, his T-shirt advertised his own shop, and his expression was dialed to Cranky Ass. Unlike Sadie, who only had a few very strategically placed tattoos, Rocco was inked from head to toe. Tattoos gave a history, a road map so to speak. There were prison tats. Russian tats. Drunken tats . . . Every one of them told a story and Rocco had started young.

Not Sadie. After high school, she hadn't been able to get an apprenticeship with a tattoo artist, so she'd gotten her esthetician license instead and started doing permanent makeup instead, working at a spa that did a lot of pro bono work for cancer patients.

It'd been eye-opening. What she'd heard most often was the devastation of dealing with the aftermath and recovery, including surgical scars.

When she'd finally gotten a chance to become an apprentice at Rocco's tattoo shop, she'd jumped on it. She'd worked under him for three years, doing whatever work Rocco had given her before getting her own clients, and she'd made her own niche. Because unlike anyone else in their shop, she specialized in covering scars.

Rocco was only five years older than her, but besides being her boss, he also considered himself her protector and her very nosy older brother.

"What's going on?" she asked.

He handed her a brown bag from the coffee shop. It was filled with Tina's famous mouthwatering muffins.

"Wow," she said. "Thanks. Is it Christmas?"

"They're not from me."

Her heart took a good hard leap against her ribs as she realized they must be from Caleb. The night before he'd had a late work night and he'd needed her to cover

Lollipop for him. She'd happily done it and hadn't expected a reward of muffins, but she would take it.

Rocco met her gaze. "I thought you learned your lesson with the last suit."

He was referring to her very-ex-boyfriend, Wes. She'd dated him for six months a couple of years back and he'd nearly destroyed her. No, correction. She'd nearly allowed him to destroy her. In any case, she had a rule, she didn't talk about him. Ever. "Excuse me?" she asked in her best PMS voice.

"Don't pull that pissy tone, you know what I'm talking about."

Yeah, unfortunately she did. All her life she'd chosen the wrong guy. Clearly, there was something in her genetic makeup that made her go for guys who treated her much like her family did, like she was someone they weren't quite sure what to do with.

Wes had been a lawyer, of all things. Cool and calm and unflappable. And into her. It'd been that to draw her in, and once he'd paid her even the slightest bit of attention, she'd fallen hard.

Stupid, stupid, stupid . . . "Actually," she said, "I have no idea what you're talking about."

"Yeah?" Rocco pointed at her. "So why then are you using your lie voice, the one that's two octaves above your regular voice? You're dating Suits, just admit it."

"I'm not dating anyone. First of all, men are stupid. Second of all, I'm a new dog mom and holding down two jobs. Do the math. No time for a man anyway. Third . . ." She'd run out of reasons, so she went with a repeat. "Men are stupid." She jabbed a finger at him. "So you're wrong."

"Old Man Eddie saw you two getting all hot and heavy up against my front door."

"That was a week ago. Your news is old." Crap. "And Old Man Eddie smoked half his brain cells gone. He doesn't know what he saw."

Rocco shook his head. "You swore off men because you make bad decisions in that arena and you made me promise to hold you back." He snatched the bag of muffins and dug in. "So this is me, keeping my promise."

She snatched the bag back and the muffin from his fingers. "I release you from that promise."

"Wow," he said. "Okay, so remind me again, when you get into a mood like this, am I supposed to give you space or attention?"

"Yes," she said.

He tossed up his hands.

"There's nothing going on with me and Suits."

"Really?" he asked, voice heavy with disbelief. "Because he's been here every day this week."

"To exchange custody of Lollipop! And let me just

say, yes, fine, I've made some questionable choices, but I own those, okay? I stand by who I am now, and it'd sure be nice if the people in my life could do the same and have some damn confidence in me." She pointed at him. "And you know what? If you're in such a chatty mood, how about we talk about you and Tyler? I can see the screen on your phone and he just texted you. Twice. I thought you'd blocked him."

Tyler was Rocco's ex-boyfriend. They'd been together forever and then one day Rocco didn't show up for work. He'd stayed away for two whole weeks, word being that he'd gone on an epic bender after a blow-up fight and the subsequent breakup. When Rocco had finally showed back up at work, he'd been even more surly, grumpy, and pissed off at the world than usual. And refusing to discuss anything.

That had been a month ago.

Rocco's scowl deepened, if that was even possible. He glared at her. "My personal life isn't up for discussion."

"Ditto."

He shook his head. "I can't out-stubborn you, I don't even know why I try. Fine, get your heart stomped on again."

She shook her head, because that wasn't going to happen. She was insanely careful about that very thing.

Letting people in, letting them get to know her, meant revealing herself. All of herself. And her track record with that, with someone loving her for her, was zip.

As for why Caleb had gotten beneath her guard, she had no explanation for that. All she knew was that she would have to be even more careful now because no matter what she told Rocco, Caleb was working his way in through her walls with his easy confidence and just-for-her smile. She was definitely in trouble.

Or at least her heart was.

Chapter 11

#TakeTheWalk

The next evening, when Sadie closed up the Canvas Shop, she was restless as hell. She and Lollipop walked the length of the courtyard in the cold misty night, the dog pouncing on a fallen leaf, barking at a lamppost, making her laugh.

It felt good to have the three-legged sweetheart for company since her own thoughts skewed dark. But even with all Lollipop had been through, she wasn't wired for dark. Every walk was exciting, a chance for a new adventure.

Sadie's phone beeped into the chilly silence. A missed call and a voice mail. She grimaced. Caleb had tried on more than one occasion this past week to see her for reasons other than exchanging custody of Lollipop.

She'd evaded.

Not because of disinterest but the opposite. She was too interested, and that was scary shit. She was working up to facing those fears, she just wasn't there quite yet, so she brought up the message with her eyes half squinted.

But the message was from her sister.

Giving you a heads-up. Mom's going to ask you to make sure your hair doesn't have any primary colors in it for the wedding. Also, she wants your tats hidden. Your friend Addie seems to think she can add a lace panel to cover the infinity sign on the back of your shoulder, but Mom's worried that the ink will make the lace look dirty, so she's thinking maybe you also wear a wrap.

Sadie closed her eyes. Took a deep breath. And then opened her eyes again and texted a reply: It's your wedding, whatever you want.

Clara's response was, What I want is to not hear Mom say, "What about Sadie?" I'm tired of this being about you, okay? It's my wedding.

With a pang of guilt, Sadie texted one more message: I'll take care of it.

And then she turned off her phone because she had no idea how she was going to take care of it. Her hair was easy enough. The color was a wash-in and would come out with a few more shampoos. Her tattoos were slightly more problematic, but she loved them and wouldn't apologize for them. She'd simply have Addie double the lace if needed.

What she couldn't change was that she didn't know how to be what her family wanted, and she'd lost the need to try anyway. All she knew how to do was be . . . her.

And she liked her, just the way she was.

Mostly. Okay, so she was working on that too. She could certainly start by being a little more . . . open. If she was, if she hadn't avoided being alone with Caleb for an entire week like a chickenshit, she might've gotten another heart-stopping kiss.

And more . . .

Whew. Thinking of sex after not having it for three years made her a little shaky. Maybe she was hungry. Maybe she just needed French fries. Deciding that was it, she headed toward the pub, making a pit stop at the pet shop on the way. Willa was thankfully working late in the back, bathing a cocker spaniel.

"What's up?" Willa asked, blowing kissy faces to Lollipop.

"I'm in need of French fries."

"And you want to leave Lollipop here while you do," Willa guessed.

"If you don't mind."

"Not at all," Willa said. "I still owe ya."

"You don't."

"Yeah, I do." Willa staggered to her feet and rubbed her baby bump. "Remember when I told you that I wasn't feeling sexy, and that me and Keane hadn't managed to have sex in two weeks? And you told me it was never too late to have my slutty phase, that it builds character."

Sadie smiled. "And?"

"And last weekend, I hired a temp to take some of the overnight dog-sitting shifts. I bought some sexy stuff and seduced my husband. He was so happy, he coaxed me into hiring the new kid as a permanent addition." She smiled. "We needed that. I mean the night before, we'd fought over the fact that he wouldn't tell me where he'd hidden the candy I'd asked him to hide from me. I didn't speak to him for twelve hours."

"You're pregnant," Sadie said. "You were going stir-crazy."

"To say the least." Willa reached for Lollipop. "I've got her covered. Go have French fries. And a drink for me, okay?"

Two minutes later, Sadie walked into the pub. It was owned by friends of hers, the O'Riley brothers. Finn and Sean were bartending when she sat at the far right corner of the bar, which they kept reserved for the tight-knit group of friends who lived or worked in the Pacific Pier Building.

Finn jerked his chin her way in greeting. "Whatcha having tonight?"

She didn't drink much. She preferred to eat her calories, thank you very much, but after thinking about Caleb and how much he made her ache for things she'd given up, she realized she needed more than French fries. "Whiskey. On the rocks."

"Rough day?"

She shrugged. "A banana is a hundred calories. A shot of whiskey's only eighty. I'm just choosing wisely."

Someone slid onto the barstool next to hers. She didn't need to look over to know it was Caleb. She could tell because her nipples got hard.

"How about you?" Finn asked her new barstool neighbor. "Rough day?"

When he didn't answer right away, Sadie turned to look at him.

"More like frustrating," he murmured, eyes on her. "Someone I wanted to talk to is playing the coy game and hasn't returned a call."

"Maybe it's not about being coy," she said. "Maybe it's about being . . ." What? Afraid? That was weak. And she didn't do weak. "Cautious," she said.

"Where's the fun in that?" As he spoke, there was a flash of something in his gaze, maybe frustration that she was being aloof. But it was instinct, a knee-jerk reaction thanks to her need to try to control her emotions, especially around him.

And for him . . .

But now that he'd had his hands on her, she was having a hell of a time controlling herself at all. And he was changing a lot of what she thought she knew of him. On the outside, he gave the world that laid-back, easygoing smile. All while holding most of himself back.

But in those sixty seconds that he'd had his mouth and hands on her, he hadn't held anything back, giving her a glimpse of a man who had depths she hadn't even guessed at.

"What'll it be for you?" Finn asked Caleb.

"Fuzzy Navel."

Finn nodded and moved away to make the drinks.

Sadie went brows up. "Did you order a Fuzzy Navel just so I'd ask you why you'd order such a thing?"

"You mean a girlie drink?" he asked.

"To be fair, I'd question *any* gender's decision to order a Fuzzy Navel."

Finn came back with their drinks and an order of fries. "To share. Play nice," he said, looking at Sadie.

"Hey," she said but Finn was gone. And okay, so she could see why he'd direct that at her. She and Caleb dug into the fries and she realized something else— eating deliciously, perfectly crispy fries with someone, sharing a big blob of ketchup, their fingers occasionally bumping into each other . . . it was an intimacy all on its own.

"So," she said, watching as he sipped his drink, which made her smile because a big sexy guy ordering anything other than beer or a badass liquor was foreign to her. "I'll play. A Fuzzy Navel?"

He shrugged. "Maybe I'm trying to get in touch with my feminine side so I can understand what a certain woman is thinking when she looks at me."

She blinked. "Is it working?"

"No. You're a closed book."

She snorted. "You're making that up. You don't care about understanding what I'm thinking."

"I care more than you know," he said easily. "You're just not open to it because you're scared." He paused while she absorbed the absolute truth of that statement.

"But you're right," he said. "I didn't order the Fuzzy Navel to figure you out. I've got the feeling that nothing but time is going to help me figure you out." He took another sip, his eyes considering her. "I ordered it because it was my grandma's fave. She drank it whenever she was stressed, which was a lot. So now I do the same. It's sort of my way of toasting her on whichever cloud she's sitting on watching over me."

Damn. That was really sweet. And when a guy like Caleb did something sweet, it was also incredibly sexy. She took another sip of her drink. "Think she was watching when you pushed me up against the brick wall in the alley and kissed the hell out of me?"

Caleb choked on his drink and set the glass down. He'd been coming out of a meeting with Hunt Investigations, the security company on the second floor, when he'd seen Sadie walk into the bar. Completely unable to resist, he'd followed her in and sat next to her. He was breaking down her walls one brick at a time—or so he hoped—but he knew he still had a long way to go.

What he didn't know was why he insisted on pursuing this, pursuing *her*, when she clearly would rather pretend there was nothing between them. Maybe it was because of *that*, he thought with an ironic grimace. The seduction of being with a woman who didn't want anything from him was too much to resist . . .

In any case, he couldn't seem to stop himself.

"First," he said, "*you* kissed *me.* And second, damn, woman, thanks for putting the image of my grandma in my head and ruining the moment."

She laughed.

And God, he loved her laugh. It was deep and throaty, and she always seemed a little surprised that she could be amused.

"Why was she always stressed?" she asked.

He didn't like to think about his past, much less discuss it, but this was Sadie, and he took the fact that she was asking as a good sign. "She was a young single mom," he said, "and then her daughter became a young single mom with a bunch of kids. There were a lot of mouths to feed."

She just looked at him for a long beat. "And you were one of those mouths?"

He nodded.

"What happened to her?" she asked.

He turned back to his drink. "She died when I was little." It'd been a whole lot of years, but she'd spent the most time with him while his mom had been gone working night and day, and he still missed her.

He felt Sadie's hand cover his. He turned his over so that he was palm up and entangled his fingers with hers.

"I'm sorry," she said, eyes and voice warm. "I'm guessing things were rough after she was gone?"

She hadn't pulled her hand from his, and he ran his thumb along hers. It'd been a long time since such a simple touch had meant anything to him. "My mom did the best she could. My sisters helped. They all put their heads down and did whatever they had to do to raise me and send me off to college."

She appeared to be mesmerized by this story, by the fact that he hadn't been born rich and successful. "And now they work for you," she said.

"Yes."

"So you all . . . like each other."

He laughed. "Yes."

This seemed to be the biggest surprise of all for her. "And you're still close."

He wanted to bring their joined hands up to rub his aching chest, because she clearly couldn't compute a family unit that was tight and loved each other. "Yes, we're close, even though they still try to boss me around. Comes with being the baby of the family."

This got a smile out of her. "Cute."

"Or annoying and unnecessary," he said. "Which I tell them as often as I can get anyone to listen to me."

"So let me get this straight," she said. "At work you run this huge conglomerate and are a well-known venture capitalist with more responsibility than I could ever manage, but at home you're the baby?"

"See? Annoying, right?"

She shook her head. "Still cute."

When he grimaced, she smiled. "So how did you go from barely getting by to . . . ?" She waved her free hand up and down, gesturing to—presumably—his suit.

"I got lucky," he said.

She shook her head. "Going to call BS. No one's that lucky."

Giving in to temptation, he brought their joined hands up to his mouth so he could brush a kiss over her knuckles. "Now who's cute?" he murmured. "And yeah, I do pretty good for myself, but here's the thing—I didn't do it alone. I had help along the way. A lot of it. No one does it alone." Again, he brushed his mouth over her fingers.

She stared at him, squirming just a little bit. Kind of how Lollipop looked at him when she was both afraid to come out from beneath his bed and yet wanted in his arms badly.

Caleb Parker, dog whisperer. Hopefully also woman whisperer.

"Does your mom still work?" she asked.

"She's retired now. Three of my sisters work for me, though one's on maternity leave. My fourth sister's an intern for me and in grad school back east. My corporation's big on decent hours and great benefits, so I get to make sure they have a good life after giving me so much of theirs." He nodded to a table in the far corner of the pub. "My family's actually here tonight, or some of them anyway. It's date night."

She looked over and he knew what she was seeing. A striking forty-year-old brunette seated next to a handsome black man who was feeding her something off his fork and laughing—Sienne and Niles. Kayla's baby bump was huge. The man next to her was holding her hand and had a baby strapped to his chest. Hannah was flashing her phone around the table and everyone waved to whoever was on the FaceTime call. And only Emory was missing. She was probably who they were FaceTiming. Or maybe it was his cousin Kel. His sisters loved and adored him.

"Looks very cozy," Sadie murmured.

Caleb laughed. "Do not be fooled by appearances. We might love hard, but we fight just as hard and as often. Give it five minutes and someone will be up in arms about something."

"Why aren't you with them?"

He held her gaze. "I'm busy."

Her breath hitched and she pulled her hand free. "No, don't let me hold you up. We're not . . ."

He went brows up, really wanting to hear her finish that sentence.

She shook her head, clearly at a loss for words as she waved her hand around. "This is silly."

Grabbing her hand, he gave it a gentle squeeze. "What happened in the alley wasn't silly."

"No kidding." She touched her fingers to her lips as if she could still feel his kiss.

He could certainly still feel hers. "Your turn, Tough Girl."

Her gaze went from his mouth to his eyes. "What?"

"Your turn to give me something of you."

She blinked. "You know plenty about me."

"Actually, I don't." He leaned in a little closer. Their thighs touched and he watched her breath catch again. "Give me something," he murmured. "You owe me now."

At that, her eyes went hooded. She pulled back, fished some money from her pocket, and set it on the bar before standing.

"Running scared?" he asked.

She stilled and stared at him. "Maybe."

Honesty at least, he thought. "I'm not looking for your state secrets." Yet. "Just tell me . . . something."

"Like?" she asked suspiciously.

He shrugged. "Like . . . what you sing to in the shower. Or your favorite piercing . . ." Reaching up, he ran a finger along the shell of her ear and all the tiny silver rings neatly lined up there that always made him hot. "Tell me what gets you out of bed in the morning. Or what your parents are like, and if you have nosy-ass siblings like I do. Or maybe a secret wish you have that you've never fulfilled."

She bit her lower lip and he thought *oh yeah*, he wanted to know her secret wish.

"Hell, tell me what you watch on TV," he said. "I don't care. Just talk to me about you."

"Maybe I don't share like that."

"Ever?" he asked.

"Anymore."

He didn't often get frustrated. It wasn't in his nature, and plus he usually didn't care enough to get there. But according to his current level of frustration, he cared more than he wanted to admit. "My turn to call BS," he said on a rough laugh. "We share a dog. We shared a moment in the alley that included a kiss, a pretty great one. And I shared about my oddball family—more than I ever do with a woman, by the way—simply because you asked. You asked, Sadie," he repeated. "And now I'm asking."

She paused. "I need to rephrase. I *can't* do this. We're not going down the road you seem to think we are."

"And which road is that?"

She looked away, glancing over at his family. "I'm

not the white picket fence, two point five kids, soccer mom kind of woman," she said quietly. "And I think you know that."

"What I know," he said, standing to meet her toe-to-toe, "is that a week ago I'd have laughed at the thought of having enough time in my life for a dog. Or a woman." He ran his fingers along her jaw. "Now I find myself making time for both."

"Your point?" she asked.

"My point is that maybe you'll surprise yourself and find that you want to make time too."

She shook her head. "I won't," she whispered.

It seemed like an automatic denial. It also seemed like maybe she regretted it the moment it left her mouth, but though he waited, she didn't take it back.

He'd struck out. He didn't want to accept that, but he knew enough about stubborn women to know when to push and when to fold. So he handed her money back to her, dropped his own to cover their drinks and the fries, and walked away instead of pressing. He knew what he wanted, and he wanted Sadie. She was a calculated risk, and though he'd been a huge risk taker all his life, banking on Sadie being willing to face her emotions was a loser's bet.

Chapter 12

#ScrewUpBigOrNotAtAll

Sadie and Lollipop took the bus home and stayed up late cuddling for some badly needed body heat and equally badly needed affection.

It was another chilly night, but Sadie hadn't wanted to sleep at the Canvas Shop tonight. Tonight, she'd wanted her own space. So she'd turned on the heat, promising herself she'd cut something out of her budget to make up for it. She didn't yet know what that would be, but she'd figure it out. She always did.

She and Lollipop shared the couch. Sadie was pretending to be thinking about her financial situation, playing with the numbers. For instance, if she stopped eating, she could keep the heat on.

But she was just fooling herself. She wasn't thinking about money. She was thinking about Caleb. She'd
walked away from him. No, scratch that. She'd let him
walk away from her.

A part of her had felt a surge of righteousness when
he had. *There, see,* she'd told herself, *you did it, you
ruined it like you knew you would. Better now than
later . . .*

But the righteousness had faded, replaced by a cold
grip on her windpipe.

She'd pushed him away.

The panic had started right around the time their
conversation had taken them to a place she hadn't intended to go. It seemed so easy for him to just be . . .
him. He had no problem sharing about himself, he had
no hidden shame and little to hide.

But she had plenty of hidden shame and lots to hide.

She wanted to think she could keep most of that to
herself and still have him, but she'd realized while listening to his story that she couldn't. He'd never accept
less than everything from her.

So she'd had to shut this thing down.

But now there were regrets. A lot of them. She met
Lollipop's warm gaze. "How am I supposed to make
big decisions when I still have to sing the alphabet in
my head to get to the right letter?"

Lollipop panted happily, as always, willing to help.

"Listen, don't look, okay? I'm about to make yet another bad decision."

Lollipop yawned and closed her eyes while Sadie grabbed her phone.

No messages.

She hadn't expected one. So she called him. She wanted to text, but that felt like the coward's way out, and she'd already taken that route and it'd been the wrong choice.

He didn't answer and she listened to his voice message.

"If you have this number, you know what to do."

She drew a deep breath and at the beep said, "Hey. It's me. Sadie." She rolled her eyes at herself. "So . . . in the shower I sing to anything One Direction." Feeling stupid, she shook her head. "Okay, bye." She disconnected.

Lollipop looked at her.

She sighed. "You're right. I could do better." She hit his number and again waited for the beep. "Me again," she said. "My favorite piercing is—was—my tongue piercing, but only because of my family's horrified reaction to it, which is why I kept it for so long before removing it last year." She closed her eyes and Lollipop licked her face, telling her to keep being brave. "What gets me out of bed in the morning is the thought of one of Tina's buttered chocolate banana muffins. No, make that two of them—shit. Okay, fine, three. I need three muffins, if I'm being honest." And she was trying to be. But here came the hard part. "My parents are regular people, I guess. Suburbanites. Normal." She covered the phone and looked at Lollipop. "That's only a little white lie," she whispered and put her finger to her lips. "And my sister's on her way to being the same. Which, if you haven't figured it out, makes me the square peg trying to fit into a round hole. My mom was a science professor before she retired a few years ago. My dad's the dean at St. Mary's, and he's every bit the old-school hard-ass his title implies. Strict. Non-verbal. Hard to please. So you can imagine how well I fit in. As for a secret wish—"

Beeeeeep.

She stared at her phone. "The voice mail cut me off."

Lollipop cocked her head to the side.

Sadie sighed. "Yeah, probably for the best, right?"

"Arf!"

And then her phone rang.

Do Not Even Think About Falling For This Guy was FaceTime calling.

"Oh shit," she whispered and stared at it through another ring. Finally, she hit accept and Caleb's face swam into view. He was in an office, suit jacket off, tie gone, standing in front of floor-to-ceiling windows, the city of San Francisco spread out behind him in all its glory.

"You cut yourself off in a hell of a place," he said with a small smile. "You were about to tell me your secret fantasy."

She took a deep breath of relief. "*Wish*," she clarified. "I was about to tell you my secret wish. Not fantasy."

"Damn." He sighed. "Okay, I'm listening."

"It's not what you think."

"Try me."

She grimaced. "I've always kind of wanted to dance in the rain."

He smiled. "Nice," he said and looked like he meant it. "One Direction, huh?"

God. He'd been listening to her messages.

Lollipop nudged the screen, wanting to talk to her dad.

Caleb smiled at her but had eyes only for Sadie. "Are you in your pj's?"

"Yes."

His eyes heated, prompting her to look down at herself. She wore an oversize Giants T-shirt and had a blanket wrapped around most of her. "Are you kidding?" she asked. "This is practically rated G. Not even a little sexy."

"We have two very different ideas of what's sexy," he said.

Her mouth went dry. Her heart was pounding. She wanted him. Now. "Caleb?"

"Yeah?"

"Come over."

He let out a breath and held her eyes with his. "You're not ready yet."

"I think I know if I'm ready or not."

He gave a slow shake of his head. "I'm not rushing this. Not with you."

She had no idea what that meant, but hell if she'd beg. She lifted her chin. "And to think, I was just about ready to tell you my secret guilty TV pleasure."

"Tell me."

"No."

"I'll bring you muffins in the morning if you tell me."

Damn. "I watch *Married at First Sight,*" she admitted.

"What's that?"

"Just what it sounds like," she said. "It's a reality show. You've never seen it?"

He laughed. "Hell no."

She narrowed her eyes. "Tell anyone, and you'll need to sleep with your eyes open."

"So you're a closet romantic."

She sputtered and he tipped his head back and laughed some more, and the sight was so sexy, she forgot to be mad for a second. But just for a second. "Seriously, eyes open, Caleb."

He rubbed a hand over his scruffy jaw and grinned. "Come at me, babe. Give it your best shot. Fair warning, you might like what you find."

Deathly afraid that was true, she closed her eyes. "I'm sorry about tonight."

"For what, standing up to me and telling me you weren't ready for me to push? Don't be sorry, Sadie. Never be sorry for telling me the truth."

Something warm went through her at that and it took her a moment to realize what it was. Affection, and also a yearning. "You're different," she said.

He smiled. "'Night, Sadie."

"'Night, Caleb."

When he was gone, she looked at Lollipop. "Okay, maybe I see a tiny bit of why you heart him so much. But just a little bit, mind you."

She tucked Lollipop into her bed and then hit her own. And apparently spilling one's guts made one tired, because she fell asleep as soon as her head hit the pillow.

Chapter 13

#TacosSolveEverything

The next morning, Sadie woke in her cold apartment shocked that she'd slept all night. She hurriedly hopped into a hot shower under Lollipop's watchful, worried eye. The dog couldn't understand Sadie's love of hot water. Or any water at all.

As she dried off, she glanced at herself in the mirror. The woman staring back at her straightened and returned the careful once-over. At some point over the years, she'd grown to accept and even love her curves, and maybe actually truly liked the way she looked in her clothes.

Quite the change from her early years.

She hadn't told Caleb about those years, or even

hinted at them. She didn't know if she ever could. But there'd been a time when she couldn't have looked at herself in the mirror at all because she hated what she'd seen as so different from the rest of her family. She'd carried around a lot of hurt about that for a long time.

Then she'd learned how to release that pain in a way that had most definitely been outside society's idea of normal. Just the occasional small slices on her upper thigh where no one but her ever saw. Until she'd been caught of course, by her mom who'd never stopped snooping into Sadie's life, needing to know all her secrets.

It'd been born out of fear for her daughter's health and safety, Sadie got that now. She did. But back when she'd been a hurting, lonely, angry teenager, she hadn't understood why her mom had freaked out and called in the cavalry to save Sadie, who hadn't seen herself as needing saving.

That's when she'd been forced into psychiatric care including the involuntary stay in a hospital, followed by counseling, a change of schools, and constant supervision. She'd tried to explain she wasn't suicidal and never had been. She hadn't ever felt the need to die, but no one believed her.

Eventually, she'd come to terms with herself and had let that inner anger and pain go. The need to cut had faded away, with the exception of a relapse a few years ago when she'd let a guy inside her head and mess her up.

Briefly.

She ran her fingers along her right upper thigh, where she had three scars, each two inches long. Two of them were old and healed, but also invisible thanks to the fact that she'd had them covered by tattoos that read like two equations:

$$\frac{\text{Heart}}{\text{Mind}}$$

And:

$$\frac{\text{Courage}}{\text{Fear}}$$

The last scar wasn't as old as the others and hadn't been covered. With the dubious honor of maturity and hitting the ripe old age of twenty-eight last year, she'd arrived at an appreciation and understanding of who she was. And also the new and improved version of herself included not giving a rat's ass about what anyone thought of her.

Fact was, she just wasn't that same person anymore.

Her remaining scar was a reminder of that, like an ex-smoker who kept a pack of cigarettes somewhere as proof she was stronger than that. It was a badge of honor and a marker place for where she was in her life right now. And as it turned out, memories—the good, the bad, and the ugly—really were what made a person.

Thirty minutes later, she and Lollipop walked into the Pacific Pier Building. Caleb had texted her that he had an unexpected early meeting and wanted to know if she could hold Lollipop until later. Because she still hadn't convinced her boss at the day spa that Lollipop would make a great emotional support dog, she took her to Willa's shop and got to work.

Late afternoon, that shift ended and she picked up Lollipop and hit the Canvas Shop to find Rocco and his two other tattoo artists—Mini Moe, a Samoan guy who was possibly the biggest sweetheart Sadie had ever met, and Blue, Moe's virtual opposite. He was as small and skinny as Moe was big and huge, and he was no-where close to a sweetheart but perpetually scowling and ticked off at the world.

They were both in the back, hunched over a tray of tacos from Ivy's truck. The scent of them had Sadie's mouth watering.

"Saved you two," Rocco said. "Better hurry before I change my mind and eat 'em all."

Knowing that wasn't an idle threat, Sadie grabbed a taco in each hand. "Thanks," she said and took a huge bite, watching as Rocco dropped to his knees and tried to bribe Lollipop closer with a piece of chicken.

Lollipop's first move was her usual *I don't trust you* growl.

"No, pretty girl, you like me, remember?" Rocco held the meat out, patient in a way he never was with humans.

Lollipop took the chicken—she wasn't stupid—and then allowed him to pet her.

Sadie looked around for dessert, hoping there was a badly needed sugar rush in her future.

"Used to be you tried to stay away from men and desserts. Now . . ." Rocco gave her a look. "You've fallen off the wagon, chica."

"Thought you learned your lesson," Blue said over his taco.

"Apparently not." Mini Moe had opinions too. "Even though she's on a self-imposed man embargo."

Working in a shop with alpha men, she'd learned early to hold her own with them and stared them all down to let them know this wasn't up for discussion. She might be the youngest, but she was for *sure* the mightiest. "Do *not* need the peanut gallery's opinion on this."

Mini Moe met her gaze, winced, and went back to his tacos. Blue was next and he rolled his eyes, grumbled something about stupid millennials, and went back to eating.

"If you think millennials are stupid," she said, "then do not ever again ask me to fix the printer or laptop."

Rocco just shook his head. "I have a point," he said. "That is that Wes devastated you. I told you what we'd do to the next guy who hurt you. You should know, nothing's changed there, no matter who he is, rich dude or not."

Mini Moe nodded.

Blue nodded.

And Sadie blew out a sigh. "Wes didn't devastate me, the situation did. And that was three years ago. I'm stronger now, and no longer that stupid. No one could get to me like that again."

"He set you back," Rocco said stubbornly. "He set you back in your recovery."

"Momentarily," she agreed. "But I got a handle on it, I've had a handle on it, and I've been fine for a long time."

At his mouth quirk, she smiled. "Okay, so 'fine' is relative. We all know I'll never be the world's definition of fine, but I'm something even better. I'm *my* version of fine."

Rocco finally smiled. "Can't argue with that." Snagging her around the neck with a beefy arm, he pulled her in for a quick hug.

She hugged him back, knowing he was worried. But she knew she didn't need his worry. She *was* fine. And luckily the discussion was now over because her first client of the day walked in.

Cal was a local PI and a repeat customer. He'd been her first client, one of Rocco's early referrals, and though she worked with mostly women now, she had a fondness for Cal because he'd been her first. They'd become friends over the past few years as she'd worked on his sleeve. Today he was having her work on the American flag low on his hipbone, and as always, once she got started, he began to talk to distract himself from the pain.

Today the topic was his current girlfriend, who he thought might be cheating on him.

"If you think there's something going on," she said, "there's something going on."

"I don't know for sure."

She lifted her head and looked at him. "Come on. You know."

He blew out a breath. "Yeah. Maybe. She said I could go through her phone and see for myself though."

"If you do it, don't bother looking for messages from

guys," she said. "Look for her and her BFF's text messages. The good shit's in there, trust me."

He sighed. "It's hard to meet the good ones."

"That's because they don't usually frequent the dives you frequent. Go to Target. The female to male ratio is ten to one and they're already looking for things they don't need."

He laughed and rubbed a hand over his eyes.

"You're tired," she said.

"I'm on a case I hate. A couple getting divorced and they're fighting over custody of their three kids. The husband wants physical proof she's cheating."

"Seems to be the theme of the day."

"Yeah." He shook his head. "I got the proof, unfortunately—a recording of her having sex with someone else." He brought something up on his phone.

It was a recording. A woman was moaning softly.

"Maybe she's just eating something good," Sadie said. "Like cheesecake."

He gave her a look of disbelief.

"Hey," she said. "I moan like that when I'm eating cheesecake. The right cheesecake's better than sex."

"Baby doll, then you're not having the right kind of sex."

No kidding. She was having zero sex.

The moaning on the recording got a little louder and

then there was a softly panted "oh yeah, right there . . . that's it, don't stop, please God, don't stop!"

Sadie froze. She hated the word *triggered*, but that's exactly what happened to her. She was thrown back to a time she didn't want to revisit, but her mind didn't care. "Turn it off," she whispered. She pointed at his phone. "Stop it." Her heart was pounding and she was having trouble drawing in enough air. She felt . . . icky. And ashamed. Not a good combination for her. Horrified, she pushed Cal. "Turn. It. Off," she said again, or she thought she did, but she actually wasn't sure the words came out. Her reaction was startling, even to herself, but that they were taking this woman's life out of context, making it dirtier than it was, seemed incredibly wrong and unfair.

And Sadie knew all about things not being fair.

Very few people knew about her past. She knew if people did know, she'd be judged just as she'd judged the woman on the tape. And at the thought, a renewed rush of blood roared in her ears and her limbs went leaden, and she knew exactly what it was. The therapist she'd seen for five years had laid it out for her.

An impending anxiety attack.

And Cal still hadn't turned off the tape. She snatched his phone, tapped the screen to cut it off and stared at him, breathing a little too hard. Shaking her head, she moved around the cot to walk away, needing a moment. She yanked the curtain aside and—

Came face-to-face with Caleb.

Lollipop was at his side, looking very happy. Not Caleb. His usual easygoing expression was nowhere in view. His eyes were tight, his mouth a little grim as he took in the sight of her. He looked beyond her to Cal still sprawled out in her chair, shirt off, pants unzipped and dangerously low on his hips, which had been the point since that's what she'd been working on.

She turned back to Caleb, who'd turned away without a word and was heading to the door.

What the hell?

"Sadie," Cal said behind her, sitting up. "I'm sorry. I clearly hit a nerve for you and I . . . I'm sorry. I was out of line." He shoved his phone away. "You okay?"

She swiped a hand over her eyes and realized that her hand was shaking. "Yes."

"Is that your boyfriend? I think he thought we were the ones having sex."

She stared at him and then whipped out of the cubicle. "Hey," she called to Caleb.

He had Lollipop on a leash and with one hand on the door, he craned his neck and met her gaze, eyes unreadable and cool, mouth grim and tight.

Yep. Cal was right. That was exactly what Caleb

thought, that she'd been having sex. With a client. At work. With other people in the place.

Unbelievable.

There were so many, many things wrong with that, she saw red. Furious, she strode across the floor until she was right in his face. Which was far better than shaking like a coward who didn't like to face her own dark, secret, twisty past.

But now that she was standing there right in front of him, so much bubbling inside her that she thought she might implode, she couldn't find any words.

Caleb just looked at her, no smile, no soft "hey" like usual, nothing. With a single shake of her head, she whirled on her heel and strode through the shop. "Need a minute," she said tightly to Rocco.

Rocco, fluent in the language of moodiness since he was the king of moodiness, gave her a single curt nod.

He'd hold down the fort.

She ran out the back door, around to the courtyard and straight for the stairs. She could've taken the elevator, but she had too much electric toxic energy flowing through her.

Five sets of stairs later, she exited onto the roof through a door only a select few in the building knew about, much less had access to, gasping for breath.

Up here, she was on top of the world.

She could see down to the marina and the glorious red of the Golden Gate Bridge against the azure blue of the bay. She could see the infamous Alcatraz, the Palace of Fine Arts, the Coit Tower in Telegraph Hill, and the new massive Salesforce Tower. She turned in a slow circle, taking in the amazing three-hundred-and-sixty-degree view as she worked at slowing her breathing, trying to consciously control her wildly ricocheting thoughts.

Still feeling shaky, she moved to the small love seat in the far corner that the owner of the building, Spence Baldwin, had brought up here. He liked to stargaze.

Sadie liked to be alone.

She sank to the love seat and covered her eyes, knowing the truth. She'd lost her collective shit, and oh how she hated that. It signified a weakness, and more than anything, she hated to be weak.

And yet she was. Three years ago, she'd been so proud of herself, feeling like she'd conquered her past, come to terms with herself. She'd moved on with a clean slate.

But then she'd met Wes. And as ashamed as she was to admit this to herself, he'd set her back. Not at first. For the first four months, it'd been great. He'd had his life together and that had been attractive to her. But work had gotten rough for him and he'd gotten moody, taking it out on her one night as he'd stripped off the tie and suit jacket she thought she loved so much.

He'd said some cruel things that night, such as he couldn't talk to her about what was important to him because she wasn't like normal people, meaning she didn't worry about job security or save for the future because the future didn't seem to mean anything to her.

None of which was actually true. At least, not true anymore, because she'd been changing, growing up, maturing, and those things had become important to her. But hearing him throw her old faults in her face had been devastating. She'd escaped into her bathroom, stared at herself in the mirror, and hadn't recognized the face staring back at her.

Her plain brown hair because Wes had thought the use of "not hair" colors such as streaks of purple meant mental instability.

No piercings except the two small hoops in her ears.

Spray tan because he thought her skin too pasty white.

Face just a little bit gaunt because he didn't believe in desserts and felt they were too big of a weakness for her.

Ashamed at what she'd done next, of the memories assaulting her, Sadie leaned her head back against the love seat on the roof and closed her eyes.

But she couldn't erase the movie playing in her head. She'd tugged her sundress up, exposing her upper thigh. She'd had her two scars tattooed over by then and she loved those tattoos. Not willing to ruin them, she'd pressed a razor blade to the skin just beneath the second tattoo.

She hadn't cut herself since age seventeen and that she'd let herself be so affected truly humiliated and horrified her. But that wasn't even the worst part of that night. Nope, it had been when she'd heard a husky male moan and looked up.

Wes standing in the bathroom doorway, videoing her on his phone, his eyes dark with excitement.

He'd fetishized her cutting.

She'd never felt so exposed in her life, and that was saying something given the time she'd spent locked away, the forced therapy, the poking and prodding of doctors to soothe her freaked-out mom.

Unable to sit still, Sadie stared up at the sky. With about a half hour until dark, it was a kaleidoscope of colors. A few clouds, one of which looked like an elephant floating lazily across the sky. Another looked like a pepperoni pizza, which reminded her that she was hungry again.

And far too antsy to sit.

Rising, she took the few steps to the corner of the

building, liking the wind on her face. Almost without thinking about it, she rubbed the phantom ache at the top of her thigh.

"Sadie."

Startled, she simply reacted to the low voice that came from just behind her, twisting, her arms coming up into a defensive pose as she led with a roundhouse kick designed to land right at a man's groin.

That man being the last man she wanted to see right then. Caleb.

Chapter 14

#SomeThingsTakeTime

Caleb dodged the foot aimed at his family jewels, instead taking Sadie's deceptively hard kick to his right upper thigh. "Damn, woman," he said, fascinated as he rubbed the spot where he most definitely was going to bruise. "You've got moves."

She didn't seem impressed by his opinion. Or by him. And he knew he'd set them back more than a few steps with whatever that had been downstairs. She was pale, her eyes hollow. "I didn't mean to scare you," he said, allowing her to keep the distance she'd put between them.

Without responding, she crossed her arms over her chest and turned away, going back to staring out at the setting sun. She was wearing a long black knit skirt that had a slit up the back and clung to her hips and legs. Her top was sheer black and gauzy, fitting loose over a soft gray camisole that hugged her like a second skin. She wore kickass boots, which matched the kickass expression on her face. If she was trying to intimidate the world, the fuck-off-and-die 'tude was a nice touch.

An icy breeze blew over them and he saw her shiver. He came up behind her, making sure to let his footsteps make enough noise that she knew he was coming. Stopping a few inches back, he shrugged out of his jacket and said, "You're chilled. I'm going to put my jacket on your shoulders." He waited a beat, but she didn't respond so he covered her shoulders.

She immediately slid her arms into the sleeves and hugged the material close to her. "Thanks," she said quietly. Begrudgingly.

"She speaks," he said lightly, when he was feeling anything but light. "Sadie. Look at me?"

She hesitated but turned to face him. Her face was closed off. She was always so tough and impenetrable, and yet in that moment also heartbreakingly vulnerable. And damn if that didn't get him right in the gut because if anyone understood having to be tough on the outside to protect yourself, it was him. "I upset you. I'm sorry."

"Why?"

"Why?" he repeated. "Because we're friends and—"

She laughed mirthlessly. "Seriously? Friends? Because five minutes ago you believed I was having sex with a client. You actually thought I'd do that, on a job—" Breaking off, she shook her head and closed her mouth.

"Listen," he said quietly. "I didn't start this conversation by saying I was very smart as it pertains to women."

She snorted her opinion of that.

"And whatever I thought when I first walked up to your workstation," he said. "It was a knee-jerk reaction and a bad one. In my defense, the sounds coming from behind the curtain . . . They really sounded like—"

"A woman eating cheesecake?" she asked.

He smiled. "No one sounds like that eating cheesecake."

"I do." She gave him a look, an indecipherable look. "Good cheesecake is better than sex."

He realized she was testing him, and that was fine. One, he wasn't going anywhere. And two, he was going to always be himself—honest, if not brutally so. "If that's true, then the people you've been with are idiots."

"It was a recording," she said. "My client's a detective and he was just messing around through the pain of getting a tattoo, playing a tape of potential evidence that he never should've played for me."

"Okay," he said. "So that explains that."

She shook her head. "It doesn't explain your reaction, or why you'd believe it of me."

Good point. He met her gaze and gave her that honesty he wasn't sure she was ready for. Guess he had some testing of his own to do. "I told you once that I have a bad habit of assuming the worst," he said. "I wasn't making that up. I assume the worst and go to a dark place."

"To mull things over," she said.

So she did remember. "And often, I'll sabotage a good thing when I have it."

She stared at him for a beat. "Why?"

He shrugged. "I guess because I don't like being vulnerable."

"Me either. And I guarantee you, my dark place is darker than yours, so I get that too." She paused. "We were a good thing?"

His heart took a good hard kick at the past tense. "Yes. Sadie—"

"I'm sorry I kicked you."

He was surprised and relieved at the words, but he shook his head. "No. Don't be. I like knowing you can defend yourself."

"Did I hurt you?"

"You've got a good hard kick, but I'll live," he said. "Next time you use a mawashi geri, extend your hip and hit with your straightened instep. And then pull your foot back faster so your opponent can't grab your leg."

She took this in for a moment. "Mawashi geri?"

"A roundhouse kick. It's a Japanese martial arts move."

She cocked her head. "Do you know a lot about martial arts?"

"Some. It's a good workout," he said.

She nodded and then hesitated, like she had something to say and wasn't sure how to say it. Employing a tactic he'd learned at the knees of too many females in his life from a young age, he held his tongue and waited her out.

"I sabotage a good thing too," she admitted. "Always have. I don't trust them, I don't believe them. So I mess with them until they go away."

Their gazes met and held. Slowly, giving her plenty of time to kick him again if she wanted, he reached for her hand. Nothing with her was ever going to come easy, he knew this and was okay with that. "I'm the one who should be sorry. I hate that I let you think I'd believe you were having sex with a client on the job.

That was shitty, really shitty. I don't blame you for getting mad. You should've kicked my ass."

She looked down at her hand in his. "I think I got mad because what you thought was happening is so far from my reality that it isn't funny. I haven't had sex with anyone for three years."

He waited until she met his gaze. "That's a long time," he murmured, wanting to know more. What had happened three years ago to so thoroughly put her off being intimate with someone?

"It didn't feel all that long." She paused and slid him an ironic glance. "Not until . . ."

He went brows up.

"We kissed." She looked at his mouth like maybe she wanted it back on hers.

"It was a pretty great kiss," he said.

"Was it?" She shrugged. "I can't remember."

His laugh was low and rough as he pulled her into him. She always went toe-to-toe with him, challenged him in a way no one else ever did. It was sexy as hell. "Liar," he whispered and cupped the back of her head, bringing her mouth to his. "But let me remind you . . ."

He kissed her, a sensuous, delicious kiss with a lot of tongue that had heat exploding in his chest and radiating out to every part of his body. It rushed north to get his heart kicking hard and south to rev up the rest of him, melting everything else along the way. Her mouth was every bit as eager as his, trailing up his jaw, teeth nipping at his ear, and then down his throat, and he just about lost consciousness. By the time they surfaced, he was more than half-gone.

And given her heavy breathing, she felt the same.

Then she shivered and he ran his hands up and down her arms, feeling like an asshole for keeping her outside in this temperature. "You're icy cold. I want to get you back inside. How much longer are you working?"

She touched her fingers to her mouth, still looking dazed.

"Sadie?"

"Right." She looked at her phone and shook her head. "Rocco just texted me that Cal's rescheduled. I'm done."

Relieved, he nodded. "Then let's get you home. You parked nearby?"

"I took the bus today."

"What happened to your car?" he asked.

"It's still out for repairs. I'm picking it up later this week."

"Okay, then let's go get Lollipop from Rocco and I'll drive you home."

She shocked him by nodding and keeping her hand

in his as they took the stairs. At the Canvas Shop, Rocco handed Sadie a container. "Lasagna leftovers. Take it," he said. "I'm going out tonight and don't want it to go to waste."

"You're going out?" Sadie asked, sounding surprised.

Rocco grinned. It was the first time Caleb had ever seen it and it was a good look on the guy.

"Got a call from an old friend. An *apologetic* old friend," Rocco said cryptically. "We're having dinner."

Sadie narrowed her eyes. "Tell Tyler if he hurts you again, I'm coming for him and it won't be pretty."

Rocco laughed. Laughed. And then nodded. "I'll pass along the message, but he said he already kicked his own ass."

Sadie hugged Rocco, kissed him on the cheek, and whispered, "Keep your guard up."

"Where's the fun in that?" Rocco asked.

Sadie was quiet as Caleb walked her out to his car, which he'd started remotely, heater cranked. When he opened the passenger door, both woman and dog sighed in pleasure at the vents blasting warm air at them.

As Caleb slid behind the wheel, Sadie's phone rang and she grimaced. "It's my mom."

"It's okay," he said. "Take it if you want."

She sighed again and answered. "Hey, Mom. Yeah.

Fresh start.

Okay." Pause. "Okay. Uh-huh. Yeah, okay." Another pause. "Okay." Still another pause. "Okay. Okay. Bye. *Okay.* Okay . . ." She pulled the phone from her ear and disconnected. "Bad connection," she murmured. "Must be the tunnel we just went through."

There'd been no tunnel. He smiled. "Tough call?"

"It was my mother," she repeated, like that explained it all.

"Where am I taking you?"

She rattled off her address, though he didn't have to plug it into his GPS. He knew the city inside and out. She lived in a neighborhood called the Tenderloin, one of San Francisco's most notorious areas. The funky colorful streets were a mix of dangerous and trendy, featuring a mixed bag of hole-in-the-wall places to eat. Nightlife ranged from dark, *dark* dives slinging beer and shots to speakeasy-style bars serving craft cocktails. Residential buildings coexisted with underground indie live theater and packs of homeless people living in tents right on the sidewalks. He managed to find a spot a block down from Sadie's building, across from the police station where a guy in handcuffs was being marched inside.

"I know it's a nutty place," Sadie said, peering out the windshield, "but the Korean barbecue on the corner is delicious and my neighbors are all really nice." She unhooked her seatbelt and faced him. "Thanks for the ride." She turned to the back, leaning in to kiss and hug Lollipop goodbye. "See you tomorrow, baby." She went to exit the car and gasped in surprise to find Caleb already outside, holding the door open for her.

She slowly rose to her feet, their bodies extremely close between the car and the opened door. "Bet that move of opening the door works on women all day long," she murmured.

"That 'move' is meant to be good manners and nothing more," he said. "It's not a pickup tool." He smiled. "I don't need it."

She laughed. "You're right. You don't. You don't have to walk me up."

"I know I don't have to," he said. "I want to." He opened the back door and let Lollipop out, holding her leash. "Lead the way."

"Look, Suits—"

"We're back to that?" he asked. "Seriously? You just had your tongue halfway down my throat. It's time to use my name. Say it."

"You're right," she said. "I did that to irritate you, so you'd get back in your car and leave."

It didn't escape him that she still didn't say his name. "If you want me to leave, all you have to do is say so. It's your choice, Sadie. It's always your choice."

She stared at him for a beat, and then another. Then she gestured with her chin and they walked to her building. She lived on the third floor and it was a walkup. At her door, she pulled out her key but didn't use it. Instead, she lifted her face to his. "Thanks for the ride."

"Open up," he said. "You should never loiter in this hallway."

She unlocked the door but then blocked his way in, bending to give Lollipop another proper goodbye. This took like five minutes. Finally rising, she met Caleb's eyes. "Goodnight to you too."

And her goodbye to him had taken a second. But he'd told her it was her choice and he'd meant it. "Goodnight."

Lollipop tried to get inside. Sadie paused, looked behind her into the apartment and then bit her lower lip. "Fine. You can come in. For a minute."

The dog was all in.

So was Caleb. He shut and locked the door behind him, taking a sweeping gaze across her place. It was small, with comfortable-looking and very lived-in furniture and colorful throw rugs scattered throughout.

Cute. Cozy. But not warm. In fact, it was freezing in here. "Something wrong with your heat?"

"No." She moved into the kitchen and put fresh

water into Lollipop's bowl. She put the container Rocco had handed her into her fridge, which was looking pretty bare.

"Just haven't had a chance to go to the grocery store," she said to his unasked question, turning away to scoop some food for Lollipop, who pounced on it and happily dug in.

Caleb kept his eyes on Sadie. He knew she wanted to think she was an island, that she was unreadable and not easily figured out, but she was wrong.

He already knew she was struggling financially. He wasn't going to be able to ignore that. He wouldn't have been able to ignore it for a perfect stranger, so he certainly couldn't for a woman he suspected he was falling for big-time. "You're pretty new at the day spa," he said.

"Yes."

"And you're still building your clientele at the Canvas Shop."

"Yes." She narrowed her eyes. "Your point?"

"I could help—"

"Wow, would you look at the time?" She strode to the door and opened it for him. "Okay, you got your little peek into my world. Time to go." She added a little chin jerk to the opened door.

Thinking the new energy in the room meant playtime, Lollipop loped a circle around them with an excited bark.

Caleb moved to the door, stopping very close to Sadie. So close that their bodies brushed up against each other. She could've stepped back, but she didn't. He decided to take that as a good sign. "Everyone struggles sometimes, you know that, right?"

"Do you offer to help everyone then?" she asked in a deceptively serene voice. Deceptive because her eyes were flashing temper.

"I help who I can." He paused. "Sadie . . ."

She closed her eyes. Reaching out, he gently shut and locked the door again, staying on the inside with her. And when he stepped even closer, she put her hands on his chest, her fingers curling into his shirt, whether to pull him closer or keep him at bay, he wasn't sure.

"You drive me crazy," she murmured. "You know that, right?"

"Yeah. And ditto." Liking her hands on him, he decided to go with optimism and wrapped his arms around her.

She pressed her face into the crook of his neck and inhaled deeply, like she craved the scent of him, and he felt his body react. "Sadie. About your heater—"

"You aren't going to be nosy and bossy about this, are you?"

"Nosy and bossy are the female Parkers, not me."

She snorted. "Okay."

Wrapping her hair around his fist, he used it to lift her face so he could look into her eyes. "So you're saying *I'm* nosy and bossy."

She laughed but pressed herself a little closer to him so he forgave her.

"Hello," she said, still smiling. "Have you met yourself?"

"So I like to be aware of what's going on around me, and—"

"*B-O-S-S-Y*," she said, spelling out the word. "And you also always need things to go your way."

"Okay, so that might be true. And you're changing the subject."

"I'm not a charity case, remember? So thank you for caring and offering, but I'm fine." She said all this without taking her hands off him. A good sign, right?

An even better one was when she nudged him up against the door at his back and pinned him there.

His hands went to her waist, slid up her arms, and cupped her face. "Sadie."

She stared at his mouth. "Yeah?"

"I'm going to kiss you now. If you've got a problem with that, tell me, okay? Don't put that lethal knee of yours into action and ruin my chances of having kids."

She looked from his mouth to his eyes, her own surprised. "You want kids?"

"Yeah, maybe. Someday." He gave a small smile when she just stared at him. "What?"

"I guess I'm just a little . . . fascinated by the idea of you being a dad to a couple of mini suits running around, taking on the world with all that effortless charm and charisma you put out there."

He smiled. "You think I'm charming and charismatic?"

"I think you're a lot of things."

He stroked a finger along her temple, tucking a loose strand of hair back from her face as he nudged in closer.

She bit her lower lip and let out an almost inaudible moan, rocking her body to his.

Yeah. For once they were on the same page at the same time.

"What are you waiting for?" she whispered.

Leaning in, he nuzzled her neck just below her ear. "Your body's saying yes," he murmured, "but that's only partial consent."

Her hands fisted on his shirt. "Seriously. You're a nut."

"Uh-huh." He kissed the spot just beneath her ear and then gently sucked, smiling when she shivered and moaned again. "But a nut you want to kiss, right?"

"Yes, very much, even if I'm still trying to figure you out."

He blazed a trail down her throat with his tongue while running his hands down her arms, to her hips, which she was still rocking into his, driving him half-mad. "Some things take time to figure out," he murmured. "There's no rush."

"Says you," she whispered and drew his head down to hers.

Chapter 15

#ShowDontTell

Sadie so completely lost herself in Caleb's kiss that when she pulled back for air, she was shocked to find she'd tugged his shirt free from the waistband of his pants and unbuttoned it. Her hands were flat on his scrumptious abs trying to decide between heading north or south.

No slouch, he had one palm full of her ass, his other beneath her shirt cupping a breast. When his teeth grazed her ear, need slid through her like fine wine. She was taking short ragged breaths, but his breathing wasn't any more steady than hers as he slowly loosened his grip on her and gulped in some air.

She'd wanted to see his control slip, and it thrilled her.

"Sadie. Tell me you want this as much as I do."

It was cold enough in her place that their breath crystallized. Staying close for body heat, she slid her fingers into his hair to tug his face back to hers. "I want this," she said against his lips and then she kissed him. "I want you tonight, Caleb."

His eyes heated when she said his name. "Just tonight."

It wasn't just a statement, it was also a question. "Yes," she said. "Is that enough for you?"

He made a sound, low and deep, which rumbled through his chest, vibrating against hers, making her nipples go hard. He looked like a man being offered a present he'd dreamed of but hadn't expected to ever have. "It's enough for now," he answered. "Be sure, Sadie."

"Oh, I'm very sure."

With a groan, he took over, hoisting her up his body, wrapping her legs around his hips, heading with her to her bedroom. Her room was lit only by a slant of light from her living room lamp. It was chilly, very chilly, but it wouldn't stay that way for long, she thought as he let her slowly slide down his body. His chestnut eyes, darkened to the deepest pools of brown, met her gaze with a dizzying amount of heat.

Then he kissed her and they both went up in flames.

She was the sexiest thing Caleb had ever seen. He let his hands settle on her hips, holding her still for him as he lowered his head, his mouth dragging wet hot kisses across her collarbone. He stopped briefly at the hollow of her throat where his tongue dipped in for a taste while he lifted her shirt over her head and tossed it aside. "It'd be warmer at my place," he said.

"Too far away. Just leave some clothes on, and I've got lots of blankets." She tried to tug his shirt from his shoulders but he was too busy working her camisole down to bunch at her waist. When he stroked a hand over the low-cut black lace bra, his fingers slipping beneath the lace to tease her nipples, her breathy moan fueled him. Then her bra fell away and she sucked in a breath. "You've got a hidden talent."

"I've got several." He'd had many, many fantasies about this, but Sadie in the flesh was better than any of his fantasies had ever been. He nudged her to the bed and followed her down, crawling up her body, leaving no question about his intentions.

She didn't shy away. Instead, she reached for the top button on his pants. "Off," she demanded.

Going up on his knees to assist, he froze when he found Lollipop in the doorway, staring at them. Specifically him, her head cocked as if she was puzzled.

"It's bedtime, baby," he said. "Go to your bed."

"I am in my bed," Sadie said cheekily, laughing when he rolled his eyes at her smartassery.

Lollipop whined.

"Ignore her," Sadie said. "She doesn't sleep on my bed so she isn't expecting that."

He grimaced.

"Are you kidding me?" she asked. "You still let her sleep with you? I told you not to do that."

"Hey, I did the research," he said. "There are lots of valid reasons why you should let your dog sleep with you."

"Name 'em."

He ticked them off on his fingers. "They keep you warm, they relieve stress, reduce depression, help you fall asleep faster, make you live longer, and there's always free hugs available."

"Wow," she said, coming up on her elbows. "Maybe we should agree to temporarily shelve how ridiculous you are and get back to you making me a very happy woman."

"Absolutely." Then, hands planted on either side of her head, he lowered himself to her and—

Lollipop whined.

"Ignore her," Sadie said against his mouth.

It was heaven, *she* was heaven, but he could feel the

weight of Lollipop's stare and he let out a breath. "She's watching."

"She has no idea what we're up to. Look, you're even still dressed."

Caleb turned his head and met the dog's knowing eyes. "She totally knows what we're up to."

Sadie nudged him off of her and sat up to look at Lollipop. "She's just afraid she's missing out on some fun."

"That's because she is."

Sadie laughed. "You're awfully sure of yourself. I'll reserve judgment until after."

A challenge, one he was most definitely up for. Wrapping his hands around the back of her legs, he tugged so that she fell to her back. He lowered himself over her again and bent to lave some attention on her bare breasts, but out of the corner of his eye, he caught movement.

Lollipop had sidled up to the bed and was bouncing up and down like she was a pogo stick.

"Don't look at her," Sadie whispered breathlessly, her fingers in his hair.

He dropped his head to her gorgeous bare breasts. "I can't believe I'm saying this, but I don't think I can perform with an audience."

Sadie snorted and pointed at the dog. "Lollipop, go to your bed."

Lollipop panted happily, and proving she didn't see herself as disabled in the slightest, took a flying leap on two fallen pillows, using them as stairs to get all the way up onto the bed. Very proud of herself, she pounced on her two favorite people in the world.

"Ohmigod, you're so effing cute," Sadie said.

"Yeah, she's the cutest cockblocker on the planet." Caleb scooped the dog up, let her nuzzle in for a minute, hugged her tight and then . . . took her out to the hallway.

"Smooth," Sadie said with a laugh when he—carefully—shut the bedroom door on the dog's nose.

"I'm motivated," he said and dropped trou.

It was now even darker in her room with the door shut, just some ambient lighting coming in from the window, but he could play connect the dots with the best of them. She'd wanted to leave some clothes on to stay warm so he tugged off her boots and bunched her skirt up to her waist. "Hold this," he said and she took the material in her hands. He admired her pretty little lace panties, before they flew over his shoulder. When he dropped a knee to the bed and crawled up Sadie's body, he took the time to kiss every inch of her he could get to. Her calf. The inside of her right thigh. Then he turned his head to do the same for her left and caught sight of some ink. Tattoos high on her thigh, written in a beautiful script that he strained in the dark to read.

Heart
—————
Mind

And

Courage
—————
Fear

He took his time there, kissing each, feeling his own heart and mind open up to her in a way he hadn't expected. But then he realized she'd frozen at the first touch of his mouth to the ink. Frozen, and then squirmed in a way that had him lifting his head to meet her gaze, which was filled with sudden nerves and anxiety.

"They're beautiful," he said, running his finger over the words. The two tattoos were lined up vertically, one beneath the other. And beneath them both was a two-inch-long scar that was at least several years old. "As beautiful as you."

She closed her eyes and he knew what that meant. Sadie retreated inward when she got uncomfortable, which was the last thing he wanted here. "Hey," he murmured, lifting himself up to rub his jaw to hers, dipping his head to press a kiss to the spot beneath her ear that he knew drove her wild.

And indeed he felt her breath hitch, felt her arch up into him, her fingers sinking into his hair. Her mouth sought his and when they finally broke apart, they were both taking short ragged breaths. "Still with me?" he murmured, his hands cupping her breasts, causing her to bow her back for more.

"Yes," she gasped, wrapping her legs around him.

"Are you—?"

"I'm sure! I'm 100 percent sure that I'm going to kill you if you stop now!"

He laughed against her and slid down her body again, nudging her thighs open so he could taste her. "I'm not going to stop."

And he didn't, not even when she went off like a firecracker, fingers gripping his hair, body arching up into his, nearly bringing him along with her and he hadn't even gotten inside her yet.

And that's when he remembered. Condoms. He didn't have any. Shit. He couldn't believe it. How stupid was he for not carrying a Just In Case condom? Though to be fair to himself, it'd been a while since he'd needed one.

"In," Sadie said in a husky voice. "In me. Please, Caleb, get inside me *now*."

There was nothing he wanted more, but he lifted his head. "I don't have a condom."

She met his gaze and bit her lower lip.

"What?"

"I have one," she said. "I have several, but you can't laugh."

"Babe, I'm about as far away from laughing as a man can get. In fact, if you're teasing me, I might just cry."

"Top drawer of my nightstand," she said.

Holding her gaze, which was a sexy mix of desire and hunger, along with a pinch of embarrassment he didn't understand, he pushed up on his hands and reached for the drawer.

Her gasp stopped him cold and he twisted back. "What?"

She covered her mouth, no longer looking dazed with lust, but like she was going to smile. "Your shirt hem rose up when you stretched. You've got a tramp stamp!"

"I don't know what you're talking about."

Dropping her hand, she laughed outright and

pointed to just above his right ass cheek. "Then explain that."

"If you're referring to the very regal, perfectly rendered—"

"—Turtle," she said, grinning from ear to ear. "You have Raphael the Teenage Mutant Ninja Turtle tramp-stamped on your ass!"

"Hey," he said. "Raphael and Nintendo got me through some really difficult times when I was sixteen, okay?"

"Someone tatted you when you were sixteen?" Her smile faded. "That's against the law."

"I lied about my age and I had a fake ID," he said.

"And some regrets?" she guessed.

He shrugged. "The incident might be the reason why I'm no longer friends with vodka. Are we done discussing my early digressions and stupid mistakes yet?"

"Not by a long shot," she said, reaching into his opened trousers and wrapping her hands around the part of him that was currently harder than any of his other parts. "But we can certainly agree to table them for the moment." She stroked him.

His eyes nearly rolled up in his head. "Oh, this is going to take more than a moment."

"I certainly hope so . . ."

He opened her nightstand drawer. There was a phone charger cord. A lip balm. A box of cookies. Correction, half a box and a few scattered crumbs. A *People* magazine. And . . .

A string of neon-colored condoms.

"From a friend's bachelorette party," Sadie said. "I won a gift basket. Seemed like a waste to just throw them away."

"Waste not, want not," he said with a smile.

Her mouth curved. "Exactly."

He tore off a condom, an eye-popping pink. Not exactly what he'd imagined for his first time with her, but he was the master of invention and making the best of any situation, so he rolled it on, incredibly aware of the way Sadie watched his every move, her breath catching in the back of her throat. At the sight of his erection encased in glow-in-the-dark pink, she laughed, low and knowing and eager, and he felt something inside him click.

Just as he knew Lollipop had been meant for him, so was this woman.

She lifted her smiling eyes to his and pulled him down to her. "Now, please," she said, the words so sweet and so utterly contrasting with her tone, which was an absolute order.

With a low laugh of his own, he slid in deep, making

her gasp in gratification. He did the same, staring down at her, into those deep blue eyes, filled with the same mix of shock and pleasure.

Like coming home, he thought, and almost lost it right then. He had to force himself to go slow. Long, slow, deep thrusts that had her fingers digging into his ass as she rocked up to meet him stroke for stroke. Reaching back for her hands, he slid them above her head, fingers entwined, so that his entire body caressed hers with their every movement. He felt her start to tremble, heard her panting his name just before she shattered.

Watching it happen, taking in the sweet shudders that shook her body, how her head flew back, her eyes drifting shut, his name on her lips . . . he let himself go.

After, not wanting to lose the connection, he rolled to his back, taking her with him. Limp and sated, she went willingly, in a way she never did when she was fully aware and in charge of her faculties. But for now, he took advantage of that, loving the way she curled into him, her heart beating in time to his as their breathing slowly returned to normal.

Sadie had no idea how long they lay there after, Caleb stroking his fingers over her cooling body, before he spoke.

"I'm curious," he said softly, his touch making her stretch and purr like a cat. "You've got the small tats on your left upper thigh, and one on the back of your shoulder and around your ankle, but that's it."

She understood the question. Most tattoo artists sported much more ink than she did. But she was as naked as she planned on being tonight. A further reveal wasn't going to happen. Knowing he'd most likely expect more than she could give, and then leave when she wouldn't give it, took down the warm afterglow quite a bit, replacing it with a wave of sadness. Rolling away, she pulled the covers up over her shoulder.

He was quiet a moment but not still. He rolled too, so his heated, sinewy body hugged up against her, his chest to her back, his legs interweaving with hers, an arm coming around her waist. "Where did you just go?" he murmured.

"I'm right here."

"And yet you're a million miles away. You don't want to talk about your tattoos, just say so."

Even though he couldn't see her face, she closed her eyes. "I thought guys didn't like to cuddle after or talk. I thought they liked to get down to business and *vámonos.*"

His hand, flat on her belly, slid up between her

breasts, over her throat to gently cup her jaw and turn it so she was looking at him. "Do you want me to go?"

She opened her mouth to say yes, but she knew that he'd do it, he'd respect her wishes and go. And though she didn't want to talk, she also didn't want him to leave.

"Sadie."

"No," she said, turning to face him, letting her fingers do the talking southbound from his chest. "I don't want you to go."

He sucked in a breath when she wrapped both hands around him again. "Because you want . . ."

"You," she said. And then she pushed him flat and straddled him to do some more of their special brand of show-not-tell.

Chapter 16

#LiarLiar

Shockingly, Sadie slept deeply the rest of the night and woke up at . . . She squinted at the time. "Nine o'clock?" she gasped. "What in the . . . ?" Okay, so it was Monday, her day off, and she didn't need to get up, but she hadn't slept this late in . . . well, ever.

She didn't have to roll over to know she was alone in the bed. Scratch that. Lollipop lifted her sleepy head and wagged her tail in greeting.

Sadie had no idea when Caleb had slipped out. After round two—no, make that three—she'd been dead to the world. Normally, her cold fingers and toes and nose woke her up, but not this morning, and suddenly she realized why.

Her heat was on.

Slipping out of the covers, she headed straight for the thermostat in the hallway, followed by a sleepy Lollipop.

The furnace, which she'd left off, was on now and set at sixty-eight degrees.

Sixty-eight.

Panic gripped her. She couldn't afford it that high. She opened her laptop and went to her account to see the usage and saw that someone had paid her bill.

For the rest of the year.

Seeing as it was February, this was a huge deal and her eyes narrowed. "Oh no he did not," she said to Lollipop, who smiled up at Sadie and sat.

On Sadie's foot.

Since Lollipop was finally putting some meat on her bones and was getting too big for Sadie to easily pick up, she dropped to her knees and cuddled the dog close. "You love me more, right? Even though he's handsome and smells good and just paid to keep us warm for the next year?"

Lollipop licked her chin.

"Thank you." Sadie moved to her fridge for the leftovers she'd gotten from Rocco, but when she opened the door, she froze in shock.

The fridge was stocked. Like fully stocked with

fruits and veggies and a whole assortment of goodies that had her just staring in disbelief. She turned to find her phone, which she knew damn well she'd left on the counter last night, as usual forgetting to plug it in.

It was still on the counter but plugged into her charger. She stared at it for a full moment and then called Ivy. "Question," she said when her friend answered. "If a guy you're *not* dating pays one of your bills and then sneakily fills your fridge with food and also charges your cell phone, do you freak?"

Ivy was quiet for a beat. "I think," she finally said very gently, "you take a deep breath and then another one, and then you set aside your pride and ego to make the decision."

"What decision? Whether or not to get a restraining order?"

"No," Ivy said patiently but heavy on amusement, "the decision on whether the fact that he's trying to take care of you in probably the only way he knows how makes you feel cared for and special, or does it make you want to set up an alarm so you can zap his very fine ass with a stun gun if he tries it again?"

Sadie sighed. He did have a very fine ass . . . "Maybe a combo? What do you think?"

"I think you're feeling cared for and special, and *that* freaks you out."

"I'm not freaked out."

"You're practically hyperventilating," Ivy said.

Oh God. She was. Because she *did* feel cared for. And maybe, dammit, special. "He can't just do this sort of thing," she said. "I'm a big girl and I take care of myself."

"Noted," Ivy said. "But you're telling the wrong person. And Sadie?"

"Yeah?"

"Have some faith. Remember my spicy chorizo and fried egg breakfast tacos?"

True story. She'd had some faith and then eaten every bite and licked up the crumbs—not so unlike what she and Caleb had done to each other in the deep dark hours of the night . . .

There were many things Caleb loved about his job. Mostly that it rarely felt like an actual job. Yeah, he had fingers in a lot of areas. Space. Energy. Climate change . . . But he'd been lucky with his investments, very lucky, which meant that he was able to push profits to areas that weren't necessarily profitable but needed to be explored, like infrastructures for developing nations, rebuilding after natural disasters . . .

If there was a downside to the job, it was that the more he diversified, the more time he had to spend

220 · JILL SHALVIS

managing everything. Which was the reason he'd just been to Idaho, London, then New York, and D.C. It was a week past the incredible night he'd spent in Sadie's bed.

Idaho had been just a stopover to check in and see Kel. His cousin had been quiet lately, too quiet, and Caleb sensed a restlessness in him.

Something Caleb could understand.

They'd ridden horses, shot the shit out of a few boxes of clay targets, and then gone at each other in the gym until neither of them could move. Kel had sisters, two of them, and Caleb thought of them as fondly as he did his own sisters, but neither had been in town so Caleb and Kel had spent the evening drinking each other under the table and swapping stories.

The rest of the trip—New York, London, and D.C.—was a blur of work. Sienne had met him in D.C. They'd had several long but productive meetings and had then flown home. After landing, they'd met up with his team in his office for a debriefing, after which everyone but Sienne left. Exhausted, Caleb leaned his head back in his chair, closing his eyes for a minute.

A flash of Sadie's lips on his skin came to him, her breath hot on his neck, followed by the remembered sensation of her legs wrapped around him, her hardened nipples pressed tight against his chest as she arched up into him. The gasp that escaped her mouth when he finally slid into her with one smooth stroke . . .

Great, and now he was getting hard at work. His eyes snapped open and he shook it off. He had decisions to make about where this was going with her, and though his heart had already made those decisions, his brain kept reminding him to be cautious.

In his pocket, his phone buzzed a text. It was Sadie and he felt a smile curve his mouth. They'd been texting during the days, calling at night.

SADIE: **I'm having dinner with Ivy. Ham and pineapple pizza. I took some grease off with my napkin, so if you see me looking skinny next time you see me, don't be alarmed.**

CALEB: Only monsters put fruit on pizza.

SADIE: **That's pretty discerning from the man who has a cartoon turtle on his ass.**

Sienne picked that exact moment to look over his shoulder and her brows vanished into her hair. "How does she know about that tattoo?"

He stood and he slid his phone away without comment and headed to the door.

"Where are you going?"

"I'm done for the day," he said.

She stared at him as if he'd just announced he was the tooth fairy. And for good reason. He never took off without a close-the-day one-on-one meeting with her. "You don't have a dinner meeting . . ." On her iPad, she thumbed her way to his calendar. "I don't see anything—"

"It's personal." He'd meant it when he'd told her that he was looking to get more of a life. Or at least better balance. He knew that was what was playing into the odd restlessness he'd been feeling. Although spending the night with Sadie a week ago now had done a number on that restlessness . . .

He wanted another night.

A lot more nights, lost in her arms, her touch, where he felt . . . well, a whole lot of things he hadn't in a damn long time, and not a single one of them related to his work.

He brushed a kiss to Sienne's cheek. "You're off too. Go see your big sexy husband and have dinner together before midnight for once."

Now she was concerned. "What's wrong?"

"Nothing. And we talked about this. You're always after me to get a life. That's what I'm doing."

He watched her go from concerned to annoyed in two point zero. "If this is a date," she said, "you didn't let anyone vet her." She brought up her notes application. "Is it Sadie?"

"None of your business."

She narrowed her eyes. "Is that supposed to make me feel better?"

"Wow," Kayla said, waddling into the room with Hannah right on her heels. "Tension's thick enough to cut with a knife in here, what's going on? Are we brawling? And why didn't we get an invite?"

"I want to be on Sienne's team," Hannah said. "She fights the dirtiest."

"Hey," Sienne said and then paused. "And true . . ."

Perfect. Caleb shook his head. "No one's fighting. I'm leaving for the night."

"Perfect," Hannah said. "Then we're going to have a girls' night disguised as a meeting so we can put it on the company card."

"I need to add something to the meeting's agenda," Sienne said. "The topic's Sadie Lane."

"No," Caleb said. "Not happening."

Sienne put a hand on his arm. "You know we vet

everyone you intend to date as a matter of course. It's called protection, Caleb, and we have a very good reason for it."

She was the only one on the planet who could make him feel like a stupid teenager. "Whatever."

"You know you've won an argument when the other person says 'whatever,'" Hannah noted.

"You used to be the nice one," he said. "And Sadie isn't like anyone I've dated before. For one thing, we're not dating." A fact he intended to fix, but that wasn't up for discussion either.

Sienne pulled out the big guns and moved in close, setting her head on his shoulder, looking up at him with deceptively sweet eyes. "We do this because we love you."

"I forgot just how dirty you fight," he murmured, but he slid an arm around her and gave her a squeeze. "Stay out of her personal life. Note that I'm not even going to bother asking you to stay out of mine. See you all tomorrow."

He drove to the Pacific Pier Building. It was another dark night but the courtyard was alight with the soft glow of the lampposts and the strings of lights.

He headed straight to the Canvas Shop, his heart starting to pick up speed at the thought of seeing Sadie.

Rocco was working on a client's upper arm. He

didn't even look up as he said, "You the one who paid her gas bill and filled her fridge?" When Caleb didn't answer, Rocco lifted his gaze, his own hard and unforgiving. "Why?"

Caleb slid his hands into his pockets and rocked back on his heels, a little surprised to be having this conversation. Not to mention the fact that his answer was complicated. Something about the tough, impenetrable Sadie made him want to take care of her. It was instinctual, much like it was to take care of his sisters—not that he felt anything close to brotherly for Sadie.

"I don't think anyone should be cold or hungry," he finally said.

Rocco's gaze bored into his and then suddenly his eyes softened very slightly and he nodded. "For the record, she didn't tell me. I overheard her talking to herself, which she does when she sketches."

This was more words than Caleb had ever heard Rocco utter in a row. He glanced toward the back. The privacy curtain was pulled across the area where Sadie worked. "Is she here?"

Just then, from behind the curtain, came a loud, furious male voice yelling *"Motherfucking, cock-sucking son of a bitch!"*

Caleb quickly moved toward the curtain, but Rocco

stopped him. "She's not in trouble," he said. "Mini Moe's just completing a Prince Albert."

Caleb felt his eyes go a little wide. "Those are real?"

"Yep."

Holy shit. He resisted the urge to cup his favorite body part as he pictured what he knew of a Prince Albert piercing. "Why?" he managed. "Why would anyone do that?"

"It can enhance your sexual experience," Rocco said.

"And you've . . . ?" Caleb gestured to Rocco's lower half.

"Fuck no."

"Where's Sadie?" he asked, hoping like hell that Rocco wasn't about to answer that she was back there with Mini Moe and his client.

"She just took Poops A Lot for a walk."

Caleb laughed. "Don't let Sadie hear you call her that. She doesn't like it."

Rocco actually grinned. "Why do you think I do it? She'll be back any second. If you want to live, I suggest you come up with a better reason for doing what you did, one that doesn't involve pity."

"It wasn't pity," Caleb said. "I care about her."

"Good," Rocco said. "But you're still going to need a better reason than that. I suggest lying out your ass."

"About what?" Sadie asked.

At the sound of her voice, Rocco grimaced at Caleb with a *you're on your own* look and then bent over his client, mouth zipped up tight.

Okay then. Manning up, Caleb turned to face Sadie and Lollipop. If he thought his heart had been locked down and the key thrown away, he was wrong. His heart wasn't locked down, not for the dog and most especially not for the woman. "Hey."

"Hey," Sadie said, quiet. Mistrustful after the partial conversation she'd overheard.

Not Lollipop. She strained at her leash at the sight of him, whining and crying to get closer after a week without him.

Sadie let loose of the leash and the dog flew through the air to get at him. He caught her up and hugged her close as she squirmed and cried with sheer joy, licking his face and whatever else she could reach.

"Traitor," Sadie said and crossed her arms. "Lie about what?" she asked again.

Caleb didn't bother to look back at Rocco for help. He was trying to figure out his best options just as Mini Moe appeared from the back. The big Samoan stood in front of the curtain, beefy arms closed over his chest.

"He needs a moment," Mini Moe said.

"Understandable," Rocco muttered.

Something on Caleb's face must have given him

away because Sadie went brows up, slightly amused. "We could get you a Prince Albert if you're interested. I couldn't do it for you, I'm not licensed, but I could assist Mini Moe."

Could one feel oneself go pale? Because Caleb was pretty sure that's what he did. "No," he said as Mini Moe looked at him with renewed interest. "I'm good, thanks."

Mini Moe went back to his client. Rocco had just finished with his own client and together they stepped into the courtyard for fresh air, leaving Caleb and Sadie alone.

"So you're back," she said.

"I am."

"And you're here."

"Wanted to see you," he said.

She held his gaze, her own deep blue eyes seeming to see straight into his head, hell, also his soul in a way no one else could. It was both thrilling and unsettling. She saw a different side of him than most. She was also one of the few people in his life who went toe-to-toe with him and could call him out on his bullshit.

They hadn't yet discussed what he'd done after he'd left her bed. She hadn't brought it up during the week he'd been gone, not in a text, not on the phone. He'd gotten the impression she'd been saving that conversation for a face-to-face, and he had no idea if she was pissed or not. She didn't make him wait.

"Thanks for what you did," she finally said. "But it wasn't necessary. I can take care of myself."

"I know," he said.

"So why did you do it?"

With Rocco's advice to lie bouncing around in his head, he went with the utter truth. "Because I care about you." He bent his knees a little to see directly into her eyes. "Is that so hard to believe? I care about you, and the thought of you being cold while trying to sleep or going to bed hungry drives me insane. It keeps me up at night, which means the why of it is really entirely selfish. I wanted to be able to sleep."

Her lips twitched. "And did you?"

"No, I didn't. I'm pretty sure it's because I'm also sexually frustrated."

She laughed. "How can that possibly be? We used a whole string of condoms!"

He smiled at her amusement. "I think it's you." He lowered his voice and ran his fingers along her jaw, liking the way her breath caught at his touch. Taking a risk, he pressed into her and murmured, "I'm not finished with you, Sadie. I want more. Go out with me."

She froze. "Like on a . . . *date?*"

"Yes." He cupped her face in both hands now. "Is that really so strange?"

"But . . . I already put out."

He smiled. "I want a date," he repeated stubbornly. "A grown-up date without using our baby as an excuse to see each other. Just you and me. What do you say?"

Sadie continued to stare at him. "I don't use Lolli-pop as an excuse."

"We *both* use her," he said. "Yes or no, Sadie?"

She looked over at Rocco, who'd come back inside. He shook his big shaggy head. "Don't look at me, baby doll. I'd say yes to him in a hot second, but he doesn't swing that way."

"This is nuts," Sadie said. "*No one* dates anymore."

"So let's show 'em what they're missing," Caleb said. "Go out with me tonight."

"*Tonight?*"

"Too soon? Tomorrow then. Whenever you want."

She stared at him like he'd lost his mind. But it was the opposite. He was just realizing how much he wanted this.

"What would we do?" she asked.

"Date stuff," he said and smiled because damn, she was cute standing there panicking at the thought of spending more time with him.

"Like go to a horror flick where I get scared and you get to comfort the little lady?"

"Are you telling me you're scared of horror flicks?"

She blinked as she gave this some thought. "No, just chainsaws."

"Well, that's just common sense," he said. "Are we going to do this, Sadie?"

She chewed her lower lip in indecision. On the one hand, she was looking adorably sexy trying to figure out if she trusted him or not. On the other hand, she'd taken a tour of his body with her sexy mouth and yet she couldn't decide if she wanted to go out on a date with him.

The odds weren't exactly in his favor.

"Can I think about it?" Sadie finally asked.

Caleb looked over at Rocco, who shrugged like, *take it, man, it's the best you're going to get.*

Probably true. "Sure, you can think about it," he said, realizing this was the first time someone had asked him that. He shouldn't have been surprised. Everything with Sadie Lane so far had felt like a first . . .

Chapter 17

#GoingToBeABumpyRide

A minute later, Sadie watched Caleb and Lollipop walk out of the shop heading for the pub.

He wanted to date her.

Before she could obsess over that too much, her client called and canceled on her. She didn't know if she was bummed or relieved and grabbed her purse.

"Running away from home?" Rocco asked mildly.

"I should," she said pointedly, but he just smiled, unrepentant.

"He'd be good for you," he said.

Rolling her eyes, she left work and stopped at a table set up in the courtyard where a Girl Scout troop was selling cookies. In her opinion, there were five seasons:

winter, Girl Scout Cookie season, spring, summer, and fall. So she searched her purse and managed to come up with ten bucks to buy two emergency boxes. Some might call eating two boxes of cookies on her own a cry for help. Sadie called it supporting young female entrepreneurs.

She opened a box and helped herself as she thought about Caleb. She'd spent a lot of time avoiding dating. That she was possibly considering jumping back in felt a little too much like her old world to her. The world where she'd been nothing to anyone, not tethered nor tied, not fitting in anywhere . . . And *that* had almost killed her. She picked up her phone and texted her friends: 9–1–1.

Not five minutes later, Ivy, Willa, and Molly met her at the fountain in the courtyard. Sadie explained the situation, trying not to freak out. "I mean what's he thinking?" she asked. "A date? With me? Is he insane?"

"I don't get the problem," Molly said. "He asked you out. It's sweet. You should go. I bet he takes you somewhere really nice and you can get dressed to kill and drive him crazy all night."

Willa nodded. "And aren't you dying to see what he looks like beneath those sexy suits?"

Sadie bit her lip because she had seen what he looked like beneath those sexy suits.

Except . . . not really. It'd been pretty dark, and so cold they'd left on a lot layers. It'd been more of a braille situation, though her fingers and tongue knew their way around his body pretty well . . .

Ivy caught her expression and went brows up. She clearly recognized there was so much more to tell but was kind enough not to ask questions with an audience.

"I know I'm with Lucas and all," Molly said. "And I'm crazy in love. But I've worked out with Caleb, and you should know, he's holy-cow hot."

This was something Sadie already knew.

"And best yet," Molly went on, "for being rich and kind of famous, he's a good guy, just really . . . normal."

Actually, in Sadie's book, "normal" was not a point in his favor. Wes had been textbook "normal." But then he'd been cruel and tried to break her down.

No. Scratch that. She'd done that to herself. And she'd walked away from men for a bit. But a bit had turned into three years and it was entirely possible she was still broken. "I don't trust my judgment," she admitted.

The girls all looked at each other. Then Molly reached out and took Sadie's hand. "I get that. There was a time when that was true for me too."

"How did you get over it?" Sadie asked.

PLAYING FOR KEEPS · 235

"Went with my heart," Molly said. "And trust me, I didn't go quietly. Actually, I went kicking and screaming. But I went. And it's been great, even if late last night we had to both get out of bed and measure it to make sure we were sleeping on equal sides of the mattress."

"I had huge trust issues," Willa told Sadie. "Keane was a huge risk for me, but now look at us . . ." She pulled out her phone. "He sends me pics of him doing household chores because he knows it turns me on."

Everyone looked at a picture of Keane feather dusting the furniture with a come-hither sex kitten pose. The next shot was him in only a pair of jeans, riding the carpet cleaner like it was a bucking bronco.

"Wow," Ivy said and they all murmured their agreement because it was true. The man looked good getting his clean on.

"I was pretty screwed up too," Molly told Sadie. "But now I'm with Lucas, who turned out to be my best friend and soul mate. And trust me, if it worked out for us, then anyone can fall in love—" She broke off to read an incoming text. "Oh hell no. Eat my molten lava cake leftovers and die," she muttered as she typed. "Sorry." She set her phone aside. "That was Lucas. What was I saying?"

"That you're with your best friend and soul mate,"

Sadie said dryly. "You said that right before you threatened him with death."

Willa smiled. "See? Marriage is great."

Ivy turned to Sadie. "How about you go out with Caleb just for fun and see what happens?"

Spoken like a person who was as single as Sadie. But could it be that easy? Could she go out with Caleb for the simple attraction and not worry about anything else? She looked into Ivy's sincere face, and then the others', who all nodded encouragingly. She blew out a breath and picked up her phone. She typed two words: Tomorrow night. And then a minute later got a response: You're on.

"Oh shit," she whispered.

"Brownie points to him for not playing coy and pretending he didn't know what you were saying yes to," Ivy said. "And nice label you gave him. Is it working?"

No. "Yes."

"See?" Molly said. "He really is a good guy, Sadie."

Sadie drew in a shaky breath and told herself to lock it down. She had twenty-four hours before she had to panic. She looked over at her friends, each of whom agreed that Caleb was a good guy.

All signs pointed to that being the truth. But whether it was bad experiences or maybe just her sheer stubbornness, she wasn't quite ready to jump into the water yet. Which was dumb. She'd already slept with him. What did she have to feel worried about?

Her phone buzzed once more and everyone's gaze went to her phone.

DO NOT EVEN THINK ABOUT FALLING FOR THIS GUY: **Bring gym clothes.**

"Gym clothes?"

Molly grimaced. "Okay, so even good guys can be stupid."

"We need to withhold judgment," Ivy said calmly. "He might be doing a misdirect for Ms. Anxiety City over here."

They all looked at Sadie.

"I'm not anxious!" she said. A big fat lie of course. She couldn't get enough air into her lungs, her face was overheated, and she was squirming. She never squirmed. "Oh my God, this is ridiculous. I should cancel—" She reached for her phone but Ivy snatched it first.

"You can do this," she said very kindly and very gently. "You're a big girl."

"A big girl wouldn't be flop sweating in some very uncomfortable places," Sadie said.

Ivy laughed and turned to the others. "A show of hands on whether or not she should go out with Caleb."

Everyone raised their hands.

Sadie felt like an idiot. But a cared-for idiot. "Fine. I'll do it."

Everyone scattered after that to get back to work. Alone, Sadie eyed the fountain. She didn't have any extra change to toss in and make a wish—which didn't matter because even if she did, she wouldn't wish on love.

Or would she . . . ?

"Fine," she admitted to the water. "I'd be tempted if I thought you were real."

A coin flew over her shoulder and hit the water with a plop.

"There you go, sugar."

Sadie whipped around and stared in horror at Old Man Eddie standing there in his tie-dyed SUMMER LOVE sweatshirt, hood up over hair that stood straight up, hands in his pockets, looking quite pleased with himself.

"What did you just do?" she asked.

He smiled.

"No." She pointed at him. "Take it back."

"Take what back?"

"The wish you made for me. The wish for love. I don't want it."

"What does it matter if you don't believe?" he asked.

She stared at him. "Dammit."

"Hear you're going on a date," he said.

"Oh my God. This entire building is a loony bin. I need to change jobs."

Eddie just grinned. "Nah. You fit here. And you don't need to talk to the fountain anymore, your wish is made now. It no longer matters whether you believe in love or not, it's going to find you."

Her heart kicked hard. "No offense," she said. "But that sounds more like a threat to me than a promise."

Eddie just rocked back on his heels with a smile. "Don't worry—"

"If you end that sentence with 'be happy,' I might have to hurt you," she said.

He laughed. "I'm a lover, not a fighter. And you know what? I think you are too."

"No way. I'd rather fight than love any day of the week."

"Well, technically speaking," he said, "some things are worth fighting for. Love is most definitely one of those things."

His words stuck with her all through the night and

the next day, through going home from work and attempting to get ready for the date with a man she realized she liked *way* too much. It put a lot of pressure on the "date," one that she was sure she would manage to mess up.

Caleb knocked on Sadie's door, not quite sure what to expect. He wouldn't have been surprised if she bailed, but she opened the door and Lollipop lost her ever-loving mind at the realization she had both of her people in the same spot at the same time. She literally bounced back and forth between them until Caleb squatted to stroke some calm into her.

The dog immediately rolled over for a belly rub and Caleb's heart rolled over as well. As surely as he'd fallen for the two-legged female in front of him, he felt the same for the three-legged one at his feet. But only one of his women was wagging her tail, thrilled to see him.

The other needed time and, he suspected, patience. Good thing he had both in spades. Slowly he stood, taking in the sight of Sadie. She wore an incredibly sexy little black dress that showed off her curves in a way that had his mouth watering. And then there were the high-heeled black leather boots that climbed up her long legs, ending above her knees and a good hand span below the short hem of her dead sexy dress. Her makeup was soft and sultry and seemed to match the dress and boots for high-volume shock value.

The sight of her literally took his breath.

She smiled when he didn't say a word. "I know you said gym clothes, and I've got them ready to go. The dress is Ivy's idea. She texted a bit ago, suggesting I render you speechless from the get-go in order to take control. So I dug through my closet for a dress worthy of the mission."

Caleb looked her over again from head to toe and shook his head. He was definitely speechless, and she was the hottest thing he'd ever seen. Liking her tactic and the reason behind it, he smiled and nudged her back so he could move inside. There he kicked her door shut and then pressed her up against it, cupping her face.

Sucking in a breath, her eyes dilated with excitement. She liked his move.

So he gave her another. He got up close and personal, letting his body speak for him.

"Oh," she breathed, at the exact height in those heels to arch into him and line them up perfectly. "You're happy to see me," she murmured and settled her gaze on his mouth, biting her lower lip.

She wanted him to kiss her.

He wanted that too, possibly more than he wanted his next breath, but they were going out on a date first if it killed him. He wasn't exactly sure why it was so important for him to do this, but he wanted to . . . well, woo her, he supposed. He wanted to show her there was more between them besides the off-the-charts sexual attraction.

From the moment she'd said yes to this date, he'd known something she hadn't, that tonight he was going to reveal himself to her in a way he never would have if she'd refused to go out with him. Lowering his head, he brought his mouth to within a fraction of hers. "Sadie . . ."

Her eyes drifted closed and her fingers slid into his hair. "Yeah?"

"You didn't need the dress to be the one in control here. One look—hell, one smartass remark from you and I'm a puddle at your feet."

She stared up at him. "You shouldn't tell me such things. I could take advantage."

"Please do," he said, smiling when she rolled her eyes. "And Sadie?"

"Yeah?"

He pressed into her a little more, wanting to see her eyes go opaque with lust for him the way they had the other night. "We're going to do this . . ."

"Yes," she breathed, nodding, tightening her grip.

"And it's going to be good."

"I know." She tried to get a piece of that "good" right now but he pulled back and took her hand, opening the front door again.

Her eyes flew open. "What the—?"

"Date first."

She stared at him. "So you were just teasing me to, what, drive me wild with lust?"

"Did it work?"

"No."

He could see her nipples trying to cut through her dress. "Liar."

She looked down at his obvious erection.

"Hey, I'm not even going to try to deny what you do to me," he said, and though he was still smiling, he was dead serious.

Her eyes were too. "So a date," she said. "And then . . . ?"

"Most definitely and then."

She nodded and walked out the door ahead of him, giving him a peek at the nonexistent back of her dress, and he groaned. "It's going to be a long night."

"Your own fault," she said and sashayed that sweet ass down the hall.

Chapter 18

#Mom

Sadie wasn't surprised when Caleb pulled up to a gym she'd gone to a couple of times on her friend Molly's recommendation. She'd actually run into Caleb here a few times, but she preferred her gym, which was much closer to her apartment.

That had been both for convenience and privacy.

Three years ago, after breaking up with Wes and losing her way again, she'd had to change her life up. She'd had to learn some things about herself. Things like self-care. For her, self-care meant working out as a drugless way to fight depression and anxiety and find some peace of mind.

And she'd needed peace of mind *badly*.

She'd also found her inner girl power at a drop-in kickboxing class. It'd diffused her pent-up emotions like nothing else. After that, she'd taken more and had kept up with it, also taking some actual MMA workshops as well. She'd learned some great wrestling moves that she'd never had to put into action but had done wonders for her butt.

Double win.

She'd given up movies, eating out, and buying new clothes for the gym membership and it'd been about two and a half years now of going at least twice a week. She was both proud and fairly confident she could kick some serious ass if needed.

She looked over at Caleb. "You're more than a little overdressed for this, still wearing your armor for the day."

Caleb turned off the car and turned to face her. They'd dropped Lollipop off at his sister Hannah's house for the night and their date had apparently officially begun. "You're big on armor," he said. "Your own. Mine . . ."

She wasn't sure where he was going with this so she didn't say anything.

There was a smile on his face but his eyes were very serious. "And you're right. I've got armor, but it's not my suit. My armor's my skin, and it's tough as an elephant hide, born of a life that hasn't always been easy."

She knew all about life not being easy, but she still didn't interrupt him because she wanted him to keep talking forever. For all his effortless charm and charisma, he didn't really talk about himself much. She was insanely curious to learn more about him—which was a self-revelation she was slowly coming to accept.

"I made a decision once I felt you softening toward me," he said. "A decision to show you the man beneath my armor."

This revealing sentence took her a moment to process. "You think I've softened for you?"

"I know you have." His gaze dared her to tell him otherwise, to lie right to his face.

And she could have. She was a good liar when she wanted to be, but she didn't want to lie to him.

He held her gaze for another beat, giving her the chance to stop this, whatever *this* was. When she didn't, he got out of the car and came around for her, taking her gym bag and shouldering it along with his. Then he took her hand and they walked toward the building.

It was located just between Cow Hollow and the marina, on the bottom floor of an old warehouse building. The front was reclaimed wood paneling and patinated decorative hardware, but Sadie bet this place had come by both naturally, weathered by time and use. It was showing its age but also a whole lot of personality with the wide floor-to-ceiling windows and open beam construction. The buildings on either side had been redone in more modern styles, but this one had been left in its original glory.

"I wonder why this one didn't get renovated."

"Maybe the owner liked it the way it was."

"I do too," she said.

Caleb slowed to a stop. "Me too," he said in a voice that had her turning her gaze on him.

He'd tilted his head back and was looking up at the gym sign hanging from the second-floor window, hands in his pockets, shoulders back in a carefree, easy stance, but something about it didn't say carefree or easygoing. He seemed far away and . . . reflective. "When I first started coming here, this place was a dojo." He took her hand, turning her to the front door.

"It's closed," she said, surprised.

"Yes, it closes early one night a week for private use." Caleb pulled a key from his pocket and unlocked the front door.

"You're the private user?" she asked.

"Yes."

"You've got connections."

"You could say that."

Since she'd been here before, she knew the front door opened into a wide room lined with windows to the street and marina on one wall, the other with mirrors and a sea of gym equipment. Near the front door was an entrance area, a front desk, the wall behind it lined with pictures of people who'd been here.

The alarm was beeping at their entrance. Caleb took out his phone and thumbed his way through an app and the beeping stopped.

"That's a pretty serious connection," she noted.

"I created the alarm app this building uses and installed it," he said.

A phone on the front desk buzzed and then a woman's voice beamed into the room. "Caleb?"

"Yep," he said.

"Just checking. Want to go a few rounds? Niles is with me and he says he wouldn't mind kicking your white-boy ass. We could be there in twenty."

"Not tonight," Caleb said. "He'll have to save that pleasure for another time. 'Night, Sienne." He disconnected whatever connection they'd had and then did something else with the app. "Disabling the security cameras," he said.

"Okay." Sadie cocked her head. "So clearly you've got more than just a connection here."

"That was my sister Sienne. Her husband and I spar

sometimes. A pass here is available to all of my employees in their benefits package."

"You own the whole building," she guessed.

"I do." He paused as if waiting for something more from her, and when he didn't get it, he said, "Gotta admit, I figured I'd get some sort of smartass comment about that."

"I was controlling myself." She lifted a shoulder and smiled. "Besides, you seem to have carved out a really great life for yourself, one that caters to your strengths. I actually think it's great."

"Yeah?" he asked. "And what are my strengths?"

She rolled her eyes. "Like you need any compliments or help with your ego."

"Humor me."

"Alright," she said. "Well, you're extremely smart."

He gave a small smile. "Is that it? I'm smart?"

She shrugged. "Started with the obvious. You're also a sucker when it comes to animals and women who can't always make ends meet—"

He opened his mouth, but she set a finger on his lips, not wanting to go there right now. "And then there's the thing I didn't expect."

At her touch, his eyes had liquefied to the color of whiskey, neat. "It's that I'm a great kisser, right?" he asked.

She liked the feel of his lips moving beneath the pad of her finger and it made her smile. As did the fact that he was right. He was a really great kisser. He liked to do it, a lot, and it showed. When he was on his game—and she suspected he was always on his game—he could make her forget things, like where and who she was. His tongue was magical and she might have whimpered a little at the memory, but she shook her head because it was more than that. "It's that you see me," she said softly.

Reaching up, he wrapped his fingers around her wrist and brought her hand to his chest. With his other hand, he stroked back a strand of her hair and smiled. "I do see you. And I like what I see. But I'd like to see more, Sadie. A lot more."

"Ditto," she whispered, the admission not coming easy. She wasn't even sure when it'd happened, and uncomfortable with the direction of those thoughts, she turned away to look more closely at the wall of pictures.

There were many from years ago when this place had indeed clearly been a dojo, and much smaller. It hadn't been the whole bottom floor of the building back then, but just one tiny corner of it. The recurring theme seemed to be an Asian man in various stages of the dojo. She realized there was also a small boy, dark hair, big eyes, skinny and awkward. As the Asian man aged in the pics, so did the boy, from young kid to teen to . . .

"You," she murmured in shock, lifting her head and meeting Caleb's eyes.

He'd been watching her take in the pictures, and gave a small smile when she figured it out. "Me. I was a scrawny, asthmatic, bullied ten-year-old, maybe forty pounds soaking wet."

Hardly more than Lollipop weighed. Sadie soaked up that tidbit and tried to picture him as anything but this confident, successful, charismatic, leanly muscled man standing in front of her.

"This place saved my life," he said. And on that shocking statement, he once again took her hand and walked her through the place.

When they got to the sparring ring, she slowed. Thanks to all her time spent in a gym not all that unlike this place on the other side of town, she felt quite comfortable here. Powerful. Extremely feminine, and . . . well, sexy. "Want to go a few rounds?" she asked playfully.

His eyes heated. "Yeah, I want to go a few rounds."

He'd used his husky sex voice and she let out a low laugh. "I meant in the ring. As long as you're not afraid?"

She knew she was poking the bear, and his mouth curved in a smile that had every single part of her body doing a happy little quiver.

Down, girl.

"Are you challenging me?" he asked.

Hell yes. "I should probably warn you, I sometimes kickbox for exercise." She shrugged. "It gets my aggressions out."

"There are other ways to do that."

That voice again. Her knees wobbled. "I prefer the mats. But if that makes you nervous . . ."

"Get changed."

She didn't often hop-to when given a demand. Okay, so she *never* hopped-to when given a command, and yet tonight she did. But only because she wanted in the ring with him so badly she was nearly humming with anticipation. When she'd been here before, she'd seen him in the ring with her friend Molly, and another time with his friend Lucas, and they'd kicked the shit out of each other. For fun.

Men were so weird, but she could admit that it'd turned her on to watch how well he handled himself. Lucas was a badass security expert and investigator who worked out of the same building she did. Caleb might be a hugely successful venture capitalist, but she'd have never imagined him to be able to hold his own against someone whose job required him to be able to kick ass.

And yet he could.

A few minutes later she was in an exercise tank and shorts, both snug to her body so she'd have freedom of movement without worrying about revealing things she didn't want revealed. Tying her hair up, she stepped into the gym area.

Caleb was already in the ring, waiting for her in what she'd seen him in the last time she'd been here. Long-sleeved performance tee and loose-fitting basketball shorts.

His warm gaze drifted over her. "You look great."

"I wasn't going for great," she said. "I was going for I-wanna-kick-your-ass."

With a heart-stopping smile, he held the ropes for her to climb in. "Show me what you've got, Tough Girl."

With a shake of her head at his easy cockiness—he was so going down—she walked around the ring for a minute, her veins pumping with an excitement she hadn't felt in a long time.

Caleb was still looking far too sure of himself as he waited for her to make the first move. "Pretty damn sure of yourself, aren't you?" she murmured.

He just grinned.

Oh yeah, waaaaay too confident. And gorgeous, dammit. "You should brace yourself," she warned.

"Bring it."

"You think I can't?"

"So far, I think that you're all talk. Hold up a sec." Then he straightened and casually pulled off his shirt.

Sadie froze. Because yes, he was leanly muscled and sinewy and perfect, just as she knew him to be. But he was also . . .

Tatted.

How had she missed it that night they'd spent together? He had tattoos across the back of his shoulders and around one bicep. Another low on a hipbone that vanished into his low-slung shorts and was sexy as hell. And then there were the words *Carpe Diem* scripted vertically down one leanly muscled side.

Her mouth had fallen open. She'd had no idea. The only thing she could think was that it'd been so cold in her apartment, he'd never taken off his shirt all the way. She was still standing there dazed by the sight of him when he took her down, flattening her to the mat.

Lying on top of her, he smiled. "You were saying?"

"Hey," she said, more breathless than she wanted to admit. "I wasn't ready. You distracted me. *On purpose.*"

He pushed himself upright, giving her a hand to

pull her up as well. "With what?" he asked innocently, knowing damn well it was his tattoos, and more than the Ninja Turtle digression. The one on his hip . . . she wanted to lick it. She wanted to lick *him*. Except he was looking quite pleased with himself.

"I didn't see them the other night and you know it," she said.

He just smiled. So he wanted to play it like that. Okay then. And knowing she could give as good as she got, she let her expression go a little sultry as she smiled and turned away, walking slowly to the edge of the ring, wrapping her fingers around the ropes, tossing her hair over her shoulder as she smiled back at him. "You really do have a nice setup here."

Coming up behind her, he set his hands over hers on the ropes and lowered his head so that he could brush his mouth along the side of her throat. She let out a pleased hum and shifted her body against his.

His breathing changed and that's when she struck, wrapping a foot around the back of his knee, causing it to buckle. Using her weight as momentum, she took him down to the mat, rolling over so that they were chest-to-chest.

"I wasn't ready," he said, mirroring her words back at her. His hands slid down her back to her butt, which he squeezed. "You have a great ass."

"So do you," she said. "Which you already know."

He rolled them so that she was once again pinned. Cupping her face, he dipped his head and she arched up, thinking he was going to kiss her. Instead, he pulled back slightly and met her gaze. "Do you have something you want to say to me?"

"Hmm." She wriggled. "Whatever's in your pocket is poking me."

His eyes darkened with both heat and a challenge that had her brain going from amused to aroused beyond belief in a single heartbeat.

They both knew there was nothing in his pocket. Nothing but Caleb. Her hands came up to his biceps, her fingers digging in as desire and a hunger for him flooded her. Wrapping herself around him, she sighed in pleasure because he was big and heated and felt amazing, and she wanted—

An alarm beeped near the front of the gym and then the door opened.

Sadie froze.

Not Caleb. He kissed the tip of her nose and then rose smoothly to his feet, pulling her up beside him. "The cleaning crew," he said.

The guy who walked in was small, wiry, and pushing a cart filled with cleaning supplies. "Hey, bossman!" he called out and then stopped at the sight of Sadie. "Whoops. Need a moment?"

Caleb's lips curved and Sadie met his knowing gaze. They were going to need more than a minute.

"You're fine, Ken," Caleb said.

Ken nodded and stayed in the entryway, bent over his cart, going through the supplies, looking like he planned to start at the reception desk.

Sadie was distracted by the Japanese character on the back of Caleb's left shoulder, just beneath a stunning living tree, and she ran a finger over the ink. "Wow. That's so sweet."

"What?"

"You've got *mom* tattooed here."

He craned his neck to eyeball his skin. "That's not *mom*."

"Yes, it is," she said. "I know because Mini Moe recently did this same character on a client."

Caleb turned to Ken, who was pulling on a utility belt loaded with spray bottles and other assorted cleaning equipment. He had jet-black hair spiked straight up and was wearing little round John Lennon glasses. "What does this say?" Caleb asked him, pointing to the tat.

"What, you think just because I'm Asian, I'll know?" Ken asked.

Caleb blew out a breath. "Shit. No. Sorry—"

Ken laughed. "Just kidding ya, bossman. I know what it is because you're putting me through that fancy-ass master degree in Japanese history and culture. It says *mom*."

"Sonofabitch." Caleb shook his head. "He told me it meant *life*."

"Who?" Sadie asked.

Caleb took her hand, looking both touched and amused, and also like maybe he couldn't decide on which one to feel. "Time for stop two of our date."

Chapter 19

#JudgyJudgerson

Sadie walked with Caleb up the front walk of a Victorian building. He'd driven them here and parked in a spot in the alley that she could never have maneuvered into, but he'd managed like a pro.

They'd both changed out of their workout clothes. She was back in her dress and Caleb was—shockingly—in jeans and a white button-down, looking good enough to eat.

"You're still staring," he murmured on the porch of the large house.

"You're in jeans."

"You've said that like ten times on the ride here."

"Yes," she said, "but . . . *you're in jeans.*"

He gave a slight head shake. "I'm never going to live this down, am I?"

"No. *Jeans,* Caleb," she teased. "Are we slumming?"

"Don't judge me by my clothes," he said mildly and entering a passcode, opened the front door and held it open for her to enter first.

She eyed the small discreet brass plaque that read CARAMEL CARE VILLAGE. Stepping inside, she took in the warm cozy vibe of the place, and the fact that there were two older men and one woman, all in wheelchairs, scattered around the room. It was an assisted-living facility, she realized. A top-notch one by the looks of it.

Caleb smiled at the nurse behind the front desk. "Hey, Dee, how's he doing today?"

"He's been watching the Rocky DVDs you brought last week." She smiled. "You always know just how to bring him back to us."

Caleb signed in for both himself and Sadie. "There are two of us today."

"No problem," Dee said. "Head on back. He's having his evening tea."

Caleb took Sadie's hand. "Fair warning," he said quietly. "He's either going to be happy to see me or pissed off. It can go either way on any given day."

Before she could ask any of the million questions on the tip of her tongue, Caleb opened the door to one of the rooms off the hallway. An older Asian man sat at a table in front of a wide picture window, a throw over his lap and legs, staring pensively out the glass.

At their entry, he turned to them and narrowed his eyes. "Who are you?"

Caleb smiled. "I'm Caleb, and this is my friend Sadie."

The man's fierce expression didn't change, nor did his black eyes soften. "I don't know you." He paused. "Do I?"

Caleb's smile didn't so much as slip, but to Sadie the smile seemed almost unbearably sad. "Yes, Naoki, you know me." And then he reached up and began to unbutton his shirt.

Naoki stared as Caleb shrugged out of his shirt and did a slow circle in front of the old man, whose sharp gaze was taking in the tattoos.

Sadie's gaze did the same and she felt her breath hitch at the sight of Caleb's broad shoulders and sleek, sinewy back. Then as he finished turning, her eyes were drawn to his chest and the defined cut of his abs, and how his jeans sat dangerously low on his lean hips, lovingly cupping all his good parts. She bit her lower lip

262 · JILL SHALVIS

because she wanted to nibble her way from his Adam's apple to his belt buckle and beyond.

Naoki finished scanning Caleb's tattoos and met his gaze.

Caleb stood there, calm, quiet, definitely searching for something in the man's eyes. She knew that sometimes tattoos could trigger memories and she hoped that whatever Caleb was looking for, he found it.

"Who are you?" Naoki asked again.

Caleb let out a breath and shook his head, clearly disappointed. "It's not important." He reached for his shirt and pulled it back on. "Do you need anything?"

"No. I'm comfortable here." Naoki stared hard at Caleb. "Are you the one who pays for me to be here in all this incredible comfort?"

"Who told you someone pays for you to be here?"

Naoki just turned away, silent now. Caleb didn't seem surprised at this, and once more he took Sadie's hand. "Have a good night."

They were at the door when Naoki spoke.

"Wait."

Caleb turned back with a look of vulnerability on his face that Sadie had never seen before. It tightened her chest so that she could scarcely breathe. She'd recognized Naoki as the man in the pictures with Caleb at the gym. He was clearly incredibly important to Caleb.

And whatever their past, the fact that Naoki didn't, *couldn't*, remember Caleb felt unbearably tragic.

"What is it?" Caleb asked him. "You remember something?" His voice was low and even. Still calm. But somehow Sadie could hear the hope in it and she squeezed his hand, wanting badly for Naoki to say yes, he remembered Caleb.

But the old man nodded to his cup. "My tea's cold."

Caleb drew in a deep breath and nodded. "I'll see to it that you get more hot water." He opened the door and gestured for Sadie to go through first.

Heartsick for him, she took a step, but Naoki spoke again.

"That tat," the old man said.

Again Caleb stilled and then turned back.

"The tree on your shoulder," Naoki said. "It matches mine exactly. And my name. It means tree."

Caleb nodded. "Yes."

"You have that tat . . . because of me?"

"Yes." Caleb moved back into the room and crouched at Naoki's side. "A long time ago, you made me strong. Strong as a tree."

Naoki studied him for a moment. "Okay. But we clearly do not share a mother. Why do you have the same mom tattoo?"

For the first time since they'd been with Naoki, good

humor came into Caleb's gaze. "Because you never told me what the character meant, only that it was very important to you."

Naoki took this in. "And because it was very important to me, you immortalized it on your body?"

"Yes." In fact, Naoki had taken Caleb to get the tattoo, which of course he didn't remember.

The man's eyes had gone from dull and quiet to bright with humor. "That was dumb."

Caleb had to sigh.

"I'm not sure how much I taught you if I didn't make sure you follow your own path and not the path of another."

"If you say 'wax on, wax off,' you can forget getting hot tea," Caleb warned.

At this, Naoki actually grinned. "You can come back."

Caleb's smile faded, but his eyes revealed the pleasure of Naoki's words. "I will."

"But you go now. You make me tired." He looked at Sadie. "Don't let him get any more dumbass tattoos. Only good tattoos."

"I'm not in charge of him," she said. "He's in charge of himself, dumbass moves or otherwise."

Naoki's smile widened and he pointed at her. "You, I like. Sassy. Salty. Smartass. You've got his back, right?"

"So you *do* remember," Caleb breathed. "You remember saving me, having my back."

Naoki nodded. "You're the boy."

"Yes."

"Small and helpless as a baby bird," Naoki said. "A weakling."

Something flashed over Caleb's face, so quickly it was gone in a blink. A haunting sadness. "Yes," he said. "I'm the weakling."

"But no longer." Naoki gestured around him. "Now it appears we've changed positions."

"You'll never be a weakling," Caleb said. "What else do you remember?"

"Your right hook is strong. Your weakness is your guard, you forget to keep it up."

Caleb's lips twitched and he took a quick glance at Sadie. "True story."

A nurse poked her head in. "Time for meds."

Caleb turned back to Naoki, but the man had fallen asleep in his chair. Head back against his headrest, chest rising and falling gently, and the most ungentle snores coming from his mouth.

This got another lip twitch from Caleb, though his eyes remained somber. "Take good care of him," he told the nurse.

"Don't you worry on that score, Mr. Parker."

Five minutes later they were back in Caleb's car.

"Naoki was your hero," she said.

"Not was. Is."

This caused another tug on her heart. "He seems like a very sweet man."

He laughed. "No. Not sweet. He's tough as nails and thinks he knows everything—which is made all the more annoying by the fact that he usually *does* know everything—the man never had a single weakness."

"You're wrong," she said softly, reaching for his hand. "*You're* clearly his weakness."

Caleb slid her a glance and then turned back to the road. "You hungry?"

"Nice subject change," she said. "And yeah, I'm starving. But in spite of my dress, I don't want fancy schmancy."

That got her a small smile. "What do you want?"

"Honestly?" she asked.

"Yes."

She bit her lower lip. "In-N-Out."

He executed a U-turn—impressive in San Francisco downtown traffic—and took her down to North Beach near Fisherman's Wharf. In the drive-thru lane, he gave her a brows up. She unbuckled her seatbelt and put her hands on his thigh to lean in and get a look at the menu—which she had memorized and didn't need to look at.

What she did feel the need to do was touch him. Soothe him. Take away the hollow shadows still in his eyes.

Their faces were only an inch apart, and incredibly aware of the weight of his gaze, she swiveled her eyes from the menu to his and stayed there while she gave her order.

Not breaking eye contact, Caleb ordered a couple of burgers for himself and added a large drink and large fries.

"It's cheaper if you make it a meal," she said.

He playfully tugged on a strand of her hair. "I know."

"So why did you—?"

"Triple the last part of that order," he told their unseen order taker.

"Will do, Mr. Parker," came a very young-sounding male voice over the speaker. "Uh, and before you ask, yes, my sisters and I did all the chores you texted."

"And your homework?" Caleb asked.

"Did you say a large drink?"

Caleb rolled his eyes and drove up to the first window.

The kid behind the register was a dark-haired, dark-skinned teenager, his eyes wary. "Okay," he said. "So I didn't do *all* my homework, but to be fair, it's stupid."

"Stupid or not, we've got a deal," Caleb said, handing over cash for the food.

The kid swallowed hard and handed over two large bags with their order. Caleb went through them and made a few adjustments before handing Sadie one of the bags and the other back to the kid. "Are your sisters in the back booth doing their homework like I asked?" he asked.

"Yeah."

"See that they get this. There's plenty for you too on your break."

The kid's sullenness lifted at the scent of the fries. "Thanks."

"Don't thank me yet. Text me pics of all your homework when it's done. And Trenton?"

"Yeah?"

"It'd better be done, and you and your sisters home safe and sound by ten o'clock."

The kid opened his mouth and Caleb merely went brows up.

The kid closed his mouth and nodded. "Yeah."

"Text me."

"I will."

Caleb nodded and pulled forward and off to the side to open the bag of food.

"What was that?" Sadie asked, stopping him. "You being a hero?"

"More like me being a dick."

She gave a slow shake of her head, leaned over the console, and kissed him. He froze for a beat, but no slouch, he then pulled her tightly into him. The kiss went wild. When they finally broke apart, both breathless, he stared at her. "What was that about?"

"You help people." She shrugged. "It's a sexy side of you."

"I have sexier sides I can show you."

She rolled her eyes and started in on her fries. "Seems to me that you take care of a lot of people."

He gave a rough laugh but didn't say a word. Not until he drove them into the Pacific Heights neighborhood where the streets were lined with big, expensive, amazingly gorgeous homes. He pulled into the short driveway of one of them, hit a button and a garage door came up. He drove inside and hit the button again and the garage door came down behind them. In the dark of the garage, he turned to her, his hand on her headrest, his fingers playing with her hair.

"You seem to have a thing for my hair," she said.

"Actually, I have a thing for you. You feel comfortable coming inside?" he asked.

"Why wouldn't I?"

"Just making sure."

She got out of the car and looked around, beyond curious about him. The garage was huge. One wall was lined with tools, all looking well used. There was a truck in the next bay and on that wall were a couple of paddleboards, a surfboard, and skis.

There was an inside door, which opened without warning, and a guy stood there, tall and big as a tree. His skin was as dark as his eyes, though he flashed a bright smile. "Just making sure you weren't a bad guy," he said. He craned his neck, looking behind him. "It's your brother and he's got the sort of company that means we're leaving."

"Is it a woman?" a woman wanted to know.

The tall, built guy grinned at Sadie and she realized she recognized him from the pub over a week ago. He was married to one of Caleb's sisters. "Yep."

"Well hurry up and let's go out the front before they see us."

"Too late."

Caleb rolled his eyes. "Sadie, this is my brother-in-law, Niles. Niles, this is Sadie. And I'll owe you big if you get the girls out of here in the next sixty seconds."

Niles grinned and the two men did one of those guy backslapping hugs and then some complicated handshake.

"Heard from my nephew," Niles said. "Thanks for scaring him straight. I'm pretty sure he's not done being a dumbass though, so don't go soft on 'em. My sister says to keep giving him hell and make sure he's good and terrified about stealing from you. She wants him to think he could go to juvie any second."

Caleb nodded. "What are you guys doing here anyway?"

"Sienne and Kayla are stocking your freezer."

"Kayla nesting again?"

"Yeah, but she needed an assist. That girl's big as a house."

"I am not nesting!" presumably Kayla yelled from inside the house. "I just don't want the people I love who have penises to starve to death or eat junk food because they don't take the time to take care of themselves!"

Caleb looked down at the bag of food in his hands and put it behind his back.

Niles grimaced and rubbed a huge hand over his bald head. "Apparently she's having trouble regulating her hormones."

"I am not!"

Niles grimaced again, fist-bumped Caleb, nodded at Sadie, and vanished inside the house.

A few seconds later, the front door slammed shut.

"My sisters Sienne and Kayla," Caleb said. "And Sienne's husband, Niles. Kayla literally goes insane when she's in the last trimester of her pregnancies."

"You guys really are close."

"We are," he said. "For better or for worse. And let me tell you, some days there's lots of worse."

Sadie followed him through the door and into one of the biggest kitchens she'd ever seen. "Wow," she said, but in truth her mind was very busy processing the things she'd learned about Caleb tonight. First, he had tattoos, which he'd not once mentioned in all the time that she'd known him. And she'd known him for a damn year.

Worse, she'd judged him for being . . . What? *Normal?*

He was the furthest thing from any of the "normal" people she'd ever known. He was smart as hell and also private as hell. Not in a negative way, but as if he'd had to guard himself all the time.

Something she knew a little something about.

But what she'd learned about him tonight was more than the fact that he had tattoos and was close to his family. She'd learned he'd had a troubled life too, and that made her a terrible person for assuming he'd had a fairy-tale life growing up.

She blew out a sigh, and that's when she saw them, on his shiny, very clean tile floor: Lollipop's food and water bowls, which caused a ridiculous tug on her heart. "I'm sorry," she said quietly.

He looked over at her.

"I'm an ass," she clarified.

"You have the best ass on the planet," he said. "If that's what you mean."

"It's not." She stalled with a few French fries. "I've got a confession."

"Is this going to be a dirty confession?" he asked hopefully.

"No! And never mind."

He took the last bite of his first burger, crumpled up the wrapping, and tossed it over his shoulder, landing it into his trash can without looking. "Come on. Tell me."

"No, forget it. You ruined it."

"Okay," he said easily. "Then I'll tell you. You want to confess to being a Miss Judgy Judgerson."

Chapter 20

#HotMess

"What?" Sadie gaped at Caleb. How the hell had he known? "I'll confess to no such thing," she said. "That's not even close to what I . . ." She trailed off when he just stood there so composed while she was . . . not composed.

Because he'd spoken the truth. She was indeed a Miss Judgy Judgerson. "It's all your suits' fault," she said.

He looked at her for a long beat, his eyes a good part amused, but also there was frustration there. "Here's what I think," he finally said. "I think that when you get uncomfortable, you look for a way out. You were uncomfortable with me from the very beginning, in the best way possible. Meaning you were attracted to me. And that scared you, so you've been looking for a way out ever since." He held her gaze. "A suit is my work uniform, Sadie, nothing more. It's business, and also about professionalism and maturity, and to a lesser degree, image. I'm not going to wear a T-shirt and jeans into a business meeting with NASA, for example. Not when we're going to sit down and discuss future projects that could add up to billions of dollars. I'm not hiding behind my clothes, but I'm not being inauthentic either."

He was right, and worse, he was as authentic as they came, whereas she tended to go for shock value, a fact that proved her immaturity more than anything else. Sagging back against the counter, she crossed her arms and looked into his knowing eyes. "It must be hard to be perfect."

He laughed. *Laughed.*

"I don't know why that's funny," she said. "And you know what else you are? Way too calm, which pisses me off."

"It's my black heart."

"So nothing gets it pumping?" she asked.

"You know exactly what gets my black heart pumping."

She felt her face heat, which really got to her, and

she closed her eyes. Because yes, she did know exactly. When he'd been buried deep inside her so that she could feel nothing but him, his heart had pounded hard against hers and it'd been thrilling. She opened her eyes and found him standing right in front of her.

Smart, sexy, *and* he moved like smoke.

"FYI, I'm not even close to perfect," he said. "I'm bossy, demanding, I don't seem to know when to give up, and . . ."

"And . . . ?" she prodded when he trailed off.

"I'm not exactly proud of this." He ran a finger along her temple, tucking a stray strand of her hair behind her ear. "But I'm also emotionally detached."

"From . . . ?"

"Just about everyone," he said.

"Except your family."

"Sometimes even them. I don't do vulnerable very well. Had too much of it growing up. So I hold back, specifically with women." His finger stroked over her earlobe now, his eyes on the movement. "My last girlfriend dumped me for it. And the one before that too. I think 'coldhearted bastard' was a common theme."

She took that in, watching him watch her from those still hooded eyes. She wasn't the only one of them who was messed up. The realization should've scared her, but instead it comforted. She glanced around at his huge house that she was pretty sure he'd not brought any of their common friends to . . . but he'd brought her. "You're testing me," she realized.

He just looked at her.

"You are," she said slowly. "You're throwing everything you've got at me so I'll realize you're just as screwed up as me and dump your ass."

He gave a slow shake of his head. "When I think about us being in a relationship, I don't picture the dumping-my-ass part."

This shut her up for a beat. "You think about being in a relationship?" she asked. "With me? Because let's be honest. Your heart isn't even close to black. But mine is."

"I like your black heart," he said. "And yes, I think about being in a relationship with you. Why does that surprise you?"

"Because I'm a hot mess!"

He smiled. "You're hot," he said, "but you're not a mess. You're strong, determined, resourceful, unpredictable—" He smiled when she grimaced at the truth of that.

But it was truly shocking to her that he remembered everything about her. He knew her, like really knew her. After living her life surrounded by people who'd barely noticed her, being around Caleb was revolutionary.

"—And," he added quietly, "apparently you haven't figured out that I like all of that, a lot."

"And yet you're still testing me. Did I pass or fail?"

"Depends," he said, "on what you do next."

She stared at him for a beat, at war with herself. *Don't do it*, she thought. *Don't.* But she set down her now empty bag of fries, licked the salt off her thumb, and strode across the expanse of the kitchen straight for him.

He didn't move an inch, just watched her come at him, eyes hooded, body on the wrong side of tense.

He wanted not to care about her.

But he did.

And she knew *exactly* what that felt like. Not stopping until they were toe-to-toe, she slid her hands up his chest and let her fingers curl into his hair. Holding his gaze, she tugged his head down to hers and took his mouth.

For a beat, he didn't budge, just let her nibble at first one corner of his mouth and then the other. It wasn't until she gave his full lower lip a nip with her teeth that he groaned and yanked her into him, hard.

"I thought you'd have run screaming into the night by now," he murmured.

She gave a rough laugh. "Look at me, Caleb. If anyone should be running scared, it's you."

"You don't scare me either, Sadie Lane."

"Well, I damn well should."

This got her another slow shake of his head. "I like you," he said. "Just the way you are."

"Now you're just trying to get into my pants."

"You're wearing a dress, a damn sexy one at that."

"My panties then," she said.

"If I was trying to get into your panties, I'd do this." He backed her to the counter and pressed his warm sexy body into hers. Cupping her face, he kissed her senseless, until she was clinging to him and trying to climb him like a tree. She drowned in the kiss, letting all the pent-up passion flood over her and take control. His hands on her body felt right, so very right as he touched her exactly how she wanted to be touched. She had no idea how he already knew her so well, but he did.

Finally, when they were both breathing crazily, he pulled back just far enough to look into her eyes. He'd tugged her dress straps to her elbows, baring her breasts, and had her hem bunched up over his forearms. His fingers were playing with the edge of her lacy thong, making it hard to pull in air.

"I can't remember what we were talking about," she managed.

He flashed a smile and she stared at him transfixed because she knew what was coming next.

Her.

She'd known what would happen from the moment she'd crossed the kitchen, and she reached for him. He lifted her, setting her on the countertop, making her squeal when she made contact with the ice-cold granite. "You're right," she gasped. "You're not even close to perfect."

"But I'm good," he said, his amusement giving way to something far more intense. His hands were on her ribcage, just beneath her breasts, his thumbs teasing her nipples, leaving her feeling like she was walking along a cliff, toying with a tumble off the edge.

Snagging one of the barstools with his foot, Caleb yanked it close. Then he rested his butt against it, giving her a look that nearly melted the thong right off of her before ducking his head beneath her dress.

"Wait," she said quickly, not at all sure why she was stalling other than the mix of how easy he was to be with and his innate sexiness had her off-balance and she hadn't had a chance to get her barriers into place. "You didn't finish your dinner. Aren't you still hungry?"

She felt him smile against her, the hands he had on her both familiar and warm. She was stalling and he knew it. "I'm starving," he said, muffled by her dress. His hands skimmed up her thighs to nudge them apart. Then the erotically rough pads of his fingers scraped the lace aside and . . .

"Oh my God," she murmured as his tongue rasped over her quivering flesh.

"Nope," he said. "Just me." This was the last thing he said.

Not Sadie. She said lots. Or rather whimpered and moaned things like "yes!" and "oh, please . . ." and "don't stop!" and when he played with her, holding her on the edge of the mother of all orgasms, there was more than one "dammit, Caleb!" And that was the thing about him. He could push buttons she didn't even know she had. And he'd clearly read her instruction manual because he knew exactly how she worked and what she needed to run at maximum capacity.

When he'd thoroughly and shockingly taken her apart and put her back together again, he gently kissed first one inner thigh and then the other, and then her two tattoos.

And then the scar beneath those two tattoos.

She stilled, but not Caleb. He rose, kicked the barstool out of his way, and produced a condom.

Not neon pink.

Leaning over her, he brushed his lips across hers
and had her fingers curling into his shirt as she tugged
it off him. His tattoos were sexy as hell and she pressed
hot kisses to every part of him she could reach as she
slid her hands inside his pants, making him do a little
creative swearing of his own.

She didn't normally have a hard time keeping her
emotional connection to a guy in check, but whenever
she and Caleb were intimate, it was impossible to control herself, much less her emotions. The gentleness
and obvious affection with which he touched her always
dissolved the best of her intentions.

"Sadie," he said huskily.

"Yeah?"

"Missed this."

"It's not been long," she managed to grate out, holding on to him because suddenly he was her only anchor
in a spinning world.

And then he was inside her.

She gasped as he filled her, his hands going to her
hips to yank her closer to the edge of the counter, allowing him to slide even deeper inside her. She bit his
shoulder to hide her moan.

"Aw. You missed me too," he said and began to move.

And just like that, like always with him, she lost herself, pulled into his force field by the sheer presence of his personality alone. Add to the mix what his body did to hers and how he looked at her . . . She'd never experienced anything like it. It'd probably terrify her if she had any brain capacity left in that moment, but she didn't. Not with Caleb holding her like she was the best thing that had ever happened to him, his body tensing, telling her he was close. But she was even closer, and even as she thought it, she fell into the abyss, pulling him along with her.

Their release was followed by a perfect moment of contentment as Caleb's kisses turned tender and lingering again. When their heart rates returned to some semblance of normal—although Sadie wasn't sure her heart would recover—he helped right her clothing. His hands were still lingering when his phone buzzed on the counter. Nuzzling at Sadie's neck, he said, "Answer."

"Honey," a woman said into the room. "The girls are coming over for *The Bachelorette* and I'm ordering pizza. Can I get you one?"

Sadie felt Caleb's chest rumble with his laugh. "Hard pass on *The Bachelorette*, Mom, but no thanks."

"But what about the pizza? You love pizza. What's wrong? You sick?"

One of Caleb's hands was in Sadie's hair. He slid it down her throat to cup a breast, letting his thumb slide over her nipple, which tightened for him. "Just . . . busy tonight," he murmured.

This got him a beat of silence from his mom, like his words didn't compute. "But you're always starving by now. Did you get dinner?"

His gaze went wicked as he looked at Sadie and she felt her face heat. "I ate," he said, and then it was more than just her face heating up. "Gotta go, Mom. Love you."

Sadie waited until she was sure the call was no longer connected. "You just lied to your mother."

"I didn't lie. I *did* eat." He flashed a dirty smile that had her halfway to another orgasm and lifted her, one arm banded around her lower back, the other sliding around the back of a thigh, encouraging her to wrap her legs around him.

Which she did, kissing her way down his throat to the emblem on his bicep. "You had a good artist."

"My cousin," he said, palming her ass, easily holding her up against him. "Like you, she normally only takes on female clients, but I bugged her until she caved."

"Why only female clients?"

Caleb shrugged. "She's not super fond of men. Says they have a lower pain tolerance."

"Men are big babies." She laughed when he looked surprised and maybe slightly insulted. "And the more alpha they are," she went on, "the lower their pain threshold. I once had a client who wanted a big badass Metallica tattoo, but he couldn't handle it. He left the shop with a single line trailing down the back of his shoulder."

Caleb smiled. "I wasn't exactly a tough guy when I got my first tattoo."

"You mean your cartoon turtle?" she teased.

"Laugh all you want, I deserve it. I was an idiot back then. An idiot who needed a couple of shots of vodka to get through it."

"It could've been worse," she said. "You didn't get the name of your high school sweetheart, for instance. Rocco makes more money covering up other tattoos, like ex-lovers' names, than anything else. If you're going to get a name inked on your body forever, it should belong to a pet, one of your kids, or—"

"—Mom?" he asked dryly.

She tried and failed to stifle a grin. "Yeah."

Apparently her grin was contagious because he was grinning back at her and they were staring at each other stupidly, and then not stupidly . . . and the room began to heat up.

He strode with her out of the kitchen and she got

breathless with anticipation. "Are we going to try again to prove neither of us is scared?" she asked.

"Yes. As many times as you can take."

"I don't have to be at work until eight in the morning." She nipped at his throat.

With a rough groan, he glanced at the time. "That gives us eight hours."

"Think it's enough time?"

"Not nearly, but I'm good at making do."

"I hope you've got a bed somewhere in this huge place."

"Yeah," he said as he strode with her into a large living room. "But we're not going to make it there."

"We're not?"

"No." The rough gravel of his voice and the look on his face turned her on way more than she'd like to admit. He dropped a knee to the biggest couch she'd ever seen and laid her out on it. "But we are going to get all of our clothes off this time," he promised and had them both stripped down to bare skin in less than a blink, and then proceeded to crawl up her body and get started making the most of their eight hours.

Sadie assumed the next morning would be awkward. After all, morning-afters weren't in her repertoire. When Caleb dragged her out of bed before dawn's first light, she told him he should prepare to die. He only laughed and slung her over his shoulder and strode into his bathroom.

She'd considered biting his very fine ass, but then he stepped with her into his blissfully hot shower so she decided he could live for another few minutes.

"You almost died," she told him.

"Shh," he murmured and lifted her up against him. "I'm not finished with you yet." Then he took his time making sure she shared in his joy of coed morning showers and she forgot all about murder.

After, she told him that maybe he might be the perfect man after all—if he cooked her pancakes. But he reminded her he couldn't cook worth shit. So whew, he really wasn't perfect.

Lollipop was in the living room attacking a pillow when they came out of Caleb's bedroom, ready for work.

Sadie froze. "Your sister's here?"

"No, she just dropped off Lollipop."

Remembering the last thirty minutes in the shower, Sadie bit her lower lip. "Think she heard us?"

He gave her an amused look. "Us?"

She smacked his chest and he laughed, grabbing her hand. "She didn't hear anything, the walls are very well constructed and nearly soundproof."

The "nearly" worried her, but she put it out of her

mind when Caleb bought her McDonald's, breakfast of champions, and then drove her and Lollipop to work, where she'd drop Lollipop off at the pet shop for doggy daycare for the morning. Before she and the dog slid out of his car, he pulled her in close for a good-bye kiss that curled her toes. His touch was sometimes playful and sometimes lust-filled, but it was always meaningful.

"Have a good morning," he murmured, smiling at the undoubtedly glazed-over look in her eyes.

"I've already had a good morning," she reminded him. "Did you wreck your knees on that hard tile floor in your shower?"

He smiled a very sexy, very knowing smile that brought her back to the steamy hot shower and how he'd dropped to his knees, slid his hands up her thighs and leaned in to give her one of the most erotic experiences of her life.

"You worried I won't be able to do it again?" he asked.

"More that I'm worried for *my* knees when I return the favor."

His eyes went molten lava and he kissed her again. When he broke away, she had to look down to make sure she was still dressed.

After what felt like a very long shift at the day spa,

she headed to the Canvas Shop. Both Mini Moe and Blue were there, as well as Cal, who was talking to Rocco.

"I'm sorry," she said to Cal. "I don't have you on my schedule for today—"

"I know. I'm just on an early dinner break. Listen, can I talk to you for a minute?"

"Sure," she said. "Come on back with me while I get set up for my first client."

He leaned back against her counter and started to pull something from his pocket and she pointed at him. "Stop right there. I don't want to hear anyone having sex."

He raised his hands. "I know. And I'm still sorry about that. I just . . ." He met her gaze, his own serious now. "I want to show you something. I was in the building the other day and also this morning. I'm interviewing for a job with Hunt Investigations on the second floor. That's confidential, by the way."

"Okay. So why are you telling me?"

"Because . . ." He broke off with a grimace and ran a hand over his head. "Shit."

"What is it, Cal?"

He accessed his photos and thumbed through, showing her two pictures.

Of herself.

One was of her walking through the courtyard with

a bag of McDonald's, which meant it'd been taken that morning. The other was of her leaving the Canvas Shop, Lollipop on her leash, and given the clothes she was wearing, it had been taken the week before. "What the hell is this?" she asked.

He took the phone back and went back to the first pic and zoomed in. There were people in the background, which wasn't odd because the courtyard was usually full of people. But there was a young woman sitting on a bench, her phone up and facing Sadie.

Then Cal scrolled to the next pic. The same woman was in the background of that one too.

Sadie shook her head in shock. "What the . . . ?"

"You either have a stalker, or you're being watched for some reason. Want me to—?"

"No," she said grimly. Because she recognized her so-called stalker, and because she did, emotions were tumbling through her like a category five hurricane. "I've got to go. Text me those photos."

Cal nodded and left her alone. She stood still for a beat, closing her eyes, trying to contain the sudden tsunami of emotions tumbling through her, battering her from the inside out.

Because her stalker was one of Caleb's sisters. Given that she was extremely pregnant, it was Kayla, no doubt backed by the others. She felt a blood-boiling temper that her privacy had been violated. This was immediately followed by humiliation, because she should have known. *Of course* to allow a woman into his life, Caleb would've had to have that woman vetted. She might have even thought of it sooner, but Caleb had pretty much locked down her good sense from that very first night when they'd rescued Lollipop. The poor dog was thankfully blissfully unaware that both of her owners were crazy.

Caleb was having her followed.

And probably doing a deep background check as well, which meant she was going to have to face facts. He'd either already learned things about her that she'd never wanted anyone to know, or he was about to learn those things.

Either way, the combo of bad temper and humiliation had her feeling like a cat with her back against the wall, claws out. She texted with her first client, who agreed to move their appointment back an hour, and strode out to the front.

In unison Blue, Mini Moe, and Rocco did a double take at her expression.

"You've been here five minutes," Rocco said. "Who's pissed in your Cheerios already?"

She couldn't tell him. She couldn't tell *anyone.* "Why is that a saying? Because it's disgusting. I mean, think about it, did someone actually piss in someone's Cheerios for that to be a thing?"

"Nice deflection," he said. "I take it you'd like me to mind my own fucking business."

"Yes," she said, never having been more grateful for his real friendship than that moment. But even real friendships had limitations. He knew some of how screwed-up she'd been, but he didn't know all of it— such as how she'd been involuntarily committed by her own parents. And if she had anything to say about it, he'd never know. No one would. "I'll be back."

"You look like you're going to kick someone's ass."

"That's because I am," she said grimly.

"Need backup?"

She stopped and moved back to him, going up on tiptoes to brush a kiss to his scruffy jaw. "No, but I love you for asking, thanks."

"Suits screwed up, didn't he."

She had to swallow the sudden lump in her throat. Not easy when it was the size of a regulation football. But there were cracks forming in her temper, allowing other, more uncontrolled emotions to squeeze through, and she couldn't have it. Not yet. Not until she dealt with this and could get herself off alone somewhere to lick her wounds.

Rocco studied her for another beat. "Do I need to kill him?"

"I've got it covered."

He nodded. "You'll call me if you need help hiding the body." Not a question but a statement.

There was some comfort in the fact that she knew he 100 percent meant it.

Chapter 21

#HowToRuinTheMorningAfter

Caleb entered his offices and ran into Sienne while getting himself coffee. "Hey," he said. "You studied Japanese in college."

She blinked. "If you mean the single Japanese culture class I took a zillion years ago because I needed the credits and it was the only class that wasn't full, then yes. I nearly failed it, by the way. Why?"

He yanked at his shirt and pointed to the Japanese character. "Apparently this means *mom*. Naoki's idea of a joke. I'd take him to the mats if I thought he remembered."

She burst out laughing. "And people call you a genius."

Rolling his eyes, he headed to his office.

"Where's the tattoo for your sisters?" she called after him. "Why aren't we immortalized on you yet?"

He locked his door.

It wasn't until hours later when he was in a meeting that he started in surprise as Sadie appeared in front of him. He halted the computer program and pulled off his virtual reality goggles.

Everyone in the huge room with him working on their latest project did the same. Spence, Sienne, the two engineers from NASA he'd been working with, and his three highest level programmers. "Lights," he said.

The lights went from dim to bright.

Sadie stood there in the same outfit she'd had on when he'd dropped her at work that morning; formfitting ripped jeans, the holes showing off flashes of sexy leg. She wore a black cropped sweater and black high-heeled boots that put her nearly nose-to-nose with him. Her hair was loose and sexily wild around her face and she was wearing enough earrings and bracelets to set off a metal detector.

But sexy as all that was—and it was very, very sexy—when his gaze met hers, he felt his breath catch. There was so much fury in her eyes he nearly missed the heart-stopping hurt.

Nearly. "What's wrong?"

296 . JILL SHALVIS

"We need to talk," she said.

"Oh boy," Spence murmured under his breath to Caleb. "Nothing good ever came from those four words. You do something stupid?"

"Take ten," Caleb said to the room, ignoring Spence while maintaining eye contact with a clearly pissed-off Sadie.

"Try thirty," Spence said with a smile to Sadie. "Sometimes a woman's got something to say and needs time to say it." He crouched low and offered a hand to Lollipop at her side, who allowed a pet, but she was all eyes on Caleb, straining at her leash to get to him.

Sadie actually returned Spence's smile, effectively proving Spence right, that Caleb was indeed in trouble all on his own. As the room cleared out, he reached for her.

She stepped back and crossed her arms. She'd locked herself up good and tight, which wasn't good. "I take it this isn't a social visit," he said and scooped Lollipop up for a big hug, accepted a face full of kisses before putting her down to concentrate on Sadie.

Not that Lollipop was okay with this. She sat right on Caleb's feet and stared up at him in adoration, giving him the *I'm still right here!* whine.

Pretty much the opposite of Sadie's greeting.

"Definitely not a social visit," she said. "I *knew*

better than to let my guard down with you, but somehow I thought you were going to surprise me and be different. Instead, you're worse than any guy I've ever dated."

"That's quite an accusation," he said mildly. "You going to tell me what I did?"

She drew a deep breath. "You were sneaky and manipulative. I mean all you had to do was come to me and ask me yourself. I'd have told you anything you wanted to know. I'm a damn open book."

She was lying. He'd never met a woman less an open book. But hell if he was going to point that out when there was steam coming out her ears. "Still don't know what the hell you're talking about," he said.

"Oh, please. And the really screwed-up thing is that it doesn't even make any sense. It's not like I wanted anything from you—or that we're even a thing."

He took a second to absorb that, realizing just how serious she was. "Okay," he said. "Well, first, we *are* very much having a thing. It started the night we rescued Lollipop, even though it took you until last night to trust me enough to lower some boundaries and spend the night."

Her eyes shot daggers. "Sex does not equal a *thing*."

"You're right," he agreed. "Which is why I didn't reference the first time we slept together. *That* was sex.

Great sex, actually, but last night was different. It was more and you know it. And now you're using it to back away and run scared."

She sputtered for a moment. "Don't turn this on me. I'm not running scared. I'm *furious*. And whatever that was last night, it's over now."

"Because . . . ?"

She drew a deep breath as if she needed it to talk instead of murder him where he stood. "Because you're having me followed like I'm some stranger you want to bang but have to vet first. And you didn't even care enough to do it yourself! I don't know what you're looking for, but I'm not some sort of con artist. I'm not going to sneak into your house and steal from you or talk to the press and give away your trade secrets, are you kidding me?"

He felt his mouth fall open. "Wait." He caught her just as she whirled to go. "Wait a damn minute. What the hell are you talking about?"

"You once told me that the people you date have to be vetted and go through a process to get cleared, a process handled by your sister."

"Yes, but that's exaggerated."

"Right, you wouldn't need to because you're having your sister do your dirty work." She shook her head. "I didn't want this, Caleb. Any of it."

She didn't say his name often, but when she did—as she had last night when he'd been buried deep inside her—it never failed to give him pleasure. Except this time. This time she said his name like it was a bad word. "I'm not having you followed. I swear it," he said at her look of disbelief. "I wouldn't do that to you." And even just saying it, he knew it was true. He wouldn't do that to her, and that's how he knew he was in deep.

Way deep.

Too deep.

Somehow when his brain hadn't been paying attention, his heart had engaged. It'd been a slow unfurling, but there was no sense in denying it. He was doing things he'd never done before, like using his awake hours for things other than working. Such as opening his home—and heart—to the woman standing in front of him, eyes flashing hot with temper and mistrust.

Which meant he'd have to have enough trust for the both of them until she understood that he wouldn't hurt her, that he was real and not going anywhere. "I'm not tracking you," he said quietly. "And . . . I *talked you into this*? I'd call bullshit on that, but I'm going to give you a pass because you're clearly upset and—"

"Let me tell you where you can put your damn pass," she said. "Sideways." She pulled out her phone.

There were two shots, both of Sadie presumably

going about her day in the Pacific Pier Building, and both featuring a woman in the background.

Kayla, in all her pregnant glory, playing the part of the sneaky photographer. He stared at it. "What the actual fuck."

"My question exactly."

He lifted his head and met Sadie's furious—and hurt—gaze. "I don't know what's happening here," he said, "but I *will* find out."

"You once told me that the Parkers act as a team," she said, "even when it's just one of you. You stand by each other, you watch each other's backs. Maybe you didn't say the words that set this in motion, but you knew it could happen and you certainly could've stopped it."

This was all true enough to make him wince. "Sadie—"

"Are you going to tell me you've *never* had your sexual partners vetted?"

"Sexual partners, no," he said. "Lovers, yes." He met her gaze, letting her know that he considered the two of them lovers and not just sexual partners, but she looked away. Whether that was because she didn't want to acknowledge it or she didn't believe it, he wasn't sure. "In the past," he said, "before I've gotten too deep into a relationship, there's been a vetting process, but always with permission. I admit, I'm in deep with you, but I haven't informed anyone of that yet."

She stared at him. "Including me."

"Then you've not been paying attention." He risked his life by closing the gap between them. "I was hoping my actions would fill you in."

"Yeah, well, I'm learning a lot by the actions of you and yours," she said, still stiff, still full of mistrust. "I just hope whatever you all found out about me was worth it." She scooped up Lollipop. "Goodbye, Caleb."

"Hold on," he said and took her hand in his when she tried to walk past him to the door.

She tugged free, and this time when she lifted her gaze to his, pain eclipsed her temper. Haunted, hollow, gut-wrenching pain, and it stopped him in his tracks. "Sadie," he said quietly, softly, wanting only to soothe, to ease what she was feeling. Because something more was going on here, he was definitely missing something.

"No," she murmured, her voice hitching. "Don't." She took Lollipop and walked out the door, Lollipop's head bouncing as she looked over her mama's shoulder to watch him.

"Arf!"

She wanted her human. "I could—" he started, but

Sadie's response was to flash him her middle finger as she left.

Right.

He could have stopped her or called down and had the front desk detain her. But he'd never do either. She was angry and upset, and she had a right to be.

He needed to fix this. First, he needed to find out what the hell had happened and why. He'd told Sienne to stay out of her personal life. When he had the 411 he needed, he'd find Sadie and lay his heart out on the line.

Sienne's office was empty.

He hit up Hannah's next and hit the jackpot. Three of them in the same spot, in fact. Hannah was sitting cross-legged on her desk eating out of a small Chinese food container with chopsticks. Kayla was in Hannah's desk chair, her plate balanced on her big belly, eating with a fork because she had no chopsticks skills and never had. Sienne was eating standing up, leaning against the desk, laughing at Kayla, who'd just dropped a pot sticker on her chest.

"Hey," Kayla said at his entrance, pulling her shirt up to her mouth to eat the pot sticker right off the shirt.

He shut the door harder than it needed to be. "Oh good," he said. "A meeting of The Coven. Let's talk."

The Coven froze in unison and then looked at each other, brows raised.

"Is it that time of the month?" Sienne asked him.

Caleb blew out a breath. "You know I had all the males in this entire company go to sensitivity training. Maybe I need to send all the females as well. And no, it's not that *time* of the month. It's the I-need-to-fire-all-of-you time of the month."

"Wow," Hannah said, taking another bite. "It's like he wants to die."

But Caleb wasn't playing. "Sit down," he said to Sienne.

"I like to stand."

"Do you like to be unemployed?" he asked.

Sienne chewed her bite and swallowed, taking her sweet-ass time about it too, but she did finally sit. "What the hell crawled up your—?"

"Which one of you approved the background search on Sadie after I told you not to?"

They all gave each other a careful look again, their faces now blank in the Parker family way when they were closing ranks.

"Someone needs to start talking," he said and met Sienne's gaze. "I pay you the most, so you first."

"You pay her more than me?" Hannah asked.

Sienne set down her Chinese food container and wiped her hands on a napkin before meeting his gaze. "I approved it."

"After I explicitly asked you not to do it," Caleb said, wanting to make sure he was hearing her correctly.

"You were—*are*—acting off," she said. "You're doing things you've never done before, like leaving work early."

"Not early," he said. "I'm just putting in normal hours instead of the usual insane overtime—something you've been after me forever to do, by the way."

"You're leaving meetings to take personal phone calls. And texting all the time. And you're so secretive about it, about her."

"Because it's private," he said.

"It?"

"Yes, and it's between me and her and not all of you. It's not about work, so leave it alone."

"But we're not just your work people," Hannah said. "We're your family. We've been doing this for how many years? Why are you upset now? What's so different this time? What is she to you?"

He was only just starting to understand the answer to that question, so he certainly wasn't about to discuss it with his nosy-ass sisters. "What does that matter?"

"It matters," Sienne said. "You know we had to

check, maybe now more than ever since you're acting so weird."

"Sienne," Hannah said and gave a single head shake. She looked at Caleb. "There's more," she said quietly. "We . . . found something."

He cut his eyes to her.

"I know you're pissed off," she said. "But—"

"Actually, I'm furious. Looking into her, *maybe* I could see. If I'm being honest, we've had reasons to do that in the past." This was a grudging admission. "But to have Kayla follow her around after I asked you not to?"

"You've never complained before," Hannah said. "What did you expect?"

"I expect you to let me live my life and let me make my choices," he said. "You went too far. I should fire all your asses."

Kayla's eyes welled up with tears and he blew out a breath. "Don't cry." He pulled her into him and pressed his cheek to the top of her head. "You've made a lot of sacrifices for me, I get that. And I appreciate all you've done, more than I can ever say. And yes, you're in charge of my *professional* life. But this is my personal life, so I really need you to hear me on this. I love you, but you all need to butt the hell out." He gave them each a long look and turned to the door.

"I'm still going to send you the file," Sienne said.

"Don't," he said.

"Okay, let me reword," Sienne said. "I already sent it to you. You should read it."

He shut the door on them and drew in a deep breath, mind spinning. To the shock of his staff, he left the building. He was headed back to Cow Hollow, though he made a quick stop on the way.

He parked and checked his phone. Sienne had indeed sent him a file this morning with the subject line:

Mercedes Lane, please read.

He didn't. Instead, he entered the Canvas Shop. Both Rocco and Mini Moe were at the front desk, elbow-to-elbow, taking up half the shop with their size, talking about the radish and grape salads they were eating.

"Hey," Mini Moe said defensively, jabbing his fork in Caleb's direction. "It's gluten-free."

"Not judging," Caleb said.

"Are you sure? Because even I'm judging us just a little bit."

Caleb refrained from laughing, knowing it was best for his physical well-being. He looked at Rocco, who hadn't said a word or uttered a greeting. "Is Sadie here?"

"Why?"

"I'd like to talk to her."

"Why?" Rocco asked, shoveling in another bite of his salad and crunching aggressively.

Caleb blew out a breath. "She told you."

"She told me things were fucked up."

"Yeah," Caleb said. "And I'm here to apologize."

Rocco and Mini Moe looked at each other in surprise.

"What?" Caleb asked. "What's so weird about that?"

"Nothing," Rocco said. "Except I don't think a guy she's been into has ever cared enough to apologize for anything."

He'd guessed as much, but hearing it made Caleb feel like an even bigger dick. "Does that mean you'll tell me where she is?"

"Apparently, he'll tell you anything you want," Sadie said darkly from behind him and he turned to find her standing in the opened doorway to the back rooms.

"And," she said to Rocco, "you know what else is gluten-free? Shutting up." She turned to Caleb, cool and remote.

"Hey," he said quietly.

Sadie didn't acknowledge this. She simply glared at Rocco and Mini Moe.

Rocco offered his fork with a grape on it.

308 · JILL SHALVIS

She shook her head. "I don't consume wine in pill form."

Rocco shrugged and went back to eating.

Caleb handed her the travel tumbler he'd stopped for, filled with her favorite coffee.

She eyed the container and the words on it:

I like my coffee black like my soul.

She gave a reluctant smile.

"Can we talk?" he asked and felt a déjà vu since only an hour ago she'd told him they needed to talk. That hadn't gone so well. He was hoping this went better.

But she hesitated. He actually thought she was going to turn him down flat, but she finally nodded and jerked her chin toward her workstation. She yanked the curtain around her area and pulled herself up to sit on the counter. Her body language said Closed Off as she sipped the coffee he'd brought her, watching him from eyes that weren't giving much away.

"I'm sorry," he said quietly. "You were right about what was happening, but I want you to know I didn't ask for you to be vetted. I wouldn't have done that without telling you first. My sisters are going to cease and desist and leave you the hell alone. If you want to be done with this, with me, I'll understand, but I hope that you'll give me another chance."

She stared at him for a long beat and he stared back, wishing he could get a bead on what she was thinking.

"Did you get filled in on whatever they dug up about me?" she finally asked.

"No." This was the utter truth and it would remain so. He had zero intention of reading the file sitting in his unopened e-mail.

She processed this for a long moment and then nodded again.

"Go out with me," he said.

She gave him a long look. "We already had a date."

"So let's check date number two off the list."

She sipped some more coffee, not nearly as composed as she wanted to be because he could see her hands shaking. "My list doesn't have a date number two on it," she said.

"What does your list have on it?"

"A lot of things." She ticked the points off her fingers. "One, men suck. Two, dump any men in my life. Three, men suck. The rest of the list isn't important right now." She set down the mug and slid off the counter.

He caught her by the hand when she went to walk away. "Are we done then, Sadie? Is that what you're saying?"

She stared into his eyes and said nothing.

His heart did a belly flop, but he nodded. He'd told her he would understand, and he stood by his word. Regardless of the way his heart threw itself against his ribcage, he let go of her hand and turned and walked out.

Chapter 22

#UnderHerSkin

Watching Caleb walk away, Sadie stood stock-still for several seconds in rare indecision. He'd told her he could be emotionally detached, and she'd believed him.

But she would bet the bank that she was better at it than he was. Except . . . normally when she detached and made a decision on someone, she never looked back. Sometimes it was an emotional cut, such as with the previous men she'd let in. They'd had to go for her mental health. Same with her family. She still saw them, she participated as a family member, but after all that had happened during her rough teenage years, she'd cut off their ability to hurt her.

The problem was, emotionally detaching in one area of her life had slowly bled into other areas as well, until she'd been emotionally detached from just about everything.

Until Caleb.

He'd come along and pulled her into his vortex, stripping her emotionally naked far before he'd ever gotten her clothes off. The truth was, she didn't want to be emotionally detached from him. But here was the thing, she wasn't sure how to be anything other than who she was. And deep down inside, she wasn't sure that who she was would be, could be, enough.

Still, she was a scrappy sort of survivor and knew how to change up a situation to her favor when she needed to. And this was most definitely a situation she wanted to change up. She'd overreacted, and worse, she'd let him walk away thinking she didn't want him. So she grabbed Lollipop's backpack, urged the dog into it, and then shouldered the pack. Then she ran out of the shop past a startled Rocco, Mini Moe, and Blue.

Rocco raised a hand with his fork in it as a salute, and Sadie ran on.

"Arf!" Lollipop said excitedly.

Sadie's phone buzzed, and hoping it was Caleb, she answered without looking at the screen while on the run. "I'm trying to catch you."

"What are you talking about?" her mom asked.

Crap. "Nothing, forget it. I've gotta go, I'll call you back—"

"You always say that, but you don't call me back. I need your confirmation that you're coming to dinner next week. It's the practice rehearsal family dinner. You know, where we practice being a warm loving family before we have to actually do it."

Damn. That was in only a week?

"Don't tell me you've forgotten," her mom said. "You know how important this practice is. We have to get in sync."

Good luck with that one. "Of course I didn't forget."

"Good. Who's your date?"

"Um . . ."

"You promised you'd have a date for the wedding."

"Yes," Sadie said. "But this isn't the wedding. It's not even the real rehearsal dinner. Like you said, it's just the practice."

"Which we're doing for you."

Sadie had to laugh. Of course they were. "Because heaven forbid I just act as myself, right?"

"Honey, I'm not in the mood for your sass. Just say you'll be here."

She stood up on one of the wrought-iron benches in the courtyard to see the entire length of it, searching for a sign of Caleb. "I'll be there."

"With a date."

"Fine, with a date," Sadie said.

"What's his name? What does he do?"

She managed not to smack her forehead with her own phone. Not *was he nice*, or *does he treat you right*, but *what does he do* . . . She was worried Sadie was going to bring someone inappropriate to the wedding and needed to get an early look at her choice. "He's a genius billionaire and he wears expensive suits," she said without thinking.

"Well, there's no reason to be sarcastic."

"Mom." She pinched the bridge of her nose. "I've got to go."

"You think I'm a bad mom."

Sadie craned her neck one way and then the other, searching for the tall, built guy walking out of her life.

"Wow," her mom said into Sadie's silence. "You really do think that."

"Mom—"

"You've got to go, remember?" And she disconnected.

Sadie might've called her back, but she caught sight of Caleb at the other end of the courtyard. She took off at a fast clip, to the huge joy of Lollipop on her back. By the time she got to Caleb, she was breathless from the mad dash.

Okay, that wasn't the truth. She was breathless because she'd nearly *not* caught him. The man was smoke when he wanted to be. But she managed to get in front of his long-legged stride and face him.

But then she realized she had no idea what she wanted to do or say. Luckily Lollipop had her own agenda.

"Arf!" the dog said at the sight of her favorite male.

Sadie wasn't going to wag her tail or give herself away in any such fashion, but she knew one thing—she wanted to believe in him. In *them*. "Mount Diablo," she said, still fighting for air.

Caleb reached a hand toward her face and her heart squeezed because it was going to be okay, he was going to touch her.

But he stroked a hand over Lollipop's head instead, although his eyes remained on Sadie. "Mount Diablo?" he asked quietly, not giving away a single hint of what he might be feeling.

Fair enough. "You asked what was on my list," she said. "Dating's not, because clearly I suck at it. But

Mount Diablo is because I've lived in San Francisco my entire life and I've never been."

He hesitated only very slightly. "Have you ever called in sick?"

"Yes, but never when I've actually been sick," she admitted.

A small smile curved his mouth.

An hour later, he'd driven them to the trailhead of Mount Diablo. They sat on top of the rock city, surrounded by a spread of cavernous caves and sandstone rock formations that took Sadie's breath away.

So did the man who'd brought her here. He had Lollipop's pack now, having relieved Sadie of the weight. Lollipop had walked a bit of the trail, but it turned out she much preferred riding on Caleb's shoulders.

Caleb had been up here before, of course. He'd been everywhere and done everything, and though Sadie liked to consider herself worldly and cynical, she had nothing on him.

He turned and studied her. "I feel like I smell something burning."

"I'm not sure what you see in me," she said and worked at not grimacing at the pathetic statement. But she really didn't know, and apparently she needed to.

He was clearly surprised by this.

"You know what? Never mind," she said quickly, turning away and pretending to study the view.

She heard him release Lollipop to run around to her heart's content and then pulled Sadie onto his lap. His arms closed around her and he kissed her shoulder, then the nape of her neck, blazing a trail to her ear.

She shivered. A full body shiver of the very best kind.

"I've been fascinated by you since the beginning," he murmured.

"Not true," she said. "We ran into each other plenty over the past year and you never seemed fascinated."

"You didn't notice because you were too busy doing your best not to be fascinated by me as well."

The sheer male ego in this statement made her laugh, but it backed up in her throat when his teeth grazed her earlobe. Then his hands slid beneath the material of her shirt and settled on her waist. "You're deflecting," she said.

"Yes, and I'm very good at it. The truth is, Sadie, you scared the hell out of me."

She stared at him. "How is that even possible?"

"Whenever I get in close proximity to you, I feel something."

She wriggled in his lap, her ass to his crotch, and felt something alright. "Yeah," she said on a low laugh. "It's called lust."

"There's some of that," he agreed, "but it's more. Before Lollipop, there was always something in your eyes that made me feel . . ." He drew in a deep breath. "Exposed. Vulnerable. And I don't typically do vulnerable. That didn't change once we got to know each other, by the way. But my curiosity and need for you overtook my fears." He smiled, though his eyes were serious. "But if the question is really when did I start to fall for you, then it was the night we rescued Lollipop. When you stood in the freezing rain with me, your clothes molded to your body, your eyes flashing. I couldn't see straight I was so turned on." He smiled in memory. "And then you proceeded to argue with me. Over everything." His laugh was low and rough. "I wanted to push you up against the wall and kiss you until you wanted me even half as bad as I wanted you, until you melted for me."

"And then?" she heard herself whisper.

"And then you co-adopted Lollipop with me. And not because you were looking to get something from me, but because you wanted to do the right thing for the dog. That's when I knew it was more than lust, and I had to walk away and plan my strategy."

"Always the venture capitalist?" she murmured.

"Something like that." His hands spread wide over her ribs, the tips of his fingers just brushing the undersides of her breasts. "You're not an easy woman, Sadie."

"I am a handful," she agreed, her pulse kicking into gear. "But that's why you have two hands."

He ignored her attempt to lighten up this conversation. "You're not easy," he said again. "You're something else entirely." And while she simmered over that, he smiled and kissed her softly. "And I like it," he said against her mouth. "I like you very much, Sadie Lane."

She sighed and tightened her grip on him. "I like you very much too, Caleb Parker. I didn't want to."

"Do tell," he said, voice amused.

She rolled her eyes and then got serious, staring up at him. "I mean, I *really* didn't want to. But you sneaked in under my defenses when I wasn't looking. And now I can't seem to shake you."

He smiled, gentle and warm. "I'm very grateful for that."

Lollipop was zooming around them like a wild woman, darting here and there and back again, occasionally tripping on her three legs, but getting right back up again, still having zero idea that she was handicapped in any way.

Sadie had the urge to stand up and run around too. Run around and . . . hide. She was a master at hiding, she'd been doing it all her life, both physically and mentally. But actually, she didn't want to hide from Caleb. She wanted to stay right here in his arms for as long as she could have him. Craning her neck, she stared up at the night sky. It was a tumultuous one, threatening rain, which she loved. When a few drops began to fall out of the sky, she stuck out her tongue to catch one.

Caleb watched, his voice husky when he spoke. "If we'd been out here a week ago, we'd have seen a rocket launch sending payloads into space."

"Yours?" she asked.

"Yes. The technology, anyway."

His world was so much bigger than hers. She'd known that. But it never failed to astonish her. "You used to travel for work all the time and be mostly gone," she said. "Before Lollipop."

"Not just Lollipop. There's a lot of reasons why I'm using SF as my home base these days. My family. And friends." He paused and met her gaze. "You."

Her breath caught audibly, and a small smile curved his lips. "I knew the day I met you," he said. "Which was just under a year ago now."

"Knew what?" she whispered.

"That I was going to fall for you and never recover."

Her chest tightened. "I don't want to ever be the thing that holds someone back."

"You don't hold me back. You make life more."

"More what?" she asked.

"More everything."

"Because I sleep with you?" she asked.

He smiled. "Most definitely."

She rolled her eyes and tipped her head up to watch the lazy drops fall out of the sky, but his fingers stroked her jaw and turned her back to him.

"And also because I *am* falling for you, Sadie. Falling hard."

She put her fingers over his mouth to hold in any more words.

"That won't make it untrue," he said around her fingers.

"Shh." She closed her eyes and tried to calm her heart down. "Just shh for a minute." Her thoughts raced in tune to her impending stroke. It was quiet around them. Lollipop was back at their feet, huffing from her exertion.

Okay, so Caleb had a lot of pretty words and those words had thrown her. He wasn't a man to toy with anyone's feelings, much less someone he cared about. He cared about her. At least he cared about the parts of her she'd allowed him to have.

But he was definitely missing some. In spite of his sisters looking into her—which they'd either not finished doing so or they hadn't filled him in on the details yet—Caleb didn't know her past. Because if he did, he'd be running for the hills. She knew this for sure.

Very slowly, Caleb slid a hand to the nape of her neck, urging her in for a gentle, tender kiss that turned very ungentle in a matter of seconds, leaving her in the same condition as always when he put his mouth on hers.

Hungry for him.

Another few drops of rain hit, and then a few more, feeling amazing against her heated skin as the last of the daylight began to fade away.

Caleb stood and offered her his hand, pulling both her and Lollipop back beneath an overhang to protect them from the rain. Lollipop climbed into her backpack and yawned.

Tugging Sadie close, Caleb wrapped his arm around her waist, taking one of her hands in his, pressing it to his chest.

"What are we doing?" she asked.

"Dancing in the rain."

That he'd even remembered it was a secret little fantasy of hers had her momentarily speechless, but she slid her free hand up his chest and around to the back of his neck, and leaned into his warm hard body, completely swept away by the moment.

She let him lead, not that they did anything fancier than shuffle their feet and sway gently to the sound of the rain hitting the rocks around them and Lollipop's gentle snores. Sadie's head rested against Caleb's shoulder, her nose up against his throat. Closing her eyes, she breathed in his scent and listened to his heartbeat. "Caleb?" she whispered.

"Yeah?"

"Take me home."

His place was the closest. The front door barely shut behind them before he pressed her up against it, kissing her hungrily.

"Arf!"

Caleb sighed and pulled free. "Hold that thought." He then scooped up Lollipop and vanished from the living room. Two minutes later he was back alone. "She's in my office with a treat. She's good for now." He pulled her into him. "Where were we?"

"Arf!"

Sadie turned, and sure enough, Lollipop stood in the open doorway, eyes bright, tongue lolling and tail wagging. Leashed to Caleb's office chair, she'd dragged it down the hall and seemed to be waiting patiently for some attention.

"Not now," Caleb murmured against Sadie's mouth. "Mommy and Daddy need a minute."

"Actually," Sadie said, staring into Caleb's eyes. "Mommy needs more like fourteen minutes, and that's only if you're really, *really* good."

"Oh, I think we both know that I'm better than good." Eyes lit at the challenge, he nipped her bottom lip. "But I'll tell you what, you can have as many minutes as you want. You can have the whole night." He unhooked Lollipop from her leash. "Don't eat the house," he said and then took Sadie into the bedroom.

She reached for the buttons on his jacket and shoved it off his shoulders. It took less than a minute for the rest of his clothes and all of hers to end up on the floor. Eyes dark with intent, Caleb gave her a little nudge. The backs of her knees hit the edge of his mattress. As she fell to his bed, he pinned her down and began to explore every inch of her body with his hands, his tongue, his teeth . . . proving to the both of them that he didn't need fourteen minutes.

But he gave them to her anyway. And many more.

Chapter 23

#FightDirty

Caleb opened his eyes a little bit later to find Sadie plastered against him, her hair in his face, an arm and leg thrown over the top of him like she'd claimed him.

Clearly, her body was on board with what her mind wasn't.

They fit like two pieces of a puzzle.

When his stomach rumbled, he remembered that they'd skipped dinner. Quietly as he could, he slid from her embrace and ended up in the kitchen with Lollipop. He found leftover mac and cheese in the fridge and put it in the microwave. While he was waiting on

326 · JILL SHALVIS

that to heat, he opened the laptop he always kept on his kitchen table and skimmed his notifications.

As usual, there were far more than he was willing to deal with at the moment, including the file from Sienne.

Lollipop was staring at him.

"Hey," he said. "I haven't opened it, have I?"

There was a text from Kel saying he'd seen in the news that one of Caleb's companies was going to be sending people into space in the next decade and he expected a free ride. Caleb responded that it was good as done because he wanted to be able to say he hired the first space cowboy. Kel responded with the middle finger emoji.

When the microwave dinged, he pulled out the container, grabbed a fork and two bottles of water, and headed back to the bedroom. He didn't expect Sadie to be awake, but she was, lying on her back, staring up at the ceiling pensively.

Setting everything down on the nightstand, he sat at her hip. "What's up?"

She blinked. "Do I smell mac and cheese?"

He handed the container to her, along with the fork. "Refuel."

She smiled. "For round two?"

He smiled back and opened a bottle of water, handing that over as well. "For me, yes. For you it'll be round . . . four, or is it five?"

She snorted and took a long drink from the bottle, but her eyes weren't quite right. He waited until she'd eaten her fill before setting everything aside, turning off the light again, and slipping back under the covers. Then he drew her into him and held her close, brushing a kiss to her temple.

She sighed. "You're good at the silent interrogation. I think it's because you're naked. You're pretty damn distracting naked. Makes me forget myself."

"Seems only fair since when you're naked, I can't even remember my own name."

She smiled but it faded quickly.

"Talk to me, Sadie."

She was quiet a moment, but he waited her out. It was his one superpower, given to him by too many sisters and a strong-as-hell mom.

"Do you sometimes lay in bed at night and relive every horrible thing you've ever said or done?" she asked.

"All the time. What are you reliving tonight?"

She sighed. "On the phone today, I let my mom think she was a bad mom."

"Was she?" he asked.

"No. I don't know." Sadie paused. "I was a bad kid."

"I don't believe that," he said. "And moms are resilient."

"Really? What's the meanest thing you've ever said to your mom?"

He laughed. "I told her she couldn't go on a date because she was ugly."

She gasped. "You did not!"

"Hey, I'm not proud of it," he said, "but in my defense, I was five and I didn't want her to leave. I wanted her to stay home with me."

"Reasonable," she said.

"Selfish," he said.

She shook her head. "I can't imagine you being selfish. If you want to hear selfish . . ." She hesitated and then spoke in a soft rush, as if needing to get it all out before losing her nerve. "When I was a teenager, my parents told me they were done with me being sullen and angry and dressing in black from head to toe all the time. They told me I needed to be more like my sister. I was thirteen to Clara's fifteen and hadn't really developed yet—much to my annoyance. So I stole one of her bras and stuffed it with those small travel-sized bags of candy I'd had stashed under my bed, and wore it under one of her favorite dresses—also stolen. It was a white sundress and looked great on her and her new curves. Being a jealous little shit, I put a coat over the whole ensemble and sneaked out of the house to go to school. Only I got called up to the front of my English class to read something and I got nervous, which meant I also got sweaty."

"The candy fell out of your bra?" he guessed.

She gave a low rueful laugh. "Yes, but first it melted and leaked through the dress, making me look like a rainbow and smell like chocolate—which was not allowed in class. I got sent to the principal's office. My parents had to come down and everyone got to take turns telling me what a shit show I was and a huge disappointment. For punishment, when I got home, I was marched to the kitchen sink to scrub the dress clean."

Caleb imagined a thirteen-year-old Sadie hunched over the sink in the M&M bra that was too big for her, scrubbing at the material of the white dress, knowing she couldn't possibly get it clean.

Or please her family.

It actually infuriated him, and the power of that took away his ability to speak for a moment.

"I didn't try very hard to clean the dress," she went on, staring at the ceiling again. "I really was a complete over-the-top, dramatic, way-too-sensitive little jerk who refused to understand my family, or the fact that they just wanted me to be more like them." She shook her head. "But with the dubious passing of time, things eventually got better."

"I'm glad," he managed to say lightly, not wanting her to dwell on shitty memories that made her feel bad, when he didn't think she had anything to feel bad about. "When I was thirteen, I stole something from my older sister too."

"Right," she said in disbelief, and made him laugh.

"I did. I stole her car."

She gasped and turned her head to face him. He took advantage of that and kissed her slow and deep, until she moaned and wrapped him up tight in her arms, which was quickly becoming his favorite place to be.

"Did you get caught?" she asked when she'd pulled back.

"Yes, because my mom called the cops."

She gaped at him. "She didn't!"

"Okay, she called my uncle Des, who was a deputy, but it was close enough. And when he dragged me back home and deposited me in front of my mom and my sister to apologize, I didn't. I told them all that I was a grown-up, I was the man of the house, and therefore I could do what I wanted when I wanted."

Sadie bit her lower lip while her eyes, those beautiful eyes, finally danced with genuine amusement. "You didn't."

"Hey, I was thirteen and on a roll."

"What happened?" she asked. "Did she beat the crap out of you?"

Hoping that wasn't what had happened to her in her youth, he rolled to his back and pulled her over the top of him, running his hands up and down her spine, forcing a light smile on his face. "My mom told me if I wanted to be a grown-up, she was all for it. She typed up a bill for my rent and food and said I could have my room back soon as I paid up." He kissed her softly. "For a week, I slept on the couch with her six crazy cats. Then one morning, I got up early and cooked everyone breakfast and begged for forgiveness."

Sadie went brows up. "You don't cook."

"I didn't say it was a good breakfast."

She smiled. "And you aren't allergic to cats, but you believed you were allergic to dogs?"

"Hey, a kid tends to believe what the people who love him tell him, you know?"

She nodded slowly. "I do know."

And she'd believed herself a fuck-up because that's what she'd been told. He hated that for her.

"Did you ever figure out why your sisters lied to you about the dog thing?" she asked.

"Yeah." He stroked a loose strand of hair from her face, running his finger along the shell of her ear, smiling when she shivered. She loved being touched by him.

And he loved touching her.

"They lied because we couldn't afford a dog," he said quietly. "They were already all working themselves half to death just to keep us fed and clothed and in an apartment that was already way too small for us."

Her expression softened. "Why didn't they just tell you?"

"They didn't want me to know we were poor."

She stared at him. "You've got a pretty great family, Caleb."

"I know."

"They supported you, and now you support them."

He cocked his head. "Who told you that?"

"You." She lowered her mouth to his. "Just now. Caleb . . . does this ever scare you?"

"You mean us?"

"Yeah."

He wondered what the right answer was. He had no idea so he went with honesty. "Yes."

She inhaled deeply. "Me too. Sometimes I like you so much I can't stand it. My heart beats crazy fast when I know I'm going to see you, and then when you look at me, I feel . . ."

"What?" he whispered. "You feel what?"

"Lucky." She hesitated. "I like you so much that I don't know what to do with it. And then when something happens, like what your sisters did, it's an excuse to back off. But I don't want to do that anymore. I don't want to back off, Caleb."

Her words were a balm to wounds on his soul that he didn't even know existed. "I don't want you to back off," he said. "You're not alone in this. I feel the same." He gave a rough laugh. "Just the memory of how you look at me and smile . . . it can make me forget whatever I'm doing. And when I know I'm going to see you, I put off so much energy that even Lollipop gets all wound up."

She laughed and he rolled again, tucking her beneath him, making himself at home between her legs. He wanted her again, still, and he was suspecting also *always*. What the two of them shared in this bed was so much more intimate than anything he'd ever had in his life. A few weeks ago he'd have said his family were the only people who really mattered. His friends too, of course, but with his family he was the baby and always would be, and with his friends, he was the guy with the party trick of being able to spin dirt into gold.

But with Sadie, he felt like . . . a partner, an equal one.

She smiled at him and slid out of the bed.

"Where are you going?"

"My hair's a frizzy mess from the rain. I need to shower and wash it before going to sleep. I'll be right back."

A minute later, he heard his shower running. With a smile, he entered the bathroom to find the sexiest woman he'd ever met standing in the middle of his rainforest shower, steam rising off her mouthwatering body, head lolled back in sheer pleasure.

"I think I'm jealous," he said.

She moaned. "You should be. I'm in love. I hope your showerhead is single."

He watched her hands run over her wet, soapy body and made an executive decision. "Move over, clearly you need some help in here . . ."

A long time later, back in his room, Sadie dropped her towel and began to gather up her clothes. She hit her knees and went ass up to fish under his bed for something, and every single thought flew out of his head.

She came up with her panties.

"You don't have to go," he said. "It's late. Just stay."

She stood and slipped into her undies.

He crooked a finger at her.

She arched a brow and reached for the rest of her clothes. "I don't know if you're aware, but it's not really PC to crook your finger sexily at a woman and expect her to come to you."

"Noted." With a grin, he rose from where he'd been sprawled out on the bed and headed to her instead. "But for future reference, you can crook your finger at me anytime and I'll come running."

"Not going to happen," she said. For whatever reason, she wasn't feeling playful anymore and turned away. "I'm going to get out of your hair. Let you have your space."

He came up behind her, and careful not to startle her, leaned in and rubbed his jaw to hers. "Feels like maybe you're the one needing her own space."

She stopped dressing and her voice went a little husky as she slowly rocked her butt into his erection. "How is that even possible?" she breathed.

"You were naked and on your knees, ass up," he said. "One of my favorite sights."

She rolled her eyes and moved toward the door.

"Stay," he said, cupping her face, his thumb gliding over her soft skin. "It's late and it's cold. You don't have to wake up with me if you don't want. I've got a bazillion other rooms and you'll be warm in any of them."

A small smile curved her lips. "Are you suggesting a sleepover of the platonic kind? Are we going to braid each other's hair and paint our toenails and have a pillow fight?"

"I'm game for the pillow fight," he murmured, brushing his mouth against her temple. "But fair warning, I fight dirty."

She gave him a playful shove with a laugh. "You do a lot of things dirty."

"Uh-huh, and you love it."

She laughed and then went serious and met his gaze. "Truth?"

"Always."

She shook her head. "I still don't know what to do about you."

He sank his fingers into her wet hair. "How about you sleep on it?"

"Only if I can take another shower in your bathroom in the morning."

She didn't know it yet, but she could take whatever she wanted. His shower, his clothes, his bed . . . anything. Because she already had his heart and soul.

Chapter 24

#JustDontScrewItUp

A week later, Sadie was working on a client, a postal worker named Irene, inking a bracelet of skulls and bones and enjoying the work.

"Are you aware that you've been smiling to yourself for an hour?" Irene asked. "It's super cute."

Actually, Sadie had noticed the smile in the mirror this morning. Caleb's mirror, since she'd spent every night this week at his house.

The smile wouldn't go away.

At first, it'd disturbed her. Why the hell was she smiling all the damn time now anyway?

But she knew.

She felt . . . different. Fuller, from the inside out,

starting in the region of her chest. Ivy had told her that unfamiliar sensation was happiness.

Her phone buzzed on the side table and she glanced over at it. Her mom. She'd tried just about everything to get rid of the perma-smile but nothing had worked.

The call did it.

She hit ignore because she was working, but she didn't need to answer the phone to know what her mom wanted.

To remind her that this weekend was the big practice rehearsal dinner at her parents' house. She was to show up with a date. The same date she was supposedly bringing to the wedding the following week.

Somehow in spite of that, she remained shockingly smiley through the rest of the workday, no doubt thanks to the orgasms she'd had that morning in Caleb's bed. And his shower. And in the kitchen . . .

At the end of her day, she left the Canvas Shop. She'd finally gotten her car back that morning, aided by a paycheck with some overtime on it—along with the fact that Caleb had paid her utilities for the year. She wouldn't need a bus pass anymore, and that was a huge relief.

She slowed at the fountain in the courtyard, drawn in by the musical sound of the water falling into the copper bowl. More than a few people who worked or lived in this building had made wishes here, wishes for love. And those wishes had come true, a fact that was both fascinating and utterly terrifying.

"Thinking of making a wish?"

Sadie turned and found Ivy watching her. Ivy went through her pockets and pulled out a quarter.

"No need," Sadie said. "Old Man Eddie already made a wish for me. I nearly dove into the fountain to yank the coin out."

"Scared it wouldn't take unless you made the wish yourself?"

"More like terrified the wish *would* take."

Ivy smiled, but she seemed muted today.

"Maybe *you* should wish," Sadie said.

"I wish all the time."

This surprised Sadie. "You're wishing for . . . love?"

Ivy shrugged. "Rumor is that it does make the world go round."

Sadie let out a low laugh. "If you believe that, then I've got some swampland to sell you."

Ivy gave her a *get real* look. "Have you seen yourself lately? You're smiling. Like all the time."

"That's not love. That's orgasms."

"I'm betting it's both," Ivy said.

"Bite your tongue." But Sadie was a little worried her friend was right. "You really want love in your life?"

Ivy shrugged. "Last year on my twenty-eighth birthday, I realized I was lonely. I figured out it was because I've never lived in one spot for longer than six months. I've never had a place that felt like home, or a person in my life from one birthday to the next. I love it here and I'm staying."

"And you want someone to share this life with."

Ivy nodded. "I do. Have you never wished for that, not once? If Caleb went away right now and your life went back to it just being you, would that work for you?"

She'd never thought about it, but for the rest of the night she thought about little else.

Because she couldn't imagine her life going back to how it had been without Caleb in it.

The next morning, Sadie woke up to Caleb's alarm sometime before the butt crack of dawn. While her mind struggled to awareness, a long arm reached past her to silence the alarm, and then the hand that belonged to that arm slid down her back to cup her ass, reminding her she was naked.

Caleb slept in the nude and he liked skin-to-skin. She had to admit she was quickly getting addicted to the feeling of being held in his warm embrace all night up against that lean hard body.

And he was right. He wasn't perfect. No perfect man got up this early every morning by choice to go to the gym and meet up with friends and pulverize the shit out of each other.

For fun.

Sometimes he'd come home between the gym and work, and if she was still in his bed, he'd go for yet another round of cardio, where, let's face it, she was more willing receiver than active participant because she didn't do mornings.

But she was slowly starting to come around to his way of thinking.

Today he came back. She heard him let himself in and she lay still, feigning sleep as he planted a hand on either side of her and leaned over her.

"Rise and shine, Tough Girl," he said.

They'd spent the long, dark hours of the night ruining each other for other people and she was still deliciously sated and limp as a rag doll. She needed another hour of sleep.

Or eight. "Hmph" was all she could manage.

"Last night you said I should come back this morning because you'd decided starting your day with multiple orgasms is the only way to go."

This was true, but she still didn't move or open her eyes. Maybe if she played dead, he'd let her sleep a little longer.

She should've known better. He grabbed a fistful of the covers and tugged them off of her.

"It's like you want to die," she said into his pillow.

With a soft laugh, he gave her bare ass a playful swat. "You'd have to get up for that."

She rolled over to find him in his usual workout gear, a painted-on long-sleeve athletic shirt and shorts, his body still shiny with sweat.

Her good parts sat up and danced because good God, he was gorgeous. Suddenly she wasn't tired. Sitting up, she gave him a crook of her finger, and with a wide grin, he lifted her off the bed. She pushed his shorts off while he rid himself of his shirt. Before she could so much as take a nibble, he scooped her up, tossed her over his shoulder, and headed toward his shower.

"Hey!"

Turning his head, he took a bite of her ass, making her squeal. Then he dumped her into the shower. The only thing that saved his life was that the water was steamy hot.

Then he proceeded to give her the best shower of her life.

Thirty minutes later, he was dressing for work as

she lay facedown, spread-eagled on his bed, thinking of never moving again. "I want to marry your shower and have its babies," she said, making him laugh.

"Dinner later?" he asked.

"Can't," she muttered into the sheets. She managed to turn her head and stare at him through the hair in her face. "I've got a family thing. I'm supposed to bring a date." She'd been dreading this for a while because he'd be the perfect date. He represented the exact kind of man her parents dreamed about her ending up with: smart, successful, wealthy. And how ironic was that? She'd spent her entire life bucking the system and yet here she was, not only sleeping with a guy they'd love, but secretly yearning for a lot more.

If she brought him tonight, her mom and dad would take one look at him and back off bugging her about finding someone. And then after dinner they'd all get into her parents' recently upgraded and remodeled hot tub that they were so proud of, which meant Caleb would take off his shirt. Everyone would see his tattoos and swallow their tongues. They'd change their opinions about him based solely on his appearance, and she'd be able to throw that in their faces, that they were judgy judgersons.

It'd be awesome.

Caleb pulled on a tie, but left it loose as he tucked

his shirttails into his pants and adjusted himself. This gave her a body quiver, which was ridiculous. Since when was she a sex fiend? And then she realized he hadn't spoken, so she sat up. "You didn't answer."

"I didn't hear a question," he said.

She just stared at him, fighting pride. Why was it so hard to ask this beautiful, incredibly smart, and incredibly out-of-her-league man out?

With a small smile, he came to the bed and sat at her hip, pushing her still damp hair back from her face. "You like me," he said, sounding quite pleased with himself.

"I do."

"A lot."

She rolled her eyes. "Maybe."

"I like you too, Sadie. A lot."

The question escaped her before she could stop it. "Why?"

"Why do I like you?"

She grimaced. "Scratch that. I didn't mean to ask that again."

"I like you," he said, ignoring her insecurity, "because you're—"

"Weird? Impulsive? Loony-toons?"

"Well, yes," he agreed with a smile. "But also smart and smartassy, and sexy and adorable—"

She held up a finger. "Okay, you're going to need to take that one back. I am not adorable."

"Sorry, but you don't get to auto-correct my opinions," he said. "You're also grumpy in the mornings—"

"You're supposed to be listing the stuff you *like* about me."

"I am. You're not the only one who's messed up, in case you've forgotten. Anyway, you're also incredibly beautiful and—"

"Okay, stop." She closed her eyes. "I know I asked, but I'm not emotionally equipped for that many adjectives."

He inched closer and waited until she opened her eyes. "I think about you," he murmured. "I think about you just about all damn day long. Yesterday, I spent hours thinking about what you'd done to me in the shower that morning and I got hard. In an office meeting about budgets."

"My knees are still sore," she said.

"I'm working on a new product. Soft, giving tile."

She laughed, and he smiled. "I'd do just about anything for you," he murmured. "Something you haven't figured out yet. Ask me what you want to ask me."

She blew out another breath. "Will you come as my date to my family's rehearsal rehearsal tonight?"

"I'd love to." He kissed her, taking his time about it

too. She was just about to yank him back to bed when he headed to the door. "Text me with details and what time to pick you up."

And then he was gone. She picked up her phone and . . . changed his contact name from Do Not Even Think About Falling For This Guy to . . . Too Late, It's Happened.

Before Caleb picked up Sadie for the evening at her family home, he made a few pit stops, the last being to Spence's penthouse apartment at the top of the Pacific Pier Building.

Spence was sitting cross-legged on the floor of his and Colbie's living room, surrounded by tools and drone parts. Colbie was sitting on their couch with a laptop, her fingers whirling away, probably hard at work at her next novel.

"Sorry to interrupt," Caleb said to her but she just waved at him.

"No worries. With this guy . . ." she jerked her chin at her fiancé, Spence ". . . I can work through a drone drop. Literally," she said dryly and went on typing.

Caleb turned to Spence. "I thought we solved your drone problems. In fact, we made a mint on the sale of the computer program."

"We did," Spence said and tossed aside two parts

he'd been holding. "I'm making improvements. Or trying. And failing." He finally looked up and did a double take at Caleb's expression. "Hey, honey," he said to Colbie, eyes on Caleb. "I need a beer. I'm going to go grab a six-pack. We'll be right back."

Caleb followed him out of the apartment. "How much beer are we getting that it takes two of us?" he asked as they took the stairs up to the rooftop and not down to the ground floor. "And since when do you keep it on the roof?"

Spence cut his eyes to him and then strode out across the rooftop right to the edge, where he sat with comfortable ease.

Caleb, not quite as comfortable with the five-story drop, remained back a few feet. Or twenty.

"Forget the beer. What's going on with you?" Spence said.

"Nothing."

"Bullshit. The last time I saw that particular look of panic on your face was when you first hooked NASA on a proposal for state-of-the-art payload software. They wanted to pay you more money than you'd ever seen for a program you hadn't finished yet and weren't even positive you could."

Caleb blew out a breath and shoved his hands in his pockets. He studied his shoes for a long minute.

Spence waited, but he didn't have the same amount of patience Caleb did. "Man, I'm hungry. Spill it."

Caleb pulled his hand out of his pocket and thrust a small black box at him.

Spence took it and lifted the lid. A giant diamond ring wrapped in a swirl of black diamonds and another swirl of white diamonds winked at them both from a velvet cushion.

Spence raised a brow. "Well, this is awkward. I'm sort of already spoken for."

"You're an asshole," Caleb said.

Spence didn't even attempt to argue this. "And?"

Caleb closed the box and shoved it back into his pocket. "You're not going to try to talk me out of this?"

"Why would I?"

"It's sudden."

Spence shook his head. "You've been falling for Sadie for over a year now. She's been falling for you right back. Everyone but you two know it."

Caleb stared at him in surprise.

"And who am I to talk?" Spence asked. "I fell in love with Colbie in less than three weeks. Hell, I fell in love with her on day one when I accidentally knocked her right into the fountain." He clapped Caleb on the shoulder. "When are you going to ask her?"

"I don't know." Caleb shook his head. "Maybe after

I talk her into loving me back, which could still be a while."

Spence laughed. "I once watched you talk your way into a multimillion-dollar deal with Google in five minutes. My money's on you."

"This isn't business."

"No, it's not," Spence said. "It's better. So don't screw it up."

Chapter 25

#PassTheRoastPlease

Sadie didn't get anxious or nervous until she and Caleb pulled up to her parents' house in Outer Sunset. The sudden pounding heart and sweaty palms were annoying. She'd long ago taught herself how to take a mental step back from her family and treat them like . . . well, entertainment. She was no longer part of the circus but just an audience member.

But tonight Caleb was going to witness the circus.

Great, and now she was sweating in other more creative places. "You brought a bathing suit with you, right?" she asked. "For the hot tub?"

He looked over at her briefly. "You've asked me that

five times, but yes, I did. You said it was tradition, after dinner you all go outside and bake yourselves."

"And stargaze." Her mom taught science. Her dad had done the same before moving into administration. They were big astronomy buffs. Which of course had nothing to do with why she wanted Caleb to strip out of his gorgeous suit . . . And as she thought it, the first little inkling of misgiving hit and her anxiety doubled. She tried to discreetly fan her shirt to give her hot skin some air.

Caleb glanced at her again, and she realized he knew her well enough to know when something was wrong. "You okay?"

"Me? I'm great."

"Uh-huh." Reaching for her hand, he gave it a squeeze, and then melted her heart when he brought their entwined fingers to his mouth and brushed his lips against her palm. "It's going to be okay," he said. "Parents love me."

She had to laugh. "Because you're cocky?"

"I was going to say because I'm easygoing and friendly."

She laughed again. "You weren't either of those things last night in bed. In fact, you were downright demanding and bossy."

He sent her a badass smile that had all her good parts quivering. "Are you complaining?"

Hell no. She'd had good sex before, and yet even good sex was somewhat predictable. But with Caleb, she never knew what to expect. He had the distinct ability to be making love to her while adding a certain level of dirty to it that kept things . . . thrilling. She never knew if he was going to get straight to business or if he'd spend long minutes worshipping her body first.

It was . . . addicting.

"Ready?" Caleb asked.

No. But it was six o'clock on the dot.

The neighborhood was made up of hardworking people and neat rows of cookie-cutter Victorian houses that had weathered the ravages of time and economic strain and gain. Caleb easily managed to parallel park into a spot that she would have never managed to get into. "Did you grow up here?" he asked.

"Yes." She stared at the house. "It's not too late to make a run for it."

He came around and gave her a hand out of the car, pulling her into him. Lifting her chin, he looked into her eyes. "Breathe, babe. We've got this."

She was so glad he thought so. Her mom opened the front door, Sadie's sister standing right behind her. Both were dressed up for the evening, wearing cocktail dresses in the color of the wedding—pale pink. Sadie had figured this would be the case so she'd dressed up too, but she hadn't gotten the pink memo. She was wearing her little black dress she'd worn on her and Caleb's first date, mostly because she liked the way his gaze heated every time he looked at her.

Introductions were made and Sadie watched her dad join the group, as well as Clara's fiancé, Greg. All of them were seemingly instantly taken with Caleb, who at one point glanced over at Sadie, eyes amused, like *see?*

She rolled hers.

"Caleb Parker," her dad said. "I just saw the episode of *Shark Tank* where you guest starred."

"And oh my goodness," her mom said, "that new app you just put out, it's going to revolutionize the way teachers teach science in the classrooms. Too bad you can't come up with a way to make sure kids won't lose the art of writing in cursive."

Her mom could barely turn on her laptop without getting six viruses or wiring half her retirement money to a Nigerian prince, but she was worried about the lost art of cursive. A thought Sadie refrained from saying out loud. Wow. Look at her growing up.

Her mom turned to Sadie next, expression dialed to confused as to how her daughter had managed to catch a guy so far out of her league. Clara was also staring at Caleb, who seemed perfectly at ease with the attention. "You're drooling," Sadie whispered beneath her breath to her sister.

Clara grinned unabashedly. "Sorry, but he's the hottest guy you've ever dated. He might be the hottest guy on the planet."

From behind Clara, Greg cleared his throat.

Clara winced. "After you, baby, of course."

Greg's eyes were laughing. "Of course. Did you tell Sadie the latest bridesmaid dress news?"

Oh God. What now?

Clara pulled out her phone and accessed her pictures. She pulled up one of Sadie in a sample of the chosen bridesmaid dress. "Do you see what I see?"

"Um . . . that question feels like a trap."

"It's actually what I *don't* see," Clara said. "I don't see my sister."

Sadie stilled and lifted her gaze to Clara, whose eyes were suspiciously sparkly. "I'm sorry, Sadie," she said softly. "I'm sorry I didn't see it in the store. You don't look like you. And I want you to look like you. So I ordered you the other dress. The light champagne-colored lace one that you liked."

"But the tattoos on the back of my shoulder and ankle will show—"

"I want them to. They're a part of you. I want you to look like you."

Sadie sucked in a breath, surprised at the wave of emotion. "Mom's going to have a cow."

"It's my wedding," Clara said simply and hugged Sadie.

It was the nicest moment they'd had in years.

At dinner, the first few moments were taken up with small talk and passing the dishes around. Unlike Sadie, Caleb didn't struggle in social situations. He could talk to a scared dog, a bitchy woman, an old guy who lived in an alley . . . He could talk to anyone and have them fall in love with him in the first ten seconds.

She admired the hell out of that skill, not that she wanted it. "Pass the roast please?"

Her mom lifted the tray and then hesitated to remove the sharp carving knife from it before handing it over.

Sadie stared at her in shock and an instant heavy tension hit the table. She didn't look over at Caleb. Couldn't.

"Really, Mom?" Clara finally asked into the awkward silence.

"What? I mean yes, she looks wonderful and happy, but I'm just playing it safe. That's what a mother does, you know."

Clara shook her head. "Sadie's therapist asked you to stop with the passive aggressiveness, remember?"

"I haven't been forced to see a therapist in years," Sadie said to the room.

They all ignored this. "I don't even know what passive aggressive means," her mom said to Clara. "And I didn't mean anything by it."

"What *did* you mean then?" Clara asked.

"I just meant what I always mean," her mom said.

Caleb slid his hand to Sadie's thigh beneath the table and squeezed in comfort, in solidarity. And that was sweet, but she still couldn't look at him. Instead, she stabbed her fork into some slices of meat and loaded her plate. It'd been years since her family had learned she'd been cutting herself and taken the control of her own life from her. The nightmare of her parents' over-reaction and having her committed under the 5585—an involuntary hold of an at-risk minor—had nearly done her in.

She'd survived, barely. And though it'd been years, her parents still did things like remove all scissors from the house and lock up the knives when she came over. Her dad had sold his gun collection. Her mom had given up knitting and thrown away her knitting needles.

"But what about Sadie?" her mom asked.

Great, she'd missed something. "What about Sadie what?"

"We need everyone to be on their best behavior at the wedding," her mom said, pointedly not looking at Sadie.

"I will be if you will be," Sadie said.

Her dad started to laugh but at a look from her mom, he turned it into a cough. Her mom knocked back her glass of champagne and gave herself a refill with the last of the bottle.

Sadie pushed back from the table and grabbed the empty. "I'll get us another."

She went to the kitchen and stuck her head in the freezer to cool herself down. She knew her mother loved her, knew that her neurosis about Sadie came from a deeply seated fear that her daughter hadn't fallen far from the tree. Her mother'd had a terrible childhood, with a mean drunk of a father and a mother who'd self-medicated with booze and pills and gone off the deep end. The fear that Sadie would do the same was very real and Sadie got that. But damn, she was tired of her mom always being on edge waiting for Sadie to crack.

Because she wasn't going to.

She grabbed another bottle of champagne. As she moved back into the dining room, she heard the low rumble of Caleb's voice but couldn't make out the words. When she entered, everyone fell quiet.

She glanced at Caleb as she sat.

His mouth quirked slightly in a smile that didn't quite reach his eyes—her parents had that effect on people—but once again he reached for her under the table. This time he reached for her hand, encasing it in his.

It was a small gesture, but it felt like a lifeline.

Her dad asked Caleb all sorts of questions about his work, and he answered with endless patience and good humor until her mom laughed and put a hand on her dad's arm. "Honey, I'm sure he doesn't want to talk about his work all night," she said. "I want to hear about how Sadie ended up on a date with him and how lucky we are that it was tonight."

Because of course her mom assumed it was a first date. "I blackmailed him," Sadie said. "Pass the bread?"

Her mom gasped in horror.

Caleb reached for the basket of bread and held it out to Sadie, pulling back slightly when she tried to take it, his brow raised.

She caved. "Fine," she said to the room. "That was a joke. I didn't blackmail him. I just didn't tell him where we were going until we parked out front in case he was a flight risk."

Caleb gave her a rather impressive eye roll and shook his head. "It's not our first date. We've known each other awhile now. We rescued a dog together."

Her mom looked even more surprised. "You got a dog?" she asked Sadie.

"Yes."

"But your lifestyle doesn't lend itself to having a dog."

Here we go . . . "Because I'm a tattoo artist?"

"Because you work all day in the spa, and then nights at the tattoo parlor," her mom said, surprising her. "You work long hours. Most people your age don't care about their career like you do. I just don't know how you'd have time to take care of a dog while you're working as hard as you are."

To say Sadie was shocked would have been the understatement of the year. "I didn't realize you'd noticed."

"Of course I notice." Her mom hesitated and glanced over at her husband. "It's been brought to my attention that I can be a little hard on the people I love."

"She means Dad's making her go to a therapist," Clara said.

Her mom waved her hands. "Enough about me." She refilled everyone's glass. "Let's toast to more dates between the two of you!" She lifted her glass. "To many, many more dates."

Sadie, still feeling a little stunned by her mom's admission, raised a glass. "How about instead we toast to Clara and Greg's happiness? And to many, many more years together. Greg, just remember, you should end every argument with three simple words—'you're right, honey.'"

Clara pointed at Greg. "You could've used that advice earlier."

"You mean when you threatened to kill me while I was making brownies?" he asked.

"You said I was fat."

"No," Greg said. "I merely suggested you slow down on the chocolate loading because you seem to always forget that your mom's cooking makes you sick and I didn't want you to make things worse."

"So now I'm fat *and* stupid?" Clara asked. She yanked her napkin out of her lap and threw it on the table as she stood. "Why are we getting married then?"

Greg calmly stood up and reached for her. "You're doing it again. Letting the pregnancy hormones drive you insane."

"Pregnancy hormones?" Sadie's mom gasped, slowly standing up as well, her eyes on Clara's stomach. "Is that why you're gaining weight? You're pregnant?"

Clara's eyes filled. "Yes!" she wailed and threw herself at Greg. "I'm sorry I'm so out of control right now. I don't know what's wrong with me."

He cuddled her into him. "I do. You're doing too much. You're working, planning the wedding, growing a human, dealing with your insane family—"

"Hey," Sadie said.

"Hey," her parents said.

"How about we all focus on the good news," Caleb said smoothly, deflating the tension as he lifted his glass in one hand and handed Clara a glass of water with the other. "To the newest addition to the Lane family . . ."

"Of course," Sadie's mom said. "And to not telling anyone about the pregnancy until after the wedding. Right, Henry?"

Sadie's dad downed his champagne. "Right. Why ruin a perfectly good bazillion-dollar wedding?"

Clara let out a low tearful laugh and looked at Sadie. "So how does it feel to not be the screw-up today?"

"Don't be silly," Sadie's mom said on a very false-sounding laugh. "You're not a screw-up. You're still getting married, right?" She looked at Greg. "Right? Someone tell me before I drink this entire bottle and throw myself off a cliff."

"Relax, Mom. We won't ruin your wedding," Clara said.

"You mean *your* wedding. It's all for you. Isn't that right, Henry?"

Henry hesitated. "I'm sorry, I lost track. Am I agreeing with you or disagreeing with you?"

Her mom shot him a dirty look, but they both got up and hugged Clara and Greg, declaring themselves over the moon with joy about their future grandchild.

They all cleared the dishes together. In the kitchen, Caleb rolled up his sleeves and began rinsing them, much to her mom's horror.

"Guests don't do dishes," she said, trying to shoo him away. "And anyway, it's Sadie's turn."

"She can stuff them into the dishwasher while I rinse," Caleb said.

"No she can't," her mom said. "She does it wrong."

"Okay," Caleb said to Sadie. "Switch. You rinse and I'll load."

"She does that wrong too," her mom said.

Sadie watched Caleb's eyelid twitch. She looked at the time. It'd been an hour. Seemed about right. By the end of the evening, they'd both be at risk for a stroke.

"That was so sweet of you," her mom said when Caleb had insisted on continuing to do the dishes until he'd finished. "If you end up marrying Sadie, knowing your way around a kitchen is a good skill to have. I'm not sure she even knows how to turn on the oven."

"Of course I do, Mom," Sadie said. "And it's a good thing too, because after we leave here, I'm going home to turn on my oven and stick my head in it. Is it hot tub time yet, Clara?"

"God yes," Clara said. "Although I can only put my legs in, dammit."

Ten minutes later, Clara and Greg went outside to check on the hot tub while Sadie and Caleb changed. When Sadie came out of the bathroom, Caleb was waiting in the hallway for her.

"Thanks for surviving dinner," she said when he pulled her into him. They were surrounded by bunches of family pics from over the years, including Clara with all her academic and band awards, and Sadie in several decades of really bad fashion choices where she often looked like she was trying out for a part in a zombie apocalypse movie. "You handled their grilling better than most."

"How many have survived?" he asked.

She pulled free and moved to lead him outside, but he caught her hand and pulled her back around, gently pushing her hair from her face. "Too personal?" he asked.

"Too embarrassing." She sighed. "Zero. I've brought zero people home. Your turn now."

He held up two fingers. "My family has met two

women. They scared away one, and I scared away the other all on my own."

She stared up at him. She wanted to know more, but now wasn't the time. "What did you say to my parents when I was in the kitchen?"

He didn't pretend to not know what she meant. "I asked your mother if she realized she hurt you with her comments and questions."

"And . . . ?"

"And she said nothing hurt you."

She searched his gaze, knowing there had to be more. *"And?"*

"And . . . I asked if she was sure about that."

Sadie's heart caught. Actually, her bones melted, leaving her nothing but a puddle. Dammit. And as always when she felt unbearably touched and didn't know how to deal with it, she reacted badly. "I don't need you to fight my battles for me, Caleb. I fight my own battles."

His gaze met hers. "I'm very aware of that. But I'm always going to have your back, Sadie."

She just kept staring up at him, realizing that he wasn't trying to fix her life. He was trying to be there for her in the only way he knew how.

Since she was now in bare feet, she had to go up on her tiptoes to brush a kiss across his jaw. Before she could react, he'd turned his head so their mouths lined up and slid a hand to the nape of her neck to deepen the kiss.

When they pulled free, she had to shake her head to clear it. "What was that for?"

"For trusting me enough to let me come here with you tonight."

"I *had* to bring someone," she said. "I thought it might as well be you."

He flashed her a knowing grin, not insulted in the least. "You wanted it to be me."

Because that was very true, and also because it made her squirm a little bit, she took his hand and pulled him down the hallway.

He took in a picture of her around eight years old looking like the little girl in the Addams family. "Cute."

"No, I wasn't cute. I insisted on wearing whatever I wanted and was practically rabid."

"Aren't all little kids?" he asked easily. "Remind me to show you a picture of me when I was eight. I too dressed myself. I favored a cowboy hat, a Superman sweatshirt, and a cape made of my mom's favorite shawl, topped off with rain boots and jeans so big I had to use a rope to hold them up. It was the only outfit I'd wear. When my mom washed the clothes every few days, I'd insist on standing naked as a jaybird in front of the washer and dryer, waiting for them to finish."

"That's not rabid, that's just crazy."

He smiled. "And yet I'm your date tonight."

"Well crazy does attract crazy."

He slung an arm around her neck. "Don't I know it."

They stepped outside together and Sadie's heart started to pound as she realized her moment was almost here, the one she'd been looking so forward to all night. She dropped her towel and got into the hot water, turning so she didn't miss the show.

Caleb was in navy blue board shorts and a long-sleeved T-shirt. He did that very male move of reaching over his shoulder and yanking his shirt off, leaving him in just the board shorts, slung low on his lean hips. Sadie's gaze went to the way they were cut with muscles that tended to make women stupid, but she knew where everyone else's gazes went.

To his tattoos.

As she watched her parents take in his ink and suck in a judgmental breath, she waited for the amusement to hit her. After all, this was why she'd brought him tonight, right? For the shock value. The entertainment. She'd known he'd charm the socks off her parents, that they would fall for him even more quickly than she had, and that they'd consider him everything they'd ever wanted for her. And she knew it would all be based off the superficial knowledge they had of him and his appearance.

And now she could say *gotcha*. He wasn't what he appeared to be. He was, in fact, *better* than he appeared.

But the joy of the moment never hit.

Instead, she felt something turn over in her gut and it made her feel a little sick. Here she'd been thinking that ever since Wes, she'd started over. That she'd actually gotten somewhere, that maybe she wasn't as damaged and screwed up as she'd once been.

But apparently, she hadn't come as far as she'd thought. Because her mom reacted predictably. She sucked in a hard breath and then met Sadie's gaze, and in them was the usual disappointment.

It was what she'd come for, so why then did she feel no sense of accomplishment or satisfaction at all?

Just shame.

Chapter 26

#MacAndCheese

When they left for the night, Caleb walked with Sadie out to his car, holding his tongue. It wasn't easy. He was good and pissed off. Sadie had brought him here, not to introduce her family to her boyfriend, but to parade him around as another bad choice.

Which reminded him, he was a complete idiot for giving her that power in the first place. He'd actually believed that she'd wanted to show off the man in her life.

Joke was on him.

Worse, what she'd done tonight spoke volumes about her level of investment in him.

He held her passenger door open while she clicked

her seatbelt into place. She tilted her face up, her eyes revealing her guilt. She opened her mouth to say something, but he shut the door on her cute nose.

Drawing a deep breath, he walked around the back of the car instead of the front, using the ten seconds to school his features into a blank expression, the one he often took with him into the boardroom when he didn't want to show his hand.

He also used it on poker nights with Kel, and he only lost when Kel was counting cards, which he did just to piss Caleb off. Hard to beat a cheater, but Sadie had done it effortlessly tonight. And yeah, she'd cheated. She'd cheated by not warning him ahead of time what tonight had been about. If she'd done that, they might have actually walked into her family home as partners.

But she hadn't wanted that. She'd wanted to throw him in her mom's face, and the minute he'd realized it, he'd also realized something else—this thing between them wasn't going work, not like this anyway.

"Caleb," she said quietly. "I'm—"

"Don't." He didn't want to hear an apology for something she'd done so purposefully.

She gave him a long unreadable look. "I get that when you say 'don't' like that, in your very serious, very authoritative voice at work, people probably shut up. But in case you haven't noticed, I've got a bit of an authority problem."

He snorted at the truth of that statement and she turned in her seat to face him, putting her hand over his before he could start the car. "And second," she said. "I really am sorry."

"For?" he asked politely.

"For using you tonight. I don't know why I did it."

He gave her a *get real* look and she sighed.

"Okay, fine. I do know," she said. "I wanted my mom and dad to fall in love with you and think you were their dream come true, and then when they saw your tats, they'd assume I was on the same old track to Loser Town."

"Why would you want them to think that?"

"Because they're going to think it no matter what." She shook her head. "But I realized that I made a tactical error. I should have done it the other way around. If they'd seen you in just those board shorts first, and if I hadn't told them your name, they'd have instantly judged you. And not in a good way. Then when they'd gotten to know you, they'd realize how judgmental they are."

He just stared at her. "Wow."

She leaned back and closed her eyes. "I know. I

heard it when I listened to myself. And now you know just how crazy I really am."

"Actually, I already knew that part."

She opened her eyes and met his and found a very small amount of amusement in them that gave her some hope. "Well you are smarter than the average bear," she murmured.

"Tell me why I watched you take the crazy to a whole new level tonight. Why do you care so much what they think?"

"Because they're my family."

He stared at her and realized something new—tonight hadn't been about her trying to stick it to her parents at all. Instead, it'd been her way of saying, *see, I'm okay, even someone like Caleb Parker thinks so,* and when he looked at it like that, she broke his heart. Letting out a breath, he took her hand in his and brought it up to his mouth, nipping the meaty part of her palm until she looked at him again.

"For future reference," he said, "when you're in a relationship, you have each other's back. Meaning if we go into a situation where one of us is being driven mad by our admittedly equally mad families, the other can be used as armor. It's a freebie. A perk."

She seemed boggled at this. "So you're saying if we

were in a relationship, tonight would've been a freebie and you wouldn't be mad at me?"

"Correct. And Sadie?"

"Yeah?" she asked warily.

"We *are* in a relationship, at least by my definition."

"And what's your definition?"

"Several mornings this week alone, I've woken up to a pair of your panties on my floor."

"Panties on your floor constitutes a relationship?"

"If it happens more than once, yeah."

"But you're still mad. Doesn't that make the relationship null and void?"

"I imagine we're going to make each other good and mad often," he said. "But no, that doesn't null and void the relationship. It's called Real Life, Sadie. Shit happens. I'll piss you off. You'll piss me off. We'll talk. We'll work through it."

"How do you know?"

"Because that's what people who are into each other do."

She appeared to chew on that for a moment. "So what are the rules of this so-called relationship?"

She'd asked the question lightly, but her expression spelled *worried*. "Simple," he said. "We stay in it for as long as it feels good."

She stared at him for a long beat. "I really am sorry for tonight."

"I know."

"I should never have"—she closed her eyes—"I'm just really sorry. I—"

He leaned in and kissed her. "I know," he repeated softly. "And thank you. But I'm not like your mom. You don't have to say it again." He started the car and got them on the road, feeling grateful and humbled to have the family he had and just a little heartbroken for Sadie that she didn't feel the same level of support and unconditional love. "Where do you want to go?" he asked. "Your place?" He knew she liked to retreat and be alone when she needed to lick her wounds.

So she surprised him when she spoke. "No, yours."

He smiled, and she rolled her eyes. "Don't get too smug," she said. "It's all about your shower, not you."

But he knew it was a little bit about him too.

A few days later, Sadie worked eight hours at the day spa and then three more at the Canvas Shop. By the time she stepped into the courtyard at the end of her day, it was eight thirty and she was dead on her feet and starving.

She'd half expected Caleb to show up between her

two shifts as he'd been making a habit of doing, but he hadn't. She looked at her phone for the tenth time. Still no messages.

He was always the one to make the move to contact her, to make plans to see her. She'd played a passive role, she realized, more than a little surprised at herself. Because she wasn't passive.

So she went to him. She and Lollipop showed up at his building and took the elevator to the penthouse level where his office was. There was a guy behind the desk, young, early twenties. He wore a headset and was on the phone telling someone that Caleb wasn't in today, but he could take a message.

"Sadie?"

Sadie turned and found one of Caleb's sisters standing in the doorway of an office.

"Sienne," his sister said by way of introduction. "I'm the oldest."

"Hi." Sadie was working hard at not wondering how much Sienne had discovered about her during the vetting process. "I'm just looking for Caleb."

"He's not in today."

Sadie had awoken that morning when Caleb's alarm had gone off at oh dark thirty. He'd had them both panting and entangled in a pile of sweaty sheets before rising and heading off to the gym and the rest of his day. He'd been fine. Better than fine if his cocky, sated smile had anything to say. "Is he sick?"

"No." Sienne hesitated. "His old sensei is."

"Naoki?"

"You know him?" Sienne asked in surprise.

"Yes, Caleb's taken me to meet him."

Sienne chewed on the inside of her cheek as she studied Sadie for a beat. Then she pulled a phone from her pocket, hit a number, and waited for a connection. "I owe you twenty bucks." She disconnected. "And I owe you an apology," she said to Sadie.

"For what?"

"I didn't think you'd be the one."

"The one what?" Sadie asked warily.

"The one to convince Caleb he doesn't have to be an island. Apparently, you're his lobster."

Sadie blinked and opened her mouth but ended up shutting it again because she didn't have words. She was completely speechless.

"Damn," a woman said, coming up behind Sienne. Another sister. "You need to stop scaring people by telling them stuff they haven't yet admitted to themselves." She took Sadie's hand and squeezed it. "I'm Hannah. The nice one. Ignore my nosy-ass sister, okay? You'll figure things out in your own time. And when you do, we'll be here waiting for you with all the 411 you could ever want to know about our baby brother, including the time he blew up our one and only working toilet when he was teaching himself advanced chemistry and physics. At age eight."

Sadie still couldn't speak. Hell, she wasn't sure she was breathing.

"Seriously?" a very, very pregnant woman asked, coming out of the elevator. "What's wrong with you, scaring Caleb's girlfriend to death?" She waved a hand in front of Sadie and Sadie felt herself blink. "Well, maybe only half to death," she corrected. "She seems to be coming around. Hi, I'm Kayla. The perpetually pregnant one."

"Hi. I've"—Sadie waved a hand toward the elevator—"gotta go."

"Wait." Sienne grimaced. "I'm sorry. Please tell me you're not going to dump him now just because he comes with a scary family."

That had Sadie relaxing enough to smile. "Trust me, you guys don't even register on the scary scale."

"So . . . you won't dump him?" Hannah asked.

"I'm going to see if he needs anything, or if there's anything I can do for him or Naoki." She turned to the elevator and then glanced back. "Which one of you makes him that homemade mac and cheese when he's had a rough day?"

"I do," Sienne said.

"Would you be willing to share the recipe with me?"

The sisters stared at one another and apparently came to some silent conclusion because Sienne had her phone out again. "I'll text it to you."

Sadie received Sienne's recipe via text before she even got to her car. It was probably for the best if she didn't obsess over how Caleb's sister had her number. Because no doubt she'd learned it—and far more—when she'd been doing her research. But clearly, she hadn't found out everything, or Caleb wouldn't still be interested in her.

And by some miracle, he *was* still interested. More than. According to him, they were in a relationship, which meant he was her boyfriend. The word seemed so tame when compared to what she felt for him.

She made a quick stop at the store and then went home to make the mac and cheese. An hour later, she and Lollipop were back on the road, on their way to Caleb's with a casserole dish, and she had to laugh at herself. No one who knew her would even recognize her right now.

At Caleb's place, she slid her hand into her pocket and fingered the key fob he'd given her last week.

"Use it," he'd said.

At the time, she'd been uncomfortable with that, with him wanting her to make herself at home there. But then she'd fallen in love.

With his shower.

In spite of the key fob, she debated knocking, but in the end, let herself and Lollipop in.

The house was dark.

But not empty.

She could sense his presence in the way her body tingled. Specifically her nipples. She'd walked through the dark living room and was halfway to the kitchen when she paused and turned back.

Lollipop gave a yip of excitement and took off as Sadie realized Caleb was sitting in one of the two big chairs facing his wall-sized TV, which was off. He was in a pair of running pants and nothing else. No shirt, bare feet. Head back. Eyes closed.

Since nothing ever got by him, she knew that he was aware of their presence, and in fact he caught Lollipop in midair.

Sadie set her things down and watched as he stroked the happy dog, who gave him one last kiss before jumping down and racing into the kitchen to check her bowls.

Sadie moved closer, dropping to her knees between Caleb's, her hands on his thighs. She studied his face, looking for clues to what he was feeling. He was exhausted. She could see that much in the tiny lines that always appeared around his eyes when he was tired. He worked a lot of hours and was responsible for so many businesses and people, she couldn't even imagine the stress he felt every day. "Hey," she whispered.

He didn't speak, but his hands came off the armrests and covered hers.

"How's Naoki?"

This had his head coming up and his eyes met hers in question.

"Your sisters," she said.

He sighed and let his head drop back again. "The Coven. They live to interfere."

"They wanted to help. And so do I."

His hands slid from hers, up her arms and into her hair. "Well, you are in another of my favorite positions . . ."

Leaning down, she bit the inside of his thigh through the material of his sweats, and he hissed out a breath. "Rough works."

"Later," she promised. "Tell me about Naoki, and then . . ."

He met her gaze again, his haunted, hollow, and very dark. "And then?"

"Whatever you want," she promised and meant it.

"Naoki's in the hospital. He fell and hit his head."

"Oh no," she breathed. "How bad is it?"

"They found him right away, but think he had a ministroke. It's not his first. They're happening more often now and they can't seem to be stopped. He's a ticking time bomb at this point."

"Caleb . . ." She felt her heart pinch. "I'm so sorry. Did you get to see him?"

"He was lucid for a few seconds. He was calm and said it was his time." His voice was gruff. Thick. "That he's ready to go." He paused. "But I'm not ready. How selfish is that?"

Shaking her head, she wrapped her arms around him and laid her head on his chest. "You love him. Love is selfish."

"Thought you didn't know shit about love."

Ignoring that for the moment, she lifted her head. "When was the last time you ate?"

He shrugged.

She went to the kitchen and brought him back a bowl of her mac and cheese. Lollipop had curled up in the dog bed next to his chair but lifted her head at the scent of the dish.

Caleb looked down at Sadie's offering and gave a ghost of a smile. "So you really did talk to my sisters."

She waited until he had a bite before admitting the

truth. "I made it," she said, knowing fully well that it couldn't possibly be as good as what he was used to. "It's Sienne's recipe, and I followed it to the letter. Well, except for the part where you have to wait a few minutes for the cheese sauce to thicken. I didn't have the patience for that part. And I might've used more butter than she does because hello, I get that our arteries are important, but so is butter."

He held her gaze as he took another bite. And then another, and another, until it was all gone. Setting the bowl aside, he reached for her and pulled her down into his lap. "I thought you hated to cook."

"Turns out maybe I do know a little bit about love after all. Or I'm learning anyway."

For a beat their gazes locked, and then he wrapped her in his arms and pulled her into him, tucking his face into the crook of her neck. She felt the heat of his bare torso and smooth, sinewy back and inhaled the innate scent of him that was better than anything she'd ever experienced. When his chest hitched, she tightened her grip, trying to give him everything she had. They remained like that, locked together, him drawing from *her* warmth and strength for once, instead of the other way around. She didn't want to ever let go.

Since that night they'd adopted Lollipop, and maybe even far before that, she'd taken comfort from him. A lot of comfort. And now she was finally able to give him some of it back. "I'm so sorry, Caleb," she whispered, her eyes stinging.

He nodded and held on, and she knew with certainty that they were working toward something pretty amazing, something she'd never imagined having for herself.

"Talk to me," he said gruffly. "Take me out of my own head."

"Okay . . ." But she couldn't think of anything. "What do you want me to talk about?"

"You. Tell me something about you that no one else knows."

He'd never asked anything of her, not once. And maybe it was that this strong powerful man could let himself be vulnerable with her, to her, that he could let himself need her, that made the difference. She took a deep breath and attempted to do the same. It was time, past time, to give him more of her, maybe even some of the dark parts she'd worked so hard to keep to herself.

So she stared out into the dark night over his head and began to talk. "You wondered why I don't have a lot of tattoos." He'd asked several times now, and she'd avoided answering. "I love creating tattoos," she said. "I also love applying my art to people and giving their skin a voice. And I love the few tattoos I have, very much.

Each represents far more than art to me, and because of that, I wanted to honor them by making them my only ones." She hesitated. "Two of them cover scars."

Caleb lifted his head to meet her gaze, his own dark, serious, and very intent on hers. "The ones on your thigh."

"Yes," she said. "And as you also know, there's a third, more recent scar I didn't cover." Because this was hard, much harder than she'd even imagined, she rose off his lap and moved to the window. The room was still dark, the only light came from the kitchen as she stared out into the night, her back to Caleb. "I was a cutter," she murmured. "Which means—"

Caleb's hands gently slid to her hips. He'd come silently up behind her, entering her atmosphere. His heat warmed her back before his chest touched it, his arms slowly wrapping around her.

"I know what it means," he said quietly.

She didn't turn to face him. Couldn't. She'd spent a lot of years being ashamed of herself, though she'd eventually gotten past that. But it was still difficult to talk about. "I started young. It's hard to explain why because I'm not that same scared, lonely, frustrated, angry, hurting teenager anymore, but—"

"You don't have to explain yourself to me, Sadie. Ever."

Relief had her shoulders dropping from her ears. Emotion at his deep understanding of her clogged her throat. "I know," she managed. "And thank you. But you've shared yourself with me, and I've held back. You've been patient, and that means more than I can say. You haven't rushed me. But . . ." She closed her eyes. "I have a dark side to me, Caleb. Sharing it is hard, but I feel like you should know." There was more, of course, but she wasn't ready to reveal it. Didn't know if she ever would be. "I cut on and off for four years," she said quietly.

A low sound of regret escaped from deep in his chest. "No one knew?" he asked. "No one was there for you?"

She turned to face him. When she raised her eyes to his, she saw genuine concern and a carefully banked anger that she knew wasn't directed at her. "No," she said, "but to be fair to my family, I was very good at hiding it. And even better at pushing them away and keeping them out of my hair. I wasn't suicidal." She needed him to know that. "It was almost the opposite. I was so sad and angry and hurting, but I had nowhere to put all of it. Cutting was . . . like releasing the emotions. I can't explain it better than that. I cut in the same two spots high on my thigh so I could hide it. And I didn't tell anyone because I knew they wouldn't understand, they'd think that I wanted to end it—" She shook her head. "But then, slowly, all those terrible, negative emotions inside of me drained away enough for me to breathe and I stopped. And when I knew I was past ever needing to go back to it, I covered the scars with the two tattoos you've seen. Heart over mind, courage over fear. It was like giving myself a second chance. A clean slate, with no reminders of where I'd once been."

"I loved those tattoos from the moment I first saw them," he said, pulling her into him. "But now that I know the meaning behind them, I love them even more." He brushed a kiss to the sweet spot beneath her ear. "Are you going to tell me about the third cutting scar, the one you didn't cover?"

Hello to yet another dark place deep inside her. She drew a deep breath. "I had a relapse."

Another low sound escaped him and he wrapped himself tighter around her as if he could protect her in the here and now from the ghosts of her past. "How long ago?"

"Three years."

His hands were gentle when he cupped her face. "Does that timeline have anything to do with why you hadn't been with anyone in three years?"

"Yes." She wanted to look away, but she couldn't tear her gaze from his steady calm one. "I met someone," she said. "Through my mom, actually. Wes was a lawyer." She managed a small smile. "He was normal, at least compared to the guys of my past, the ones that were so bad for me, so I thought I'd give him a try. He was fun, charming, sweet . . . He wore suits." She grimaced and let out a low laugh. "My parents adored him."

She felt Caleb draw in a deep inhale. "What happened?"

"He . . ." She closed her eyes. "This is really embarrassing."

"Sadie, it's me." His hands were warm and tender on her face. "You can tell me anything."

Yeah, she was starting to get that. But she still couldn't imagine telling him the whole story. "When he saw the tattoos on my thigh, he was fascinated by them, and I admitted that they covered my cutting scars." She shook her head, still envisioning how he'd reacted.

"Tell me he didn't care," Caleb said. "That he didn't dump you because of that."

"No." She actually found a low laugh. "He didn't say anything about them at all. But as it turned out, he liked my dark side, a little too much."

"What do you mean?"

"He, um . . . wanted to watch."

Caleb went very still. "You mean he wanted to watch you cut yourself?"

"Yeah. I guess it's a fetish thing."

"Jesus." Caleb dropped his forehead to hers. "Did you—?"

"No." She swallowed hard. "Not intentionally. One night after a fight, I . . . I thought I was alone, but he'd come in and was watching. I . . . it was a private thing, I was feeling sad and vulnerable and a little down, but when I realized he was watching and was really into it, it freaked me out. I dumped him." She closed her eyes. "But I let him set me back." She shook her head. "No, that's not fair. I set myself back. That's where the third scar comes from. I fell back into that pattern for a few months before I realized that I'd let a guy bring me back to that place. So I stopped. That was three years and a lifetime ago. Or so it seems."

"Is that why you specialize in tats for women and covering scars?" he asked.

She lifted a shoulder. "It's not easy to tattoo over a scar. I just want to be able to do the same for others if they need."

Whispering her name softly, he kissed her, sweet, lingering but just warm lips, no tongue. "Thanks for trusting me enough to share that part of you," he said quietly. "I won't ever break that trust. I know you're not sure about us yet, but I'm sure enough for the both of us. You can take your time to tell me the rest, I'm not going anywhere."

"How do you know there's more to tell?"

"Because it's still in your eyes."

And he wasn't going to push. He was okay with her having her dark side. He was okay with her keeping it to herself if that's what she needed. She'd never met anyone like him. Going up on tiptoes, she met his kiss with one of her own. The kind of kiss that did involve tongue. The kind of kiss that led to soft moans and hot hands and losing clothes and rolling across the mattress to their mutual satisfaction.

An hour later, Caleb was sprawled flat on his back, fast asleep and maybe comatose. He looked sated, which she knew he was, and . . . content. And it was that which had doubts surfacing. He didn't know it yet, but she wasn't the right one for him. She was too jaded, too stubborn, too broken—

"I can hear your brain spinning," he mumbled, reaching for her without opening his eyes. "What's wrong? You hungry? You want to fondle me in my sleep? I'm here for you, babe."

A smile formed without her consent at the drowsy quality of his deep voice. Even half asleep he was still in tune to her completely and it vanquished her wavering confidence. "I'm okay. I'm just going to go into the other room so I don't keep you up."

"Nope." He'd already dragged her into his embrace and now he tightened his grip, settling his face in the crook of her neck, kissing her there before falling back asleep.

She waited until he was all the way out this time. With a sense of feminine pride for having put him in that state, she slipped quietly out of bed.

Her intention had been for some more of the leftover mac and cheese, but she slowed at the kitchen table because Caleb's laptop was open, sending a glow into the room.

She didn't mean to invade his privacy, but her gaze slid to the screen. It was open to his e-mail program and she couldn't help it. One of the subject lines of an e-mail jumped up and grabbed her by the throat. She froze to the point that she wasn't even breathing. What the actual hell. Her feet took her closer until she was standing at the table, staring at the subject line:

Mercedes Lane, please read.

Chapter 27

#OhNoHeDidNot

Caleb didn't know what woke him up the next morning, but as he reached out and felt the cold sheets around him, he knew he was alone. He sat up and listened. The house was silent.

Even Lollipop was gone.

What the hell? He thought they'd gotten past this, past Sadie running scared. Just last night, they'd shared more of themselves than they ever had, and when they'd gone to bed . . . Well, the sensual, erotic memories would be fueling his dreams for a long time to come.

So why had she left without a word? And, he realized as he rose from the bed and saw her discarded outfit scattered across his floor, without her clothes? *What the hell?* Had she gotten a call? Was there an emergency? Grabbing his phone from the nightstand, he activated the screen. Nothing from her, not a call, text, or e-mail. Nothing but work, a text from Kel, and an e-mail from Naoki's night nurse that there'd been no change in his condition.

Caleb strode through his house, but his gut was right. Sadie was gone. Moving quickly back to his bedroom, he pulled on the sweatpants from the night before and a T-shirt. He jammed his feet into his running shoes, grabbed his keys, and took off after her.

It was too early for her to have gone to the day spa for her shift, so he went to her place. He got to her door and knocked.

From inside, Lollipop went apeshit. She knew it was him.

But Sadie didn't open the door. Most likely because she too knew it was him.

What the actual fuck?

He knocked again, knowing the barking would drive Sadie nuts.

Finally, the door whipped open and there she stood, the mystery of how she'd gotten home without clothes solved. She was wearing his overcoat belted tight around her waist, bare legs, and bare feet. Her hair was morning wild, just the way he loved it because it reminded him of how he'd had his hands fisted in it only a few hours before. He was pretty sure there was a beard burn on her throat, but when she caught his eyes going there, she yanked the collar of the coat closed. "How can anyone sleep with this racket?" she demanded.

"They can, after they answer the door."

She slammed it shut.

Okay. Call him a little slow, but he was starting to realize there hadn't been any sort of emergency, and she hadn't just gotten anxious because they'd gotten too close last night. Nope. She was pissed off at him for something else, but hell if he knew what. She rocked his world in ways he hadn't known were possible, but she also aggravated him to the ends of the earth. Tired of this game, he pulled his keys from his pocket and unlocked her door, only to come up against the chain. "Sadie. Let me in."

"I'm sorry, but hell hasn't frozen over, so no."

"Are you going to tell me what's going on?"

"Like you don't know."

"Arf!"

He looked down to find Lollipop staring up at him with bright happy eyes, tail wagging. At least there was one female happy to see him.

But then the dog was scooped up and vanished from view. "Sadie—"

"Go away."

"Wait." He put his foot in the door just as she tried to shut it. Grateful he was wearing the trainers that he'd actually designed for astronauts because this meant she couldn't squish his foot, he held firm. "Talk to me," he said. "What's going on? A few hours ago you were in my bed panting my name and—"

"—I most definitely did *not* pant your name."

"Yeah, you did. And you begged too, very sweetly."

The one eye he could see through the chained door narrowed. "Hey," she said. "You did some of your own begging too, you know!"

"I did," he agreed. "And afterward, we fell asleep wrapped up in each other's arms. But then I woke up alone, which is odd because you never wake up before me, much less functioning enough to get up and out of the house—without your clothes, no less. Which means you basically ran out of there like your ass was on fire. So I'm going to ask you again, what is going on?"

"I saw what you did." She undid the chain and opened the door to stare at him in his coat, and, he could see now, wearing one of his T-shirts which fell to her mid-thigh. Her eyes were filled with so much emotion it took his breath. Temper, most definitely, but hurt too, and it was that that killed him.

"Sadie," he said softly. "Tell me what you saw, what did I do?"

"You have an e-mail. The subject line says, *Mercedes Lane, please read.*"

He stilled. He had no idea how she could have seen his unopened e-mail—until he remembered his laptop on his kitchen table.

She was watching his face. "So it's true."

"It's not what you think," he said. "I—"

"No. Don't you dare try to explain this away. Now move your damn foot before I call the police."

It wasn't the threat that had him moving his foot. He did it because her eyes had gone suspiciously bright and her breath hitched, and he knew she was nearing meltdown status and didn't need to feel bullied while that was happening. "Okay," he said, lifting his hands as he pulled his foot back. "But—"

But nothing because the door once again slammed in his face.

Before he could decide what to do, the door opened again and his coat and his T-shirt hit him in the face. Then, with a flash of sweet bare-ass naked curves, she once again slammed the door.

Sadie headed straight to her bedroom for clothes. It was damn hard to maintain control when one's bits were out in the breeze. She pulled on the first things she came to, a pair of black and gray camo leggings and a camisole, and then added a denim jacket because she was suddenly cold all the way to the bone.

Lollipop came running for her, and at the sound of the little pitter-patter of her paws scrambling on the floor to get to her, Sadie's eyes stung. Her precious little dog sat at her feet and stared up at her solemnly, her huge doggy eyes filled with concern.

"Don't worry," she said. "Just because I broke up with him doesn't mean you did. Nothing will change for you, I promise."

The knock at her door made her grimace. "Gee, wonder who that could be." She peered through the peephole and sighed.

"I never opened the file," he said through the wood.

"But you *have* the file. You didn't trust me enough to believe whatever I told you about myself." She opened the door. "You didn't take me at face value."

"Wait a minute," he said. "Are you going to tell me that you've always taken me at face value?"

"Yes."

He gave her a long look. "You called me Suits for the entire first year you knew me."

And though he was right, this only made her all the more mad because she'd never been able to handle someone shoving her own shit in her face. He was the one in the wrong here, dammit.

"Sadie," he said quietly, seriously. "You know my sisters have been running background checks on the new people in my life for a very long time. This was a matter of course, and I stopped it soon as I realized, which was when you came to me with the pics of Kayla stalking you. We've already argued about this. I never saw the contents of the file. I never wanted to."

"But you *have* the file. You didn't even tell me."

"And I should have," he said. "I'm very sorry I didn't. I won't make that mistake again. But I never read it, Sadie." He looked into her eyes and a grim set came to his mouth. "I need you to believe me."

No, that was asking way too much. "You swore to me you weren't having me followed," she said. "And I believed you."

And wasn't that the kicker. She'd been stupid enough to trust when she knew better. Shocked to find that she was suddenly feeling not good enough for him, a sensation she hadn't experienced in a long time, she slipped into her boots, slung her purse over her shoulder, and handed Lollipop's leash over to Caleb. "It's your day and I won't rob you of that," she said. Bending low, she cuddled the dog and whispered, "See you tomorrow, baby." Then she stood. "Goodbye, Caleb."

"Where are you going?"

"Out."

"But this is your place."

"Yes, so if you'd please lock up when you leave, I'd appreciate it. Don't be here when I get back."

Chapter 28

#PlayingForKeeps

Caleb worked hard in his life to avoid making bad decisions and being actively stupid.

But he'd screwed up and he knew it.

He honestly hadn't thought about how it would look to Sadie, him having the file. He hadn't thought of it because he'd had no intention of ever reading it. Except that by not telling her, he'd hurt her.

He'd made a mistake, a bad one, and he had to fix it. Not quite sure how yet, wanting to honor Sadie's request that he be gone when she got home, he went to his office. His plan was to cancel his day and figure out how to make things up to Sadie. He needed to somehow convince her that even though he was an idiot, he was worth taking a shot on.

He was exiting the elevator on the penthouse floor of his offices when his cell buzzed an incoming call.

Sadie.

He picked it up so fast his head spun. "Sadie," he said in huge relief. "You okay?"

He heard a soft sigh.

"Okay," he said. "You're not. Where are you, I'll come to you and—"

"No. Don't. I'm . . . fine, but I didn't want to do this. I didn't want to have this discussion with you, but I realize now I have to."

The foreboding that filled him made his knees wobble. "Sadie—"

"I need you to know that I'm not that same person I used to be," she said. "I've grown up a lot and moved on, and I don't want to be defined by who I was."

He was straining to hear her quiet voice while being followed by two admins and a sister from the elevator to his office, all of whom wanted a piece of him before the morning got started. He shook his head at them all, signaling he needed a moment, and then shut himself in his office. "No one should be defined by who they used to be," he told her.

"That's easy enough to say when you don't know who I used to be," she countered. "The file in your possession . . . It undoubtedly exposes things that I never wanted exposed, things that will change how people think of me. How you think of me."

Sienne opened Caleb's office door and tried to come inside but he pointed at her to get out. This time he locked the door. He'd pay for that later, but at the moment he didn't care. "Sadie, to me you've never been, nor will you ever be, whatever that damn file says," he told her. "The file's been deleted from my computer. From my server, in fact." He'd done that first thing. "No one can ever see it, including me, I promise you that."

There was a pause while she hopefully considered the fact that he was being honest, that he'd truly never read the file and never would.

"But at least one of your sisters knows everything in it," she said.

He closed his eyes. True. And he'd promised not to lie to her. "Yes. But—"

"See, the thing is that secrets don't work," she said. "We can't . . . we can't do what we were doing with your sister knowing things about me that you don't."

"I don't care about that," he said.

"But I do," she said. "Secrets hurt, Caleb. I'm not going to be the reason maybe something happens to your relationship with your family. I told you about the cutting. About how my parents caught onto me when I was sixteen. How they freaked." She drew a shaky breath. "I told you about me being forced to get help."

It was the second time she'd used the word *forced* when she'd talked about that time in her life, and he sat down—again—because he realized she was going to tell him what he was missing, and that he wasn't going to like it.

"What I didn't tell you was that I was detained under the 5585 hold," she said. "It's a psychiatric hold—"

"For minors," he said quietly, feeling anything *but* quiet. A 5585 hold was an involuntary hold for seventy-two hours minimum, and could be done against the minor's will. For someone who was at risk or in danger from themselves, it was a good thing. But for a teenage girl who hadn't been suicidal, just mixed up and trying to figure out how to navigate a family who hadn't understood her, it would have been . . . Jesus. He couldn't even imagine. Terrifying probably didn't begin to cover it. "How long did they keep you?" he asked, unable to keep the emotion out of his voice.

"The first seventy-two hours were to evaluate my so-called mental health crisis," she said. "But because I was"—she let out a mirthless laugh—"stubborn, to say the least, and refused to communicate, I was held for an additional fourteen days before being able to convince my medical professionals that I could be released on my own recognizance and not be a danger to myself."

Two weeks in a strange place with medical professionals deciding your every move and no say or control over anything. For anyone, it would have been a living nightmare. For a girl like Sadie, who thought and acted outside the box, who'd been misunderstood all her life and felt like she had no one on her side, it would have nearly killed her.

"If I wasn't certifiable before," she said, "I was certainly close after."

Her voice sounded hollow and he felt furious and also devastated for her. And sick that he'd brought it all back to her. "Sadie—"

"I assume that something like that is exactly what your people are supposed to weed out, right?" she asked. "So consider me weeded out, Caleb."

And then she disconnected.

Christ. He'd done this. Driven a wedge between them, made her feel like she couldn't trust him. And he had to pay the price for that. He unlocked his office door and opened it. As suspected, Sienne nearly fell inside.

She took one look at his face and closed the door at her back. "What is it?"

He pinched the bridge of his nose and drew a deep breath.

"It's that bad that you're trying to figure out how to tell me?" Sienne asked.

"No, I'm trying to figure out how to kill you and get away with it."

Sienne made a show of looking at her calendar for the day. "Sorry. I don't have time to be murdered today. Want to schedule it in for next week?"

"Don't."

At his tone, she dropped her playful one and stared at him. "What's wrong?"

"Mission accomplished."

"What are you talking about?"

"You did it. You wanted to make sure I was protected, and you did. Because when Sadie found the file you sent me, she dumped my sorry ass."

"Oh shit." Sienne moved farther into the room and dropped into the chair in front of his desk. "What was she doing in your e-mail?"

"I had my laptop open at my kitchen table."

"Are you shitting me?" she asked. "We put all these safeguards on you to keep you protected and you do something stupid like leave your laptop open where anyone could get their hands on it? Seriously?"

"It wasn't just anyone, Sienne. It was Sadie."

"Okay," she said. "That was bad, but surely if you explained—"

"—Explain what, exactly? That you ran her life through background checks more regimented than the military, even after I promised her I wouldn't do that?"

"Well, that was a stupid promise."

"The file brought up bad memories for her about her past, very bad. As I'm sure you know."

Sienne's expression softened. "She told you?"

"She felt she had to. She didn't want to be a secret between you and me."

Sienne sighed. "Dammit." She shook her head. "I like her. I like her a lot."

"She dumped me."

"Oh, Caleb. I'm so sorry. Maybe if I called her—"

"Don't even think about it," he said. "What I need from you is what I already asked you for—stay the hell out of it." His phone buzzed. It'd been buzzing consistently all morning, which was nothing unusual. "I'm canceling today. I only came up to yell at you. I'm out—"

"You can't cancel the whole day. Or at least you can't cancel this morning. The NASA guys are already in conference room A. You need to make that deal happen and then you can go to Sadie."

"No. As of right this minute, you're in charge."

Her mouth had dropped open. "Of the meeting?"

"Of the entire project. You wanted to take more on, you've got it." He headed to the door. "Don't blow it."

"But—"

But nothing. He shut the door and hit the elevator. He was going to find Sadie and do whatever he had to do to get her back.

When Sadie hung up with Caleb, she left the day spa and strode through the courtyard. She had an hour before she had any clients on her books, which was good because she needed sustenance—the only cure for heartbreak that she knew.

Actually, nothing was a cure for heartbreak, but it might help her survive it.

She walked straight to Ivy's taco truck. She'd texted ahead so Ivy was waiting for her. At the moment, The Taco Truck was up and running early, serving breakfast and lunch only, closing by early afternoon. When Sadie arrived, Ivy finished serving the two customers ahead of her and then handed Sadie an egg, potatoes, and chorizo taco.

Her favorite. Sadie felt her eyes fill.

"Oh shit," Ivy said. "This is more serious than I thought." She added a second taco. "On the house." She came outside the truck and was wiping down the two picnic tables where her customers often sat and ate. "Tell me everything."

"He betrayed me."

"What?" Ivy gasped in shock and clear surprise. "Caleb?"

"No, the tooth fairy. *Yes, Caleb!*"

Ivy was instantly on her side without any details, the sign of a real friend. "That ratfink bastard!" she said angrily. "Why do men need to sleep with more than one woman at a time anyway? I've never understood—"

"No." Sadie shook her head. "He didn't sleep around on me."

Ivy looked confused. "Okay. Then what did he do?"

"He allowed his sisters to do a background search on me. A deep one."

Ivy stopped wiping down a table and looked at her. "I don't understand."

"They looked into me like I was applying for credit, only this wasn't for credit, it was to see if I was worthy enough to date Caleb Parker!" Sadie was stuffing her face with tacos and crying at the same time. "I'm just so mad."

Ivy brought her a stack of napkins and gave her a minute. "Honey, you know who he is, right? He's like . . . Elon Musk. And there's a lot on the line with a man like that. Surely you can understand why his people would be very, very careful."

Sadie just kept eating.

Ivy just watched her for a moment, and then sat. "Sadie—"

"Hey," said a man coming up to the food truck. "I need tacos."

"And I need a million bucks," Ivy said.

"I mean it." He went hands on hips. "I can't go to work until I've had your eggs, avocado, and queso fresco tacos with a drizzle of your amazing chipotle crema. I can't get it anywhere else, not like you make it."

Ivy nodded. She got that a lot. "Two minutes," she said. "They'll be worth the wait, I promise." She turned back to Sadie. "Okay," she said quickly and quietly. "I want you to just listen and not react for a minute. Can you do that?"

Since Sadie wasn't actually sure, she took another bite.

"Is it possible you're just really scared here and maybe, possibly, looking for a way out?" Ivy asked.

Suddenly full, Sadie put down her taco. "No." She paused. Dropped her head to the table. "Maybe, yes."

"Aw." Ivy stroked a hand down her back. "The best of us are."

Sadie lifted her head. "Not all of us. Caleb's got his

shit together. He's faced his demons and beaten them back. He doesn't let the dark get him and he doesn't angst. He lives. There's nothing messed up about him except for one thing."

"What's that?"

Sadie felt her eyes fill. "I think he loves me."

Ivy gaped at her and then turned to the guy waiting on her. "You know what? We're going to have to make that five minutes." She shifted back to look at Sadie.

"Shut up," Sadie said.

"I didn't say anything."

"You said it with your eyes."

Ivy smiled. "Okay, if you're so smart, what did I say?"

"That I'm completely overreacting and most definitely using this as an excuse to run-not-walk away from one of the best things that's ever happened to me."

"Hey," Ivy said, lifting her hands. "That was all you."

"Not helping." Sadie once again dropped her head to the table and this time banged it a few times.

"Stop, you're going to knock something loose." Ivy slid her hand between the table and Sadie's forehead. "Look, we both know we don't need someone in our life to make it complete, but let's be honest. Having someone who knows your dark and angsty side and yet isn't scared off . . ." She shook her head. "It's the greatest gift ever."

"Is this from personal experience?" Sadie asked, knowing it wasn't. Ivy's past hadn't been good or easy, and she was possibly more dark and angsty than Sadie and that was saying something.

"Not personal experience," Ivy admitted. "It's from reading a whole lot of really great romance novels. But that doesn't make it any less true."

"She's right." This was from the guy still waiting on the drizzle of chipotle crema. "My wife reads romance novels all the time. She gets good stuff from them. Especially the bedroom stuff."

Ivy looked amused. "Good for you," she told him. And then she looked at Sadie. "You gotta follow your heart."

"And your good parts," the guy said.

"That's actually true," Ivy said. "You know what you've gotta do, right?"

"No."

Ivy went hands on hips.

"Okay, fine," Sadie said. "I know what I have to do."

Ivy narrowed her eyes. "Do you really?"

"Sure."

Ivy shook her head. "You don't have a clue, do you?"

Sadie's eyes filled. "No," she whispered.

"You *follow your heart.*"

"And your good parts," the guy said again. "That's important too."

Sadie stood up and hugged Ivy in thanks. She didn't hug the chipotle crema guy, but when he held out a closed fist, she bumped it with hers in solidarity.

"Good luck," he said with sweet sincerity.

She was going to need it, because the truth was she had no idea how the hell to follow her heart, an organ she hadn't made much use of and had actually never listened to.

Caleb got stuck in a traffic gridlock due to a construction blockage on the way to the Pacific Pier Building. He could've walked the four miles faster than he made it by car. By the time he strode through the courtyard, heading toward the day spa, an hour and a half had gone by since he'd spoken to Sadie on the phone.

He didn't often let emotions get the best of him. It was counterproductive and a waste of energy. But his emotions were getting the better of him now, all of them.

He entered the spa and about fifteen women's heads swiveled his way, both staff and waiting clients, some of whom he realized he knew. The women were sitting around the plush couches sipping champagne beneath floating balloons that said HAPPY BIRTHDAY ELLE!

Great.

Sadie was with them. She had the spa's brochure in one hand and a bottle of champagne in another to serve the women as she was explaining what their day at the spa would entail. At the sight of him, she stopped midsentence and met his gaze, looking surprised.

And not the happy kind of surprise.

"What are you doing here?" she asked.

He hesitated, mostly because he still hadn't worked out his strategy in Project Grovel, and in the silence came several whispers from their peanut gallery.

"Looks like he's in trouble . . ."

"When they're packaged like he is, they're always in trouble."

"I always thought he was so smart . . ."

Caleb ignored them and had eyes only for Sadie. "Can we talk?"

Everyone's gaze swiveled to Sadie.

"I'm working," she said, gesturing with the brochure and the champagne.

"I can wait."

Sadie gave a slow shake of her head. "After this I'm going to work at the Canvas Shop."

"I can give you a ride home after."

412 · JILL SHALVIS

"I've got my car back, remember?"

She could avoid him forever if she wanted. They both knew that she was stubborn enough to do it. And the longer she managed to put him off, the easier it would be for her to forget what they were to each other. Which meant he needed to get through to her now, right now, and make sure she knew she was numero uno in his life, no matter what her past entailed. No matter what her future entailed.

All in front of a live studio audience.

He drew a deep breath. "I made a mistake," he said. "A big one. I'm probably going to make a lot more because, well . . . I'm male and also sometimes an idiot. But I'm incredibly sorry, and if I could take it back, I would. I love you, Sadie. Ridiculously. And I think you love me too."

"I think so too," someone in the group whispered.

"Hell, *I* love him, and I'm already happily married," someone else whispered.

Caleb concentrated only on Sadie. "What we have is way too important to blow on my stupid mistake," he said. "I don't want to lose you."

No one moved. No one blinked. Including Sadie.

"Maybe you should say the part where you're an idiot again," someone helpfully suggested. Tina, he thought.

Sadie bit her lower lip, whether to hide her amusement or agreement, he had no idea, but she stood up. "Excuse us a minute."

"Ah, man, she's going to take it outside," someone complained. "We're going to miss it."

"No worries, the windows are open," someone else said.

Sadie shut the windows hard enough to rattle them and then jerked her chin at Caleb, gesturing to the front door. He stepped outside with her and the last thing he heard from inside before the door was shut was "Ten to one his body's never found."

Sadie had been practicing all her life at playing it cool, at making sure no one knew when she was ruffled, much less down for the count, but all her skills had deserted her.

Caleb not only had admitted to making a mistake and apologized for it, he wanted to make it up to her. But even that was eclipsed by what else he'd said.

He loved her.

He'd even said so in front of a bunch of people. He wasn't afraid of the emotion nor of letting anyone else know about it.

The magnitude of that—he'd *chosen* her!—had her heart overflowing so that she could barely breathe,

414 · JILL SHALVIS

much less speak, but she had to try. "First," she said, "you're not the only one who's made mistakes."

She absolutely had his attention. His eyes held her prisoner, his entire body still. "I'm not?"

She gave a slow shake of her head. "I used what happened as an excuse to run away. And actually, that's a bigger mistake than yours. Because your mistake showed faith in me, in us. Mine showed a distinct *lack* of faith. And that's what makes it so bad because it's not true. I have faith in you, in us. I was just scared."

"Sadie," he breathed quietly, reaching for her hand to pull her into him. "I get being scared. What we have took us both by surprise, you're not alone there. But you need to know that what you've told me about you, about your past, whatever you haven't told me about your past . . . none of it could ever change my opinion of you. If anything, what you've gone through makes me feel even more for you. You're one of the strongest people I've ever met."

She stared up at him, afraid to hope. "I'm pretty sure I'm going to make a bunch more mistakes too. It's how I'm programmed—"

"I love how you're programmed." He cuddled her into him and she looked over his shoulder at Lollipop who was lying in a toasty, sunny spot, looking like she had no plans to move unless she was physically relocated or until she burst into flames.

Sadie felt the exact same way being in Caleb's arms.

"Do you have any idea what you mean to me?" he asked, sliding a hand to the nape of her neck, thumb extended to nudge up her chin. "Everything," he said in a heart-stopping voice. "You mean *everything* to me. I didn't know how to face the fact that I might have scared you off forever."

A not-so-small lump formed in her throat. She'd spent so much time ignoring her feelings for him, and in return it seemed she'd also managed to ignore his feelings for her. She'd convinced herself that this was just a diversion, but it was so much more. She shook her head, marveled at the fact that she had this man in her life. "I can't believe I almost let the guy I love walk right out of my life."

He stilled and pulled back to see her face. "You love me?"

She froze in shock that she'd said the words, and he smiled. "You do," he breathed. "You love me."

She dropped her forehead to his chest. "Maybe a little."

He lifted her off her feet. "You *love* me."

"Yes," she whispered, terrified, throwing her arms

around his neck. "I love you, okay? I never meant to, but I kept feeling all the little broken pieces of my heart give themselves to you. It's terrifying, Caleb," she said to his smile. "I've never really given my pieces away before, at least not to someone who could protect them and take care of them."

He kissed her gently. "I've got you, Sadie, I promise you. Give me all your pieces, I can take everything you've got." He kissed her again, long and deep, until she broke off, breathing heavily.

"We get to have a round of makeup sex now, right?" she asked hopefully.

"Sadie, this is leading to a lot more than just a round of makeup sex," he said, voice thrillingly rough.

Her heart hitched. "*Two* rounds of makeup sex?"

He smiled. "More."

She bit her lower lip and stared at him, taking in the affection and teasing in his gaze. And love. So much love. She was never going to get tired of that. "As much makeup sex as I want?"

"Yes," he said on a sexy laugh. "But tell me that you want more from me than just makeup sex."

"I do," she said very seriously now, sliding her fingers into his hair to pull his head down to hers. "I want it all."

Epilogue

A few weeks later

The wedding reception was in full swing. Ten minutes ago, Sadie had stood at the edge of the dance floor watching Clara and Greg as they slow danced in each other's arms. Her mom had come up to her and they'd watched together.

"You look very nice tonight."

Sadie had turned to look at her mom in surprise.

Then she'd felt Caleb come up behind her and his arms slid around her as he leaned in and nipped at her ear. Her entire body had quivered, and the next thing she knew, they'd taken a time-out from the wedding.

Now, with his fingers still digging into her hips, he held her tightly to him. When they could finally breathe without gasping, he said, "I knew we'd end up here someday."

"Naked and sweaty in the back of your Audi?"

He laughed. "Yes, but I was referring to something else." He stroked the damp hair from her face while from not too far away, the music of the reception got louder. "Do you want one of these, Sadie?"

"An Audi?"

He grinned. "A wedding reception. But I'd be happy to throw in whatever car you want."

Her heart was beginning to pound in her chest again as she searched his gaze, which was serious in spite of the warm smile on his mouth. "Did you just ask me if I want to get married?"

"Might be fun," he said.

"Are you insane?"

He smiled. "Obviously." He pulled a small black velvet box from a pocket and held it out to her. "But I don't see why that should stop us."

Her mouth fell open. "Oh my God." Her fingers, acting independently from her brain, took the black box and opened it, and then she was staring down at a gorgeous white—and be still her heart, also black—diamond ring.

Caleb slowly slid it on her finger. "Feel like a good fit?"

She stared at him. "*You* feel like a perfect fit."

With a smile, he kissed her tenderly. "Is that a yes?"

"Yes." The minute she said the word, a sense of warmth slid over her. Warmth, and the hope she'd held at bay. "You realize you should be worried," she said to his goofy smile.

"I'm the opposite of worried. I'm more at ease and happier than I've ever been." He pulled her into him, wrapping her up tight against him so that she could feel the steady beat of his heart. Hers was flopping all over the place, but his calm infused her and settled her down.

After a few minutes, he stirred first. "Did I ever tell you I knew that very first night when Lollipop adopted us that you'd be mine?"

She pulled back to give him a baleful stare. "*Yours?*" she asked.

He kissed her again. "Don't worry. I'm yours too. In fact, I've been yours since *before* that night."

"But I was so bitchy to you before that night."

"Only before?" He smiled when she rolled her eyes. He cupped her face. "I *knew*," he said with quiet certainty.

It took her a while to find her voice thanks to the emotion that clogged her throat. Because she hadn't known. She hadn't dared to even hope they'd end up here, and to be honest, she was still shocked that they were. "Really?" she breathed as his lips traveled along her jaw toward her mouth. "You always knew?"

"Always, Sadie," he said. "It's always been you."

Her eyes filled. "And it's always going to be you."

They grinned at each other and he reached for her again, but she held him off, doing her best to smooth down her bridesmaid dress. "We've got to go back in before Clara kills me. How do I look?"

"Perfect." His eyes never left hers. "You look like the rest of my life."

JILL SHALVIS lives in a small town in the Sierras full of quirky characters. Any resemblance to the quirky characters in her books is, um, mostly coincidental. Look for Jill's bestselling, awarding-winning books wherever romances are sold and visit her website, www.jillshalvis.com, for a complete book list and daily blog detailing her city-girl-living-in-the-mountains adventures.

THE NEW LUXURY IN READING

We hope you enjoyed reading
our new, comfortable print size and found it
an experience you would like to repeat.

Well – you're in luck!

HarperLuxe offers the finest in fiction and
nonfiction books in this same larger print size and
paperback format. Light and easy to read, HarperLuxe
paperbacks are for book lovers who want to see
what they are reading without the strain.

For a full listing of titles and
new releases to come, please visit our website:

www.HarperLuxe.com